FOREWORD

Spirits of the Mighty Oaks

Is a book about Cajuns on the Gulf Coast of Louisiana's marshes and bayous.

Armade`ous a half Indian half white privateer and his wife Sara Fina Delande` captured by pirates at the end of 1850.

Their abandoned son Alphe Peltier endured abuse and neglect at a young age and grew up to be a strong willed, hard fighting, straight talking, wielding dealing individual as the result of having to fend for himself. His story spans 86 years and touched the lives of a variety of people.

Travel with Cajun Al as L`eau Noir, the voodoo prince of the bayous, Magic Jack Callahan the gambler and his woman Fadoe reader of tarot cards, the Cajun Priest, the Cajun Barber, The Banker, Eli secret keeper of stones, Gabriel the slave girl, Uncle Bud, Daniel, Sanchez the underhanded scoundrel, Henry-Henry the peg leg pirate and Miss Mary Irlanda and others come to life.

Mary Jane Fitch Peltier

Privateers

1850

    Africans were a proud race of free people who had respect for the laws of nature. They took only what they needed to survive. Although there were many tribes and each protected its members there was an unwritten law that certain boundaries were not to be crossed. Sounders were stationed as look outs to alert the villagers of any intruders.
    Privateers on the other hand knew no boundaries and had learned that humans were a valuable commodity on the auction block. They did not discriminate in their captures, dark skin, brown skin nothing mattered not age, race, gender, status, nothing! They came by sea and quietly landed on the African shores. Before any alarm could be sounded the villagers were invaded. Some escaped into the jungles but, because they were so heavily outnumbered by an enemy with modern weapons, others were captured and placed in chains. Once the Privateers were satisfied that they could capture no more of these people they all returned to their ship, THE SOUTH WEST PASS, where the Africans were stored below deck, stacked like the usual smuggled cargo not living, breathing human beings. Some stood, some sat, others were made to lie flat but the misery was the same. Ship rats were better off, at least they could move about.
    Unable to understand what was happening to them, they almost lost their minds. They had never been on a ship and some became sea sick. During the seemingly endless voyage none were allowed to go on deck for fresh air. They were forced to remain in filth; they were given little or no water and fed molded bread. Many did not survive the horrors and those who did suffered many more indignities. The Privateers figured the captives could not speak any English so whom could they tell. Nobody cared.
    Finally THE SOUTH WEST PASS stopped moving but there were all sorts of odd noises and more people yelling. The overhead door opened and a white man who said nothing

motioned to them to climb the stairs into the sunshine. This in itself was another misery because they had been in the dark so long it was painful to open their eyes to the light of day. Another white man began throwing buckets of cold seawater on each of them to try and remove the stench. Privateers and auctioneers had learned a few tricks of the auction trade such as a clean slave sold for a little more money, or a young black male who's arm and chest muscles had been smeared with grease appeared stronger thereby increasing his value, or touching young black females inappropriately made them scream signaling a sure sign of virginity to the sick minded auctioneer who laughed and thought it increased their worth.

    The most painful part of their experience was possibly never seeing their children and family members again. Very few who happened to be captured together remained on the same land. One by one they were placed on the auction block and sold like trapped animals to any wealthy white man. Health, gender, age and looks were always a determining factor of sale price. Tall, muscular young men were sold for use as laborers; older females were sold for use as cooks, house keepers and mammies to raise the children of the masters; slave children were sold as live dolls for the masters children and as foot warmers on cold nights; the beautiful young females were sold and used for the masters pleasure until he tired of them or they became pregnant. They were then sold again because after all, he could not keep black children born of him out of wedlock who possibly, in changing times, could lay claim to part of his estate. This sale was considered a very good deal because the new owner got two slaves for the price of one.

    The blending of the beautiful black trapped Concubine and the rich white man commonly known as a whoremaster became an unspoken, accepted, standard practice and brought about a lighter skinned slave, a Mulatto. The pleasure of the whoremaster was likened to a sore that would not heal. He had an itch that he wanted to scratch. He obsessed over any black beauty. His offspring were like spirits he could not see but he knew were there. The white whoremasters were so troubled by desires and greed that they bonded together and created a law stating that any person who had black ancestors was to be considered black, legally. They were not to pass themselves off as white. To do so meant they were to be jailed or hanged from the nearest tree wearing a sign saying, " black is black". The new law was convenient for these master trappers. They were confident that any threat of a hanging would be a strong reminder that blacks, no matter what shade of skin color would never be white.

    Although slaves quickly learned to speak English they continued to suffer, mostly in silence. They had been beaten into submission and taught obedience. Black Concubines continued to have children for wealthy white men. It became so common that the joke around the card table in any gambling hall was, " Do you want to put cream in my coffee?" Only the master said with whom the Concubine lay, she had no choice in the matter not even if she was in love with a member of her own race and wanted to marry.

Gabriele

Wives of the masters were always addressed as mistress and expected to instruct slaves as to their household duties, to plan and host parties and always to maintain their dignity in polite society. Most suspected their husbands infidelity but dared not speak openly about it for fear of being beaten. Servants weren't the only ones made to suffer submissive obedience. The sad, lonely mistress of one home in particular often unburdened herself of her heartfelt thoughts while gently being tended to by her personal slave and hairdresser she had named Gabriele. The mistress pretended she didn't know Gabriele was her husbands Concubine and Gabriele never repeated anything her mistress told her. Because the two were alike but yet different they became friends in a strange way. It was as though the mistress had eyes but didn't see and Gabriele had ears but didn't hear.

Memories of Africa sometimes came to the forefront of Gabriele's mind and saddened her a little but at the same time seemed to give her strength. This time while the mistress had her hair done, Gabriele did all the talking. The great land of Africa is a beautiful place much like your country. There are rules in each village that must not be broken but these rules help everyone. Your skin is white and mine is dark. In Africa you would be free and in your country I am trapped, why? Are we not women?

The mistress admitted that she could hardly go on living with herself because she seemed to have lost all self-respect. Dependency means a slow, silent death to people like her who sit around and do nothing. Nobody is totally innocent. An eye for an eye really does make everyone blind to the real problems at hand. The simple truth is that right is right and wrong is wrong. We must quit looking the other way while suffering in silence. Don't we all have a brain and two hands, men and women alike? Somebody has to take hold and fight. When will our strength come, next week, next month, next year?

The mistress began to weep because she realized her strength had arrived; right here, right now, this minute. Suddenly without warning a flood of emotional thoughts came pouring out from her mouth as she openly exclaimed her inner most feelings She rose to her feet and with fierce, dramatic affirmation declared that she was no longer at war with herself; she was taking the fight to the enemy and directing her anger where it belonged. She would have to take baby steps at first but it was on! There was a bone to pick and she planned to pick it clean! Gabriele stared at her mistress with her mouth wide open. She was speechless and shocked. Could this be her gentle, kind, quiet friend standing before her like a great warrior? The mistress suddenly seemed to have heard her own spoken words and she likewise was shocked. They began to laugh as reality set in and they were back to taking baby steps.

As she and Gabriele became closer friends she realized that she alone could help both of them out of bondage. They would have to come up with a plan but it would have to be a good one because failure could mean certain death or prison for both of them. They could not put the cart before the horse. They had to stop and think. Should they act alone or should they gather strength in numbers? Should they leave now or later? They decided to be patient until the time was right. They were still chickens, not yet eagles.

   The mistress said that maybe by allowing Gabriele to run unsupervised errands people would be accustomed to seeing her out and about all alone and would not sound any alarms of a runaway slave. So the mistress convinced her husband that Gabriele could be trusted and wouldn't do anything to disrespect him. He agreed and the mistress said to herself, "Good". She counted on his lustful, roaming eyes to do their job. The master began to pay less and less attention to the time it took to run these errands because he had become more interested in another slave on the auction block. Most men become wise with age but not this old fool. He simply became more and more obsessed with his black beauties. He had so many of them that he didn't even think about Gabriele anymore.

   One evening while sitting by the fireplace deep in thought the mistress suddenly remembered that one night long ago when her husband was half drunk and in a generous mood he gave her, in writing, legal authority over their household slaves. She searched the chest where she kept her valuables and found the document that she never realized would become the key that would unlock the door to her dreams. She decided to write a letter to whom it may concern of her intent as of now and forever to set free her African slave, Gabriele, thereby making her a free person of color for the rest of her natural born life. She rang for Gabriele and explained everything as she signed it, gave it to her good friend and told her to keep it with her always because it was the most important paper she would ever have. It wouldn't be long before the attorney received by mail the mistress's letters of freedom for the remaining household slaves. These two friends were not aware that because of the changing times more and more lighter skinned slaves were being set free. In all probability there would be little or no questions asked of Gabriele.

   The little taste of freedom for one to run errands and the power of the pen for the other had awakened two brave souls.

They realized that there was no need for a plan. They cried, hugged each other for a moment and agreed to hold onto their dreams. They felt unstoppable. Gabriele and her mistress simply packed their bags and left. Once they reached the city the mistress boarded a ship bound for who knows where and Gabriele traveled the bayous from one settlement to another.

Gabriele didn't know at the time that this journey would be a teacher, an educator in this game called life. There are many things to learn and how you play the game matters. Be true to yourself; truth will always be your best weapon of defense or attack. Always remember there are no secrets. Never do unnecessary harm either physically or by word. Learn to subdue your passions; no good decision is made in the heat of any moment. There are times you must speak up but mostly you must listen and be aware of your surroundings. Day by day lessons are valued and passed on whether learned in pain or pleasure.

Unfortunately Gabriele had learned all too soon in her young life some painful lessons brought on by slavery. She was trying to put the past behind her as she traveled the settlements along the bayous but it was as though slavery was a heavy noose around her neck that she had to drag everywhere. She was free and had papers to prove it but the constant evidence that others of her race weren't free made her feel guilty.

Gabriele was naive and saw evil as white on black but it had sadly become black on black. She was shocked and felt so sad and helpless this morning when she saw a black male auctioneer beating a crippled, black, male slave on the auction block. Some poor, stupid, loud mouth, white men yelled, " That's it Thomas, show him who's boss!" Gabriele whispered to the black lady standing next to her, "How can this be?" The lady explained that years ago when Thomas, a black slave, was on the auction block he learned quickly how to beat the white man at his own game. He was smart enough to know that resistance was deadly. He also knew that the rich white man had an ego as big as the Mississippi River. So a whole lot of flattery, kiss up, brown nose, boot licking or anything else you wanted to call it was Thomas' weapon of choice and over time it worked. Because Thomas had quickly proven his loyalty and could be trusted, he rose to the plantation position of overseer and was paid a small salary. Thomas was worse than the white slave owner because in order to make himself look good Thomas would mistreat the other slaves especially when the master was around. The master became so impressed at how Thomas maintained control over the other slaves that instead of paying the overseer a small salary he decided to unburden himself of the responsibility of slaves he considered to be damaged goods and give them to Thomas to do with as he pleased. The master had simply used Thomas' weapon of choice and slyly did a little kissing up himself. Suddenly Thomas not only had control but he now had "THE POWER'. Poor Thomas was proud and didn't realize he was being used as a common disposer of what had become the trappers' Mulatto trash. Gabriele thought surely their God was saddened by some of his children calling the others trash.

    Some of these Mulattos had limbs missing, some were half blind, some were simple minded and some of the old females were pregnant. Thomas suddenly became Master Thomas and insisted on being addressed in that manner. He saw the females as his mistresses and the males as his servants. It didn't take long for Thomas to realize that he didn't have the means to care for these poor unfortunate souls so he decided he would be an auctioneer in his spare time. Thomas thought that some Privateers, smugglers or other scoundrels would pay money or maybe border for them. No matter what, Thomas felt he came out ahead. The lady said that their people call him Monster Thomas behind his back rather than Master Thomas because rumor is that he is creating damaged goods hoping that the master will give him more slaves for his auction block. Men folk say that if ever the master catches on to the scheme Thomas will be dead Thomas, the dumb ass. Both ladies wept at the horror of it all. Gabriele went for a stroll along the dock to clear her mind. Hours passed but the thought if it all lingered.

Armade`ous

    Armade`ous Peltier was one of many in the long line of descendants that made up this harsh, un-yielding, dark, swampy bayou country. Their heritage made them a strong mixture of Indian, French, German, Spanish, English, African and many others who ended up here. All had one goal in mind-----survival. They didn't realize they would do it by any means necessary and at any cost.

Armade'ous was tall with a body resembling that of a mighty tree trunk. He had dark hair, cold, dark, expressionless eyes and his face revealed strong features indicating his Indian bloodline. Despite his appearance that struck fear in many before he even uttered a word, he was known to have a heart of gold and a strong belief in family. He enjoyed a good laugh but was quick to lose his temper. He believed anybody had the right to say anything and he enjoyed a good argument but he never allowed anybody to attack his family members, verbally or otherwise. If you were bold or dumb enough to try it, it meant a fight to the death and in no gentlemanly fashion.

One day Armade'ous was hanging around the dock of the bayou looking for a good deal. He was always thinking about how to make a profit on anything he saw, but today for some reason he was more relaxed as he slowly and quietly observed his surroundings. Children ran around like wild Indians because they knew their mothers didn't have time to make them behave. People were all over the place and they seemed to enjoy the beautiful day by simply looking up at the sun high in the sky or taking a deep breath and remarking about how a gentle breeze brought in the wonderful scent of the gulf. Some were fishing from the dock, some were sitting on bales of cotton chewing tobacco and others gathered together real close, tightly grouped in secret conversations. Seems like women weren't the only ones who liked to gossip when they had a chance. Cargoes of cotton bales, barrels of flour, sugar, coffee and whiskey arrived on barges by way of the bayous and were loaded and unloaded by any man looking for work. Delivery day was always exciting because many people did their shopping for anything they couldn't make or grow.

Gabriele took notice of Armade'ous. He was troubling to her because she knew she had seen him some place before, but where? His commanding presence was breathtaking. Right away she knew that nobody bossed him around and that he was not afraid to do the right thing. He was everything she wasn't and like they say, opposites attract. She saw first hand just how right she was. While she was standing on the dock still day dreaming about Armade`ous, a white man came up to her and shoved her in anger for the simple reason that she was a black person who was blocking his path and did not step aside. She and Armade`ous made eye contact for a brief moment but that's all it took. Armade`ous calmly, quietly, slowly walked towards that man like a great African Lion. The bully trembled in fear as he waited for the Lion to punch him in the face knocking him to the ground saying, "You know what to do!" The bully had publicly been reduced to the scared mouse that he was. He rose to his feet, tipped his crumpled hat to Gabriele and asked for her forgiveness as he assured her that this would never happen again. Gabriele smiled in acceptance as she proudly walked away, heart pounding at the thought of maybe one day thanking this mighty Lion who helped her feel like the eagle not the chicken.

    Gabriele's feelings of excitement calmed a little and she began to wonder what to do. How could she survive? Where should she go? Suddenly, seemingly out of nowhere who appeared but Armade`ous. It was as though he could read her thoughts but she hoped not because this could easily allow her to release her passion. He had cast a spell over her and she was willing to trust him no matter what, after all she had to start somewhere, why not with a protector.

    Armade`ous introduced himself and asked her if she needed his help? She smiled, blushing a little and told him that she really did and that she felt she had seen him someplace before. He told her that he was around when she arrived on the slave ship, THE SOUTHWEST PASS and he often wondered what had happened to her. She told him that she had not been free for a very long time but now she was. He smiled and told her that he had always been free and nobody dared take that from him. They talked for a time then decided they would stick together for now, free and easy, no commitments. Armade`ous said, "Wherever I go you go."

They shared a good life for a long time and learned much from each other.

Lately she felt restless as a strange thing began to happen. Each time Gabriele felt a breeze across her face she also heard a faint whisper of the prayer songs of her people. She was the daughter of a tribal spiritual leader in Africa and maybe he was reaching out to her, guiding her path. It was as though Mother Nature's breeze took care to gently nudge her on because this life was not meant to be; this was not her time, not her place.

Gabriele again asked Armade`ous to help her by letting her go. She told him that she looked on their life as a beautiful time that brought forth much happiness. She loved him but just as any other eagle she too must soar. Armade`ous was saddened but he hugged her and told her to go and not to dwell on her past because if she did she would surely miss her future.

When she arrived in a new settlement, this time a little farther away from the bayous, she realized that she was pregnant with Armade`ous's child. Many thoughts went through her mind and as she roamed about she noticed a little church up the street so she went inside and sat a minute. After a while a man dressed in black robes came up to her and introduced himself as Father John. They talked for a long time, mostly about God and how he loves all of his children and is forgiving of all sins. He told her she was welcome here anytime whether to attend mass or sit in peace.

After much thought she decided it was best to tell people that her husband had died of a fever. She knew Armade`ous was a free spirit and she loved her Lion enough to let him be. Gabriele used the money Armade`ous had given her to open a dress shop. At first she did mostly mending but soon she was filling specialty orders for clothing and became fairly successful but very lonely.

Finally her son was born and she named him Daniel. He was big, healthy and very light skinned. With each passing year Gabriele could see how much Daniel was like Armade'ous, strong but kind and fair. She felt guilty that neither one knew about the other but she also felt that if God wanted them to meet they would, but for now it was just the two of them and they were happy.

    Armade`ous never revealed his deep, inner feelings to anyone. He was always torn between good and evil. He knew it was better to listen to his honest side but hardships made it easier to listen to his bad side, the side that constantly thirsts for quick riches and a better life. He began earning a little extra money by helping smugglers but he soon realized his knowledge of the bayous made him better at it than they were. He could hide and deliver any cargo at any given time and do it quicker than anyone. He knew bayous connected and led everywhere but not just anybody had the map. You see even as a young man Armade`ous was wise. He had figured out that he should make a mental chart of this land and its waterways. Nobody else thought it was worth the effort at the time, but he knew better. It wasn't long before he had a reputation of being the best. No body said openly what he did for fear of being arrested or worse yet, fear of suffering the wrath of Armade`ous because smuggling was illegal. When some were asked where he got his money they simply whispered, "I'll tell you but don't tell nobody."

Sara Fina Delande`

One night Armade'ous was returning from a meeting with fellow smugglers. He knew who he was dealing with so he was deep in thought trying to be sure in his own mind who was cheating who. There was a light, misty fog that hugged the ground and seemed to slowly flow like a wave as it moved across the water. He walked along the bayou and was usually at peace in these woods but tonight he began to think about Gabriele and hoped she had found happiness even if he hadn't. He was very lonely and often thought how wonderful it would be to have a wife and children. He had a long, miserable day and was so tired and sleepy that he thought the woods whispered to him " rest with us, we'll take care of your loneliness." Could Miss FAYDOE, the old lady of the bayou who some thought of as a witch be trying to tell him something? He stopped walking, rested his arm on the barrel of his gun and slowly looked around. There was nothing new just the same old creatures, bullfrogs, snakes and alligators. He listened and thought he heard a very faint rustling sound among the marsh grass. Armade'ous turned and walked toward the noise that had become louder as though someone were struggling.

With his large weather beaten hand he pushed back the marsh grass and found a beautiful olive skinned female in a weakened state but desperately trying to survive. Armade'ous took her by the arm and brought her to the bank of the bayou. She clung to his muscular body as though her very life depended on him and it may have. Being a protector seems to be one of his best qualities. When she calmed down a little, he asked her what was she doing there. She told him that she is Sara Fena Delande` and that she was hiding from the privateers who had captured her and made her their slave. She was very submissive and her spirit seemed to be broken. Armade'ous brought her with him to his house on the bayou. He warmed her with his favorite deerskin hide, fed her chicken gumbo to help her regain her strength and over come some of her fears. They became friends and after a few weeks Armade`ous decided to marry her and dared anyone to say anything about it.

They were drawn to each other, not by a fiery, passionate, physical attraction but in a very comforting way. Theirs was a love born out of compassion and loneness, but it gave them peace and happiness. Each time Armade`ous walked in the woods near the marsh grass where they first met, he picked some wild iris and marsh lilies and brought a small bouquet to Sara Fina. The pleasant scent was a private unspoken reminder to both of them of a special moment in their lives.

It wasn't long before they brought a son into the world. They named him Whitney because Armade`ous thought he would have a sharp whit just like him. How right he was. Everything about him was just like Armade`ous especially his kind heart. Armade`ous was very proud of Whitney and taught him everything he knew but vowed that Whitney would grow up to be a better man because there would be no need for smuggling or cheating in order to survive. He would instill in Whitney the importance of doing the right thing so that your family can be proud of you. Every morning when a man shaves he has to like who he sees in the mirror and has to vow that today he will be a better man than yesterday. Armade`ous felt so blessed to have a son who liked the wilderness. They went everywhere together, hunting, fishing, trapping even a little trip to the tavern every now and then, which by the way, they saw no reason to tell Sara Fina.

Armade`ous had secretly hoped for more children but he was so thankful for what he had that he didn't dwell on it. Ten wonderful years of family life went by before they were happily surprised by the birth of twins, a boy and a girl. Armade`ous yelled out, Cajun Al welcome to my world. Sara Fina asked what should we name our girl then said, I know. Her name will be Alfreda after my very own mother. I will teach her to be a lady just as my mother taught me. This was the first time there was any mention of her family.
Armade`ous smiled and said that he liked the name and maybe she could write stories about her life in Spain and she could read them to the children. She gave her husband a big hug, told him it was a wonderful idea and cried tears of joy.

The twins were a handful, always running around getting into things. Alfreda always wanted to play rough. Sara Fina began to wonder if she would ever be lady like. Al on the other hand liked looking at bugs, butterflies, mosquito hawks, etc. even if he didn't yet know what they were. Whitney loved teasing them a little but he mostly liked the look in their eyes when he taught them something new. At the end of each day Armade`ous always played with the three of them and gave them a bear hug before kissing them goodnight. The children thought Armade`ous could do no wrong. He was their big, old bear and they loved him.

During his life as a smuggler Armade`ous made many enemies, some he knew and others he didn't. The enemy he knew best was his friend Paul Ed. Several times in the past he had caught Paul Ed stealing from him and bad mouthing him to privateers. There always seemed to be an underlying jealous hatred for Armade`ous that he didn't hide very well especially when women were around. He wanted their attention but they only had eyes for Armade`ous. On one particular night of wine, women and song, Armade`ous had not yet started drinking as he played his fiddle and overheard Paul Ed, who was drunk, letting it be known that if it were not for Armade`ous, he would have Sara Fina. This brought to mind the old saying, " A drunk man says what a sober man thinks". Suddenly there was dead silence in the room. Armade`ous was stunned. Years ago he befriended Paul Ed. He was slow of mind and people in the settlement shunned him, so Armade`ous protected him and saw to his survival needs. They had been friendly enemies for many years and since his friend was very drunk and would forever be slow of mind, he would let the insult go and thought no more about it. He played his fiddle and the dancing and laughter continued through out the night.

Cajun Al

But it seemed that truer words were never spoken because a few weeks later, Armade`ous died suddenly one night at the supper table after making a toast to his friend, welcoming him to his home. Armade`ous in a suddle way was trying to reassure Paul Ed that there were no hard feelings in the family towards him. Al remembers that it was the last time Al's dad drank his favorite drink that he made from the root of a sassafras tree. He called it root beer.

Sara Fina was devastated and wondered what would happen to her and her three children. Her first born, Whitney was old enough to soon venture out on his own, maybe even marry but Al and his twin sister, Alfreda were little and would have to be taken care of for a long time. Sara Fina decided she would think about that later because right now they had to make arrangements for the funeral.

Friends and family were so busy with the preparations that nobody realized that Al was not told that his dad was dead. He had seen his dad fall across the table but he thought he was sick. Al's mom held his hand as they entered a gloomy, candle lit room. There were several old ladies sitting in chairs along the wall on both sides of their living room and they were crying saying, "poor little thing". He and his mom walked forward towards a big wooden box in the corner. She lifted Al and told him to kiss his dad goodbye. At first Al thought his dad was sleeping but then he said to himself, "why in this box". After he did as he was told and kissed his dads cold, stiff face he knew that his dad was dead. Al did not cry then and not later. He understood what loss meant, real loss and the helpless feeling of not being able to do anything about it.

This misery of dealing with death was not over. He now had to help bring the wooden box, he learned was called a coffin, to some place else they called the cemetery. They were very poor so the only way to get the coffin to this cemetery place was by way of the bayou, which was their roadway. Some men carried the coffin and placed it on a pirogue. It was so dark that nobody could see where they were going so a few ladies lit some candles and placed them on the coffin, the family got in Armade`ous' pirogue and the rest of the people got in theirs and followed down the bayou. People remarked how strange it was that even in death Armade`ous led the way to a place some towns people had never been. Many attended as a show of respect but some attended out of curiosity. Gossipers wanted to later assure those who weren't there that they knew what they were talking about because they saw everything with their own two eyes. Many pirogues arrived and people called Mourners, were softly singing a song in French {AMAZING

GRACE} as they stepped ashore and formed a narrow candle lit road. Whitney, Paul Ed, one Privateer, one Smuggler and two very old men dressed like trappers carried the coffin down this little road to a big hole somebody had dug called a grave. A priest was waiting there holding a book and praying out loud. This place felt good and holy because of the candles, the singing and the priest but at the same time it felt cold, scary and evil sort of like voodoo stuff. Al wondered who was in these graves good people or bad people. The whole cemetery was lit up. Everyone was sad and crying as the priest said a few more prayers. Then they buried Al's dad in the grave and left. That was it. Nobody held Al, nobody tried to explain anything, and nobody told him everything would be all right. All he knew was one day his dad was here and one day he was gone forever. He didn't blame his mom for not helping him understand because she was so sad, but this was really tough.

He seemed to be growing up fast mentally and had many emotions and inner conflicts to deal with. He wondered why his dad died. Did God just take him, did somebody kill him, what? Al was young but smart and began to reason out a few things. He remembered his parents' talking about how Paul Ed was attracted to Sara Fina. He was as people said, somewhat simple minded, but at the same time a bit dangerous. People felt sorry for him and most of the time gave him his way rather then deal with trying to make him understand something. Al remembered that on the night that his dad died, Paul Ed did not drink any root beer when his dad made a toast to his friend. This was unusual because wherever Paul Ed went he was known to eat and drink until there was nothing left. He also remembered seeing mud on his shoes. This sticky, brownish green mud was only found along the bayou where the poison hemlock grew. Al was now convinced that Paul Ed was so jealous of Armade`ous that he poisoned his root beer in order to have Sara Fina for himself. Al tried to tell people but they felt Armade`ous was dead and buried and it was time to move on. No use stirring up trouble.

Sara Fina knew long before Al that she would have to marry the only man in town that would have her in order for her children to survive. Now that Armade`ous was not around to protect her the evil, razor sharp, gossiping tongues of the good respectable so called Christian women of the settlement just ran a muck. All they did for entertainment was talk about the pirate whore of the bayou. Men, although attracted to her, did not come forward and defend her for fear of being run out of town. Sadly there wasn't a real man amongst them. That's when Sara Fina realized how special Armade`ous really was. He knew no fear, stood up to anybody, told them what he thought whether they liked it or not and never let anything get out of hand. Many times he helped these witches and their families. They would have starved had it not been for her husbands' charitable, kind heart especially towards children. She had grown to love him and missed him so very much.

The first person in Al's life to become trapped by an evil trapper was Al's mother. Paul Ed came to her with a marriage proposal knowing full well she could not refuse. He promised her he would be good to her two children and that they would never go to bed hungry. Al's brother had found a lovely, caring girl and they were happily married living in a cabin somewhere along the bayou. Sara Fina hesitated for a moment then agreed and married him the next day. In her heart she knew they would be miserable and she was right. Life was much worse in every way. He abused on the family. He contributed nothing and ate everything in sight. He just sat there day after day barking out his orders, telling everybody what to do and how to do it. His way of doing things was always the better way even if he didn't know what he was talking about.

Al thought to himself that most Cajuns had a lot of kids so that they had their own free labor but not this lazy, good for nothing, bayou marsh rat. He said he could not have kids. Al thought he was probably too lazy to even do that and end up with the responsibilities of his own.

Al and his mother were very close and she would often tell him the same story over and over about how she was from Spain and had been traveling on a ship when privateers attacked them. She was kidnapped and became a slave on this new ship. She had to cook, clean and wash clothes. She was tall, thin, had olive skin, dark eyes, long dark hair and a nice smile. She was very beautiful, frightened and homesick. There was one privateer who was not like the rest. He seemed to be more gallant and gentlemanly. His kindness towards Al's mother helped her get through these terrible times. At night when the other seafarers were asleep, he would tell her of his adventures. Suddenly he said, "I don't even know your name." She smiled shyly but proudly said, " I am Sara Fina Delande`, daughter of the Governor of Spain and you sir?" He removed his plumed hat, bowed from the waist and introduced himself as Jean Lafitte, pirate extraordinaire of all the seas, at your service. May I have this dance?" They laughed and for a moment she forgot her misery and they pretended they were at the Governors Ball in Spain having a wonderful time. She knew he was not Jean Lafitte because she had seen very, very old wanted posters of Lafitte hanging everywhere in Spain but she said nothing and enjoyed the moment.

    Lafitte, the imposter, suddenly had an odd, cold feeling come over him as though the spirit of the dead plunged him into his grave. He told Sara Fina he sensed they were all in danger and he may be killed. She smiled and tried to change the subject but he was so serious that she began to pay attention. He gave her a map drawn on goatskin that marked the route to buried pirates treasure. He said there was a fortune in gold. If she survived she was to hide it in an old oak tree along the bayou where this battle took place. They would meet again but she was to be careful and trust no one! She hid the map on her person and they retired for the night.

    Suddenly she was awakened by very loud, thundering sounds. BOOM. BOOM. Cannons were being fired and fighting began amongst pirates and privateers. They were being viciously attacked. Ships were sunk and many men died. She survived and floated to shore on driftwood. When she landed she immediately hid the map in the opening of the first oak tree she could find.

Secrets

    She pushed it deep inside then made her way along the bayou, hiding in fear of being captured again. She was so scared at the time that she does not remember where she hid it, only the general area and that the driftwood had SOUTH something or other written on it. It was during this time that Al's father found her and took her for his bride.

Story time seemed to be the only pleasant time Al's family had. His mom made them feel special by having a separate secret story to tell each of them. Al never found out what stories she told his brother and sister in the past but he was sure they were happy ones. Al saw his Mom suffer in silence as little by little she became so run down physically, mentally and emotionally that she could hardly manage a smile or even a hug for him or his sister any more.
   One day she remembered that she had Armade`ous' fiddle hidden in an old chest. She decided to give it to Al because he loved it so and she knew Armade`ous was planning to teach him how to play it. She knew the family was in need and she should have sold it but sometimes doing the right thing is more important than doing what is necessary. She was right. The look on Al's face was a happy memory she would take to her grave.
   Al always thought the worse thing that could have happened to them had already happened! But there was more pain to come, much more. Paul Ed finally told Sara Fina that Al would have to go. They couldn't afford to feed and clothe him. He convinced her that Al would be better off. Although Al's mom was a nurturing person and loved her children very much, she had low self esteem, no inner strength, no fighting spirit to be able to stand up for herself or her children. She thought to herself, nothing could be worse for Al than this and she said a silent prayer to the saint of the impossible to please take care of her baby boy and help him find peace and happiness, maybe even the pirate treasure. Paul Ed told her he had hired Al out as a field hand and he wouldn't be coming back. He said he would tell Al himself; it would be easier that way. But what he really told Al was that his mother didn't want him any more and wanted to give him away and keep his sister and that Al had to go and work on the farm up the road. They would take care of him. He pushed Al out the door and slammed it behind him. Al didn't believe him but left anyway to try and find a better life and maybe return later to rescue his mom and sister. He went to the barn and didn't let Paul Ed see that he was taking his

harmonica and pocketknife his dad had given him before he died, and the precious fiddle his mom gave him because surely he would have taken them from him. Al knew Paul Ed only wanted a girl child but Al was too young to understand why. Al asked God every night from then on to keep his twin sister safe.

Although a mere child at this time, Al was given from one farm family to another. He was passed along and traded as though he were a good mule. Finally one farmer kept him but he was treated with less compassion than this farmer gave his animals and he was made to work twice as hard. His meals consisted of cornbread and milk sometimes cornbread and water.

As a means of survival, Al had learned early in life to read the signs of nature signaling animals and plants of things to come. When he noticed all the cows in the field turning their backside to the north he knew a cold spell was coming bringing more misery to him. He had no shoes to wear so in wintertime he would follow the cows around the field hoping to bury his feet in a fresh cow paddy for warmth. But all too soon he would hear what he considered to be the call of the wild, " Al come here". He knew he had better hurry, cold feet or not because the razor strap would be used across his back.

As time went on and Al grew older he became braver and decided he could not take this cruelty any longer. No matter how hard he tried he could never please these people so he decided to run away. He remembered that when he first came to live on this farm he got up at night and went exploring. Then he would let his imagination take him to another time and place but now this was a real time, a real place, and he had a real problem. He took his secret path known only to him and maybe the dead pirates of the bayous. It lead to a partially sunken pirate ship named "THE SOUTH WEST PASS". Al cleverly used muscadine vines to tie some of the floating logs together hoping to lift the lower side, which was below water, but it didn't work so the logs became a raft. He climbed on board and crossed Bayou Chene to freedom. The runaway was a very daring move because he spoke little or no English but he had good, strong character with a little snake oil to boot.

When he finally stopped running he became a little depressed and saw everything as being cold, dark, damp and dreary. He heard a scary, splashing sound. Was it an alligator or a human sloshing in the bayous? He had learned to recognize the scent of a water moccasin and saw one evade his steps.

He heard hooting owls in the trees and from a distance he could see egrets and herons standing around like guardians. As he moved on he was startled by a couple of frogs and muskrats. He knew this was his test as a man and it would make him or break him. He had drawn his line in the sand and was determined to survive. He had an inner mental strength that always told him do or die; there was no turning back. He heeded nature's warnings signaling him there was bad weather brewing and he realized he needed shelter. He spotted a high and dry area amongst some trees on a levee so he set about preparing a make shift camp for the night. He used a few dry branches and palmetto leaves which he bonded together with vines to make a lean-to. He then gathered a little moss for bedding. He felt safe enough hiding in the thickets. His sleep was not so peaceful because it was a bit scary out there.

Soon the weather was clear and as he saw the sun rise and shine he thought to himself, what a great day it was to be alive. Suddenly he heard a growling sound but he began to laugh because he realized it was his stomach calling for food not a wild animal looking for food. He knew eating berries would not sustain him and that fishing would be the quickest way to get food. He found an oak branch about six ft. long and three quarters inch in diameter. He built a small fire and began burning one end of the stick to slowly fashion a point thereby making a spear for fishing. Al knew that when bayou water rose in a shallow area garfish, flounder and catfish would be plentiful. He found the perfect spot, used his new spear and ate well that day. His dad always said that nothing seemed to taste as good as some good old catfish fresh from the bayous.

Al figured he had not traveled far enough to really feel safe, after all he was considered a runaway. He moved on and came across a very, large, hollow oak tree. As he stood inside he thought to himself, "What a good hide out" He set about making his first home. He again gathered moss for a bed and this time used dry wooden branches, palmettos and vines to make a makeshift door but fashioned it in such a way that it blended with the scenery. He hung his spear on the wall as he began to realize how really big his home was. He placed his pocketknife and his harmonica on a tree stump he used for a table. Al sensed that he was not really alone because he felt that the large, strong, old oak protected him from the weather and from the creatures of the marshy bayous, maybe even from humans who might be trying to find him. While he lay down and began playing his harmonica a strong feeling of sadness crept into Al's thoughts. He had really hoped with all his heart that those farmers would be like family and love and care for him. As long as he kept busy he didn't allow himself to think about how lonely he was and how much he missed his poor Mom and sister, but during quiet time he couldn't seem to control the sadness, not now anyway. He hoped his brother had a good wife and a happy home, wherever he was. He said his daily prayer for his sister and today asked God to please help him not to dwell on the past, not to have such evil thoughts towards Paul Ed, after all he figured God knew what to do about him. He also asked God to please help him to be strong, good, kind and caring. AMEN

    That old stomach began to growl again. This time he wanted to eat something different. As he sat about thinking, a branch suddenly fell from the oak tree. Could the mighty oak be telling him "I'll help you"? Maybe! He noticed the branch had a curve in it and he decided he could use it for hunting. Al said, "Thank you Mr. Oak," and he began to smooth it out by using his pocketknife. Finally he felt it was perfect and began to practice throwing it at different targets. Soon he felt his aim was good and so was the little spin technique he used. He quietly hunted and killed a rabbit. What a celebration. He cooked the meat over an open fire. It was pretty well done, burnt actually but he didn't mind. Al was so full from eating so much that he could not move and hoped nothing tried to chase him because he would be a goner. He climbed the mighty oak and lay across one of the large branches and fell asleep while being cradled by the moss.

When he woke up he played his harmonica and from his high perch stared out at the vast marshland and marveled at the peaceful beauty of it all. After a while he climbed down and hung the rabbit skin on the outer trunk of the tree to dry while he explored the area. Al came across a baby raccoon that, like him, was alone. He named him T-Coon. They adopted each other and he followed Al everywhere. Sure was nice to have a friend to talk to even if he couldn't talk back, maybe that was a good thing because there was no argument to settle. When the rabbit skin was dry he placed it near his bed for T-Coon to sleep on. They sure were cozy and happy.

 Al decided cooking would be easier if he had a black iron pot and a few things from a kitchen. The only way to get them was to sneak back to the farm and steal them. He was not proud of what he was about to do but he could think of no other way since he remained at large. He used his same secret path and traveled by the light of the moon. When he arrived he noticed that the place was a bit rundown. The fences needed mending, the gates were broken, the barn stalls needed cleaning, the vegetable garden was over grown with weeds, the house needed a white wash and the porch had a few rotten boards. As he looked around he said to himself, "I'll bet the old buzzard really misses me. Sure are a lot of cowpaddys around." He went in the barn and found his dad's old fiddle. Thank god it was still in good shape. Everyone seemed to be asleep inside the farmhouse when he arrived. He quietly entered the kitchen, took a medium size pot and saw a fresh baked blackberry pie on the shelf. Just as any other youngster tempted by a sweet tooth, Al couldn't resist. He decided one pie and one pot was all he needed. He then noticed that the dagger he had made when he first came to live on this farm was lying in the open drawer of the food cupboard. The blade was fashioned from the leaf of a wagon spring and the handle from animal bone thereby making it very sturdy. These things were all he needed. On his way back across the pasture he saw a salt lick and took it also. Al knew it would help preserve his meat and fish. Later that night Al and T-Coon sure enjoyed that pie. The old lady baked often but never let him have any, not even a small slice. Al thought, " I guess she wasn't happy so she never wanted me to be happy, not even for a few minutes."

    Al was very good at fishing and hunting but now he began to think more like a trapper. He worked on an idea he had to snare animals. He gathered pal meadow leaves and separated the strands from the long leaves. He rolled them between his large fingers and made lots and lots of twine, which he stored in the oak tree. Then he and T-Coon began to hang out along the Intercoastal Canal waiting for tugboats to go by. As the tugs made their way Al would yell out, " Throw me an apple Mr." The deck hands did and Al jumped in the water after them. Al did not eat all the apples. Instead, he brought some to the camp and planed to use one in his snare. The idea was to hang an apple from a cypress tree branch which extended away from shore then tie a large twine loop from the same tree branch but closer to shore. The deer would try and reach for the apple, stick his head through the hidden loop, realize he was caught, pull back quickly trying to get away but the noose would tighten and the deer was snared. Al was so excited because the first time he tried the snare it worked. That salt block came in mighty handy in preserving the meat.

    There wasn't much else to do but swim, eat, sleep, wander around, play his harmonica and think of new ways to hunt, fish and trap. He had not yet learned to play the fiddle. One day he watched T-Coon reach for small fish in a shallow area of a bayou. The fish were very small but T-Coon kept trying to catch them anyhow. Suddenly Al had a new idea. He would catch small fish, tie a piece of twine to a stick, shove the stick down the mouth of the fish then throw the fish out in the water where it would float Al would hold the other end of the twine while lying in wait for water fowl to eat the fish. Seemed like a good plan to Al. He soon learned that the plan was not perfect. Al had to be well hidden and ready to jerk the twine just at the right time in order for the stick to get caught in the fowl's throat. The best thing Al learned by using that plan was patience. The first few tries didn't work because he moved too fast but he soon mastered the technique. Mother Nature provided all he needed to make one heck of a duck gumbo in that old black iron pot much the same as his own mother would have done for him.

Al knew that bayous led just about everywhere. In order to make his adventurous travels easier he needed a good old-fashioned pirogue and in order to have one he would have to make it himself. He looked around and found the perfect cypress tree lying on the ground, apparently recently struck by lightening during a storm. He whittled the outside of it as best he could with his dagger. He became exhausted and while resting and playing his harmonica he thought, "FIRE". Suddenly again full of energy, he built a fire and laid the tree across until the massive trunk was mostly ashes throughout the center. He removed it from the flames, turned it over and began to easily hollow it out. Now, all he had to do was fix up the ends of the best pirogue ever built. He called it Tee Pee in honor of his Indian ancestors. Getting food and bringing it to his camp had become a whole lot easier.

During one of Al's explorations of the area he heard several men on horseback yelling back and forth to each other. He couldn't quiet understand what they were saying but he had a feeling they were trouble. He ducked down and remained hidden as he made his way back to the safety of the mighty oak. After several weeks went by, Al decided he had been gone long enough to take a chance showing his face in town, after all he was a little older now and had changed somewhat in appearance over the years. Besides, maybe he could find out what that group of horsemen was after. Were they looking for Al because of what had happened a few days before he left the farm? As Al thought about it he remembered the farmer was a hard man but the farmers' wife was mean, just plain mean to the bone and had taken to beating Al. She could not stand up to her husband and get away with it so she kept a small whip handy and took her anger out on Al and from the look on her face, she enjoyed every minute of it. Well, she came after Al once too often and like any old dog backed into a corner Al exploded, grabbed the nearest thing handy, which happened to be a window screen and hit her over the head with it then ran away that very same night. He just had to know what these men were looking for. So he again used the secret path and when he got to town he overheard a few men talking about those marsh hunters he had seen. It seemed that some rich men were very angry with runaways. It didn't matter who ran away from them, or from a plantation owner, or from a small farmer. It didn't matter why they ran. It didn't even matter if they were black or white. The only thing that did matter was the rich man considered them to be somebody's property and wanted them back dead or alive. Maintaining total control was power and power was everything to these men. They felt the need to feed their inner beast never realizing the great feast actually created a small man.

People were so poor in this area that men hired on with the marsh hunters for pay even if they knew this was a terrible thing to do. The marsh hunters became a vigilante group known as the CLAN. They met in secret places to discuss plans to commit evil acts while hiding their faces behind hoods made of gunnysacks thinking that nobody knew who they were. But guess what, there are no secrets in ERATH, everybody knows that. The more money they were paid for their services the larger the group became. The larger the group the more powerful and indestructible they felt.

Al was very troubled when he heard a story about several black runaways. Like Al, they could not read or write and like Al they had been abused but worse than Al, much worse. The abusers had no feelings towards other human beings and pushed the blacks so close to the breaking point that they seemed to have lost their will. A few whites became afraid and thought that maybe they were possessed by voodoo and the spirit prince of the bayou, the one they called "L'eau Noir". Late one beautifully clear night some of the blacks started a very small campfire. The full moon shone brightly as the flames reached higher and higher for the stars. Cracking sounds grew louder and more intense, but were they sounds of fire or of breaking bones of slaves past and present. Finally the ashes cooled and a very faint, dark cloud rose towards the sky while many stars seemed to twinkle. Without uttering a sound some blacks ran out into the night, some walked slowly but all moved as though they no longer felt pain. Whites wondered if L'eau Noir called them to his kingdom along the bayou in the marshy swamps never to be seen again?

Al hoped that over time people would come to their senses and put an end to terrorizing the poor. He was making his way back to the mighty oak where he felt safe and sane when suddenly out of the corner of his eye on THE SOUTH WEST PASS he saw a shiny, sparkling thing in the mud. He bent down to pick it up. Oh my God, he yelled, it's gold! He put the coin in his pocket, climbed onto his raft and went on to the camp.

Finding the coin made him happy but he suddenly became angry and bitter at the hand life dealt him. He felt less than human. It was as though he went from being a boy to being an animal. Having both instincts he never knew which he would call on or how far he would allow either to take him. He was alone all the time, no friends, and no family. He constantly had to think, " SURVIVE, SURVIVE, SURVIVE". He was so upset that he tired himself out and fell into a deep sleep. He dreamed of meeting Jean Lafitte, only he was a ghost. The pirate treated him with kindness when he needed it the most. He and the ghost walked along the bayou as the ghost listened to him for a very long time before fading out like fog. Al then knew that Cajuns don't really die. They stop breathing but they don't die. They just move on in timeless spirit to be a part of a different kind of settlement, a member of a fog village. Some experience remorse for many things just before they quit breathing and are allowed to remain on earth as peaceful spirits to comfort the troubled minds of good breathing people who have been repeatedly wronged in life. If a Cajun does not feel remorse before he stops breathing he does not become a spirit of a peaceful settlement but a prisoner of L'eau Noir the voodoo spirit prince and remains trapped, weighed down as though carrying the evils of the world on his shoulders. He feels fear, anxiety, every emotional and physical distress he helped inflict while breathing. There is no peace of any kind and his spirit roams forever in pain making the sad, lonely, sometimes creepy moaning night music of the foggy, marshy, swampy bayous.

Al awakened with a whole new outlook on his life. He realized this was the life God meant for him to have and that things happen for a reason. Everything was beautiful, sunny and peaceful. Maybe this was heaven and he didn't even know it. He thought to himself, "for now I come first and it's up to me if I am a good, happy man or if I become a mean, bitter, unfeeling man who doesn't care about anybody or any thing." Surely God has told Sara Fina not to worry anymore because her baby boy aims to be the best.

More time passed and Al, the man, emerged as his confidence grew. He decided to use his gold coin to buy what he needed to begin trapping alligators and furry animals for the hide and meat. He had become very good at it because in his heart he was truly a man of the marsh and bayous and felt free. He had a pirogue and a make shift camp along this bayou or that bayou depending on where he felt like stopping at the time. You see, Al was his own boss and answered to himself. After the trapping season ended he returned to civilization and sold his furs and hides. The profits, no matter how little were his alone and he liked the idea.

Gabriele Continues

One day a gentle, quiet, shy man came into the shop and wanted to have a shirt made. Gabriele smiled as she took his measurements and then told him it would be ready in about one week. The next day he again came to the shop wanting to have a second shirt made. Gabriele smiled and told him it would be ready in two weeks. Well, wouldn't you know that the next day this man came to the shop again and wanted a third shirt? This time they both laughed and Gabrielle said, " Would you like to sit and have coffee with me before you go broke?" He said, "Yes. Thank you kindly." He went on to say that his name was Uncle Bud and he had a little place just outside of town. He knew Daniel because they fished at the same fishing hole on Saturdays. Danny boy had told him that his Mom was beautiful but lonely and Uncle Bud seemed lonely too so why didn't they get together. Uncle Bud said he liked a straight talker so he decided to maybe take his advise. Once he saw how nice and kind Gabriele was he just had to keep coming back and since the cat had his tongue when he was around her all he could manage to say was, "I need a shirt." Gabriele said, "Well Uncle Bud you come around any time and you don't need an excuse. I find your company very pleasant, in fact why don't you stay to supper?" That was the simple beginning of a beautiful friendship.

Uncle Bud was assertive, confident and well respected by all. Perhaps this was part of his attraction. He was like Armade`ous but different, not as bold, not as quick to his feet in times of trouble but a problem solver just the same. Turns out that Danny boy was wise beyond his years because Uncle Bud and Gabriele were married that very summer. Gabriele still called him Uncle Bud not honey or baby or dear. He liked that because when she called his name he could see the love in her face, especially in her beautiful eyes. He raised Daniel as his own. He knew the whole story about the two of them and felt that sooner or later the truth always comes out no matter what.

Gabriele was so busy these days that she hired a very young girl, named Lucille to help her clean up. All of the customers liked her because she was so sweet and polite. Lucille eagerly learned to mend socks, sew buttons, and do other alterations. She and Gabriele soon became a team. One day Gabriele was busy sizing a dress for a customer and Lucille was in the back room doing some mending when the customer began to talk about a man who had married a woman who had two small children. Word of mouth seemed to be the newspaper of bayou land and believe you me there was most definitely a gossip column. Gabriele took offense to gossiping and never engaged in it but she had no choice but to listen to her customers because she couldn't afford to offend them and maybe lose their business. She felt that by not passing on anything she heard she maintained her dignity. The customer went on about how this man was a lazy; good for nothing that gave the woman's son away to a farmer but kept the girl child. The woman was never the same after that, all sad and lonely. The customer went on to tell that the first husband protected everybody especially children. Nobody could boss him around, he wasn't afraid of anybody and boy was he good looking. Too bad he had to die. The customer said that she wouldn't be a bit surprised that the good for nothing had killed him. Gabriele suddenly knew, she just knew but held her breath as she asked if the customer knew their names. The unsuspecting customer told her that the dead man was called Armade`ous, the wife was called Sara Fina, oh and the boy was called Al. She didn't remember the girl's name. Poor little Al, I don't know where he is. When the customer left Gabriele gathered a little strength and told Lucille to close the shop. Lucille was concerned and asked if she was all right and if there was anything she could do but getting no response Lucille did as she was told and went home. Gabriele began to cry as she quietly, with love in her heart said goodbye to her mighty, fearless Lion, her first love. Later she told her husband the sad news but chose not to tell Daniel. Maybe one day she would but not now.

Years and years went by and the secret was still a secret. Daniel was now full grown, a man all three parents could be proud of. As a child he was shy, but as a man he was big, bold, loved Cajun country life, worked hard on land he now owned and had little time for fun. He was so driven to succeed that he often hired himself out as a field hand on other farms for extra money. Gabriele often told him to loosen up and not be so serious all the time. His reply was always the same," Life is hard, fun is for children." Uncle Bud would tell Gabriele to leave the boy alone, everything in due time. He knows what he's doing.

Poor Daniel, it wasn't in his nature to ignore anyone who needed help. It seemed that every time he was just about caught up with his own responsibilities he learned that a friend or neighbor's barn burnt or the fence was down or the crop needed harvesting before the storm hits, etc. He never waited to be asked, he just showed up asking, "What can I do to help?"

The farmers' wives thought that Daniel was getting on in age and was too good a man to be single and lonely. The farmers were of a slightly different opinion. They loved their families but were secretly envious of a single man viewing him as representing freedom. Traps come in many forms and the human animal is not always spared. As the men sat around at the watering hole known as CRABBYS, which was so named because of the old men who had coffee there every morning and boiled crabs and beer most afternoons, they began kidding around about how women have changed over the years. One man laughed and said, " Maybe the chase is different but the end is the same!" He went on to describe how the young, beautiful, female of today reaches a point in her life where she knows what she wants and doesn't wait, she goes after it. She is smart and uses no physical force. She first stalks her man like a black panther; silently appearing in the back ground wherever he goes. She fixes her hair nice, she dresses nice, she smells good, smiles a lot and acts all shy and helpless. When he's talking she pretends to be interested in everything he has to say all the while thinking," just a little closer, I got what you need and I know you want it." She wiggles a little when she walks away, not too much so as not to appear easy. Then when the man finds enough courage to ask her out she plays hard to get by having other plans for the time he chose but she takes control by naming another time, another place, all the while sporting a beautiful smile. She talks softly, moves in close but very careful not to touch, always leaving the man wanting. Most men always want what they can't have. The haunting smell of her perfume and her shy, sweet smile is all he thinks of. The spell is cast and he dreams of her night and day moaning, "I do, oh baby I do." On the last I do he wakes up standing before God and witnesses at the altar, in a church and is trapped for life. Most of the time, just as in our day, the beauty turns into a witch when the honeymoon is over because the spell has been broken and the poor man usually has a rude awakening realizing he said," for better or worse until death do us part." Some men become so miserable that the death part crosses their minds as they wonder if they should help it along rather than let it come natural. The farmers had a good laugh and said, "poor Daniel." However they had to admit they were no prizes either and there are two sides to anything. There is give and take in any good marriage, as well as anger and happiness but over all it is a wonderful union and children come along as sweet fruit from the trees. They make anything worthwhile because they are innocent and see beauty in all things. Children see their parents just as they saw each other in the beginning; the hero and the beauty, side by side against all odds, knowing no fear, doing no wrong. One of the farmers said, " Maybe God in his wisdom sends children along to serve as a reminder to us that it's not about sex, it's about unconditional love."

Daniel was humble but proud and farmer's wives felt he would never find a wife because he worked all of the time, so they began praying in the form of a request, "God, you know Uncle Bud's son, the one they call Daniel, well we think he needs a wife, can you please help?" As usual these well-meaning women took matters into their own hands because they thought even God was too slow with a response. They tried just about every invitation they could think of to accidentally, on purpose have Daniel meet their single relatives and friends but there was no spark, no heat, only frost.

These nice ladies just thought God was asleep but he wasn't. He set his own plan in motion and made rough and tough old Daniel slowly look with soft eyes to see the lovely Lucille who had worked in his mom's shop since she was a child. She had a crush on Daniel ever since she could remember. Everyone was so use to having her around that they never noticed that the quiet, shy, soft-spoken Lucille had become a beautiful butterfly.

Uncle Bud was a kind man who smoked his corncob pipe and listened to the conversations going on around him. He never took part in gossip and never preached dos and don'ts to others. He patiently waited for and witnessed first hand the change in his son. He always thought Daniel and Lucille were good for each other. He knew in his heart that there was romance in the air, no trap, just pure love. The young couple took great pleasure in the simple things of life. It's as though they were one because they were so much alike but where one was weak the other was strong thereby weaving a strong bond. At long last Daniel was young not old, not hard and worn out before his time He hoped they would marry soon and give him lots and lots of grandchildren.

Everyone was happy for the young couple and wished them nothing but the best life had to offer. Eventually they were married in the church by Father John who was also a witness as the couple joined hands and jumped over the broomstick to complete the outdoor ceremony in honor of their ancient custom. All the ladies claimed that they were the ones who brought Daniel and Lucille together. The men couldn't help but poke fun by asking what took so long? Wasn't she under their very noses when they were searching so hard? Everyone had a good laugh because after all, the truth is the truth. The ladies openly thanked God for answering their prayers and admitted that God knew what he was doing all along. Father John rose from his chair, raised his glass of blackberry wine and proposed a toast to the bride and groom after which the guest left and the young couple retired to their home to begin their new life together.

In the past Daniel always resented his friends nagging him about having fun because they thought getting drunk and womanizing was what it was all about. Daniel saw them react to hangovers known to the wicked as hangarounds because the miserable after affects of the alcohol seemed to hang around the next day for hours and hours. It wasn't until Lucille came along that he understood. Real fun is experiencing a simple, happy time in ones life that becomes a cherished memory as time goes on. He often thinks of how he and Lucille laughed when they went on a fishing picnic and after eating he was trying to teach her how to fish but they both slipped in the mud and fell in the bayou. They were in and out before the gators knew the two had hit the water. Sure is amazing how fast a decision can be made when faced with fight or flight?

After they were married a few years there was a short period when times were rough and they were miserably short of money. Due to a few unfortunate circumstances they hit bottom so hard that there was no place else to go but up. They held onto each other tight, real tight because each of them knew neither one would walk away. Starting over made them reach deep down inside themselves to come up with a plan to survive and survive they did, together. Every morning Daniel and Lucille sit on the back porch and take time to watch the sunrise while sipping a cup of good hot coffee. Daniel secretly thanks God for sending him Lucille and prays that she will always be with him for better or worse because after all, he is who he is and try as he may to improve he is still just Daniel.

Mr. Batiste

Mr. Batiste was a poor Cajun farmer. All he had ever wanted was to provide for his family and work the land. He took his time and carefully made sure that the area he chose had woods for timber, enough acres for grazing and hay, a body of water, and a large section to grow a variety of farm crops. He staked out several acres and registered the farm as his own and called it Big Woods. He felt that spiritually he and Mother Nature had a deal. She would provide earth, water and sunshine and he would provide labor and tools; one could not function well without the other. A good crop was the secret. Together they would care for all of her children, animal and human alike. He always knew the golden rule of farming. Work very hard and all will be fine and good but become too confident, too weak or too lazy and the deal is off. There will be no mercy. Mother Nature has many methods of destruction at her disposal, drought, flood, hurricane, pestilence or a little of everything. Slowly she could and would take back what was hers.

He built a home, barns, fences and what ever else he needed to create a working farm. He sold crops, hay, timber; produce and leased water rights to neighboring farmers for a fee. He did whatever it took to make it self-sufficient and became very wealthy.

With wealth comes power and control. Control of humans is possible and sometimes necessary, many men make use of it. They call it saving the day, or taking over for one good reason or another, or in some cases to abuse the weak whether human or animal. In Batiste's case he was rich but not an enforcer, not a leader, not a controller. Little by little things were slowly going bad. The farm, because of its production and sale of bi products, needed many hands to continue on the path of success. But just because you hire these hands does not mean they are working hands as Batiste eventually realized.

He lost the battle as soon as the farm started to grow because he could not say what he meant and mean what he said. He was not smart or trusting enough to hire a foreman who could, one who was a leader of men, a controller. The new hands were lazy and always threatened to quit on the spot if they didn't get a raise or if they had to work late or sometimes if they had to work at all. Batiste became more and more frustrated and miserable. The spider web began to unravel slowly and just as she promised Mother Nature took back what was hers He had to sell the farm to his neighbor for just enough money to clear his debt at the feed store, etc. He had been taken advantage of, ridiculed and humiliated most of his life and now he left just as he had arrived, only more humiliated. He became cold hearted and bitter. Some would say down right mean. He made a vow that it would never happen to him again and he would do onto others, including his wife and daughter, before they could ever do onto him. They had no voice in any matter and were submissive to any of his commands, they were to be seen but never heard. He felt justified in ruling his own household with an iron fist and with much practice he became very good at it.

    He decided he would move to Erath and get rich again but this time he would use his brain not brawn. He learned everything he could about banking and he opened the first bank in Erath and named himself as its President. Everyone was excited because this meant their little settlement was growing and citizens were very proud to have a bank in town. It was small but it was a bank. The first part of his plan was to make personal contact with as many people as possible; people who could then say to others, " I know him personally." These four little words fed the ego of the poor man who wanted nothing more than to exaggerate his importance. Batiste held an open house, introduced his family and provided free drinks, tea and lemonade only, no hard stuff. The word free seems to be the most important word in the English language, but no poor person ever asks what it really means. Is there really nothing to pay? The devil doesn't think so. He'll gladly accept your conscience as a down payment and your soul as payment in full.

Mr. Batiste seemed well educated and this alone gave him an edge. The poor were and still are always blindly impressed by anyone who could read and write and held any position of importance in any community such as a lawyer, doctor, banker, or priest. Mr. Batiste always had a smile, always shook your hand and patted you on the back as he walked you out assuring you that if you were ever in need he could draw up a loan, after all, what were friends for. He had a way of making every person feel like they were the president of the bank and he was their servant. He was the servant all right. Many times he served himself a piece of their farm or business. More often than not he took the whole thing and had no conscience about doing it. He soon became known as a shady character, you know, one of those good old boy trappers.

   Not everyone knew about his method of operation. Heck even a rattlesnake warns you before he strikes but not egg snake Batiste, he just swallowed you whole. Many unsuspecting farmers had a bad crop this year due to hurricanes and could not feed their families or replant their fields. They were broke. They went to the bank; secured a loan in order to buy seed to plant new crops. They put their mark on the paper and happily left the bank with peace of mind. Mr. Batiste knew that this inner peace would be short lived and he seemed to relish the thought of the shocking misery he had the power to inflict upon the poor, unsuspecting farmer and his family. He had control!

   As usual just before it was time to harvest the crops the bank foreclosed and legally seized the farms for non-payment. The banker then had their lands and the added benefit of selling the crops leaving the farmers in shock and disbelief. The banker had always avoided answering the farmers questions about the loans knowing full well that the farmers did not understand that payment was due in full the month before harvest time. The banker became richer and the farmers became poorer. Surely the banker must have known that sooner or later everyone has to pay the piper! One day his luck would run out.

Because Mr. Batiste was so obsessed with wealth and power he made sure he used every opportunity to promote himself, including having his wife and daughter with him at public events. Projecting himself as a good family man couldn't hurt. But the truth was that he spent less and less time at home. Mrs. Batiste figured her husbands' absence gave their daughter Marlie a better chance at life. She saw her own loneliness as penance for being the wife of an evil man. Her marriage vows bound them together in sickness and in health and lord knows Batiste was now mentally ill. She remembered that as a young girl all she dreamed about was getting married. She would make the man in her life so happy that he would never leave her. They would have children and things would be perfect. Dreams are fine but why doesn't a mother, a friend or a priest tell the young couple the truth about how hard it is to live with another person and adjust to the ups and downs of real life as the physical attraction finds it's place. It is said that love is blind but is it really, or is it the idea of being in love that causes blindness. Nothing prepares you for married life, especially not the obey part. Hopefully when the new priest arrives she can confess her true feelings and make him understand how important it is to her that he explains about life, in general, to Marlie.

A Cajun Priest

Each of us looks into a mirror every day. If we were to place a divider between the left and right side of our faces we would notice a difference. One side has a look of a lighthearted, pleasant person and one side has a look of a heavy hearted, angry person. This serves as a constant reminder that good and evil exist within each of us. It is up to us which side we listen to, which path we take, what choices we make in life

Most Cajuns had strength, wisdom, and their faith to overcome and survive on their own, but some were just the opposite, weak! The few who did nothing. They sat and waited. Some felt somebody owed it to them to step in and take care of their problems; others tried everything they could and felt beaten because with every step forward they took, life caused them to take two steps backward. These were the easy prey that grew into a flock who blindly followed anyone who had realized he could easily rule over a little kingdom, because you see, when humans have difficulty evil comes calling.

Cajuns placed their personal lives in the hands of their priest and blindly gave him their complete trust because they believe God spoke to him and then he told them what God wanted them to do. To the Cajun he was a comforter, a wise man who spoke French, English and some other Holy sounding language called Latin. They were highly impressed by the priest they thought could do no wrong. Some never knew that sometimes the person they turned to was the evil they feared.

Most men enter the priesthood with good intentions. They want to comfort the sick, help the needy and encourage goodness by spreading Gods word and guiding people on their path to heaven. Some men however quietly enter from the dark side with all the thoughts, acts and deeds that evil can bring forth and secretly unleash on the unsuspecting.

As Cajun people from different walks of life traveled and lived together some grew weary and settled in the swampy, marsh lands but others continued on and as they bonded they decided on just the right spot to settle and raise their children. The first thing one particular group did was build a proper church in which to worship, marry and baptize their children. It had small living quarters in the rear for a priest, and it also served as a Town Hall where they gathered and decided to call their community, ERATH. They then appointed leaders; a Mayor and a Sheriff; any other appointments would come later. Their first order of business was to write to the Bishop with a request. Their little community was growing due to the migration of more Cajuns and was badly in need of the services of a Priest who could stimulate their conscience to silently do battle with their evil side. Although they were only a small settlement in Vermilion Parish located almost as far south as one could travel by land, they realized that faith and spiritual guidance was just as important if not more so than law and order in a civilized society As they waited for a reply together they built their homes, a small bank, a jailhouse and began working on a schoolhouse.

Mail delivery was a very long and difficult process. It was more likely than not that response time to any inquiry could take months sometimes as much as a year. Just as the community began to give up hope on ever having their own priest, a freight wagon arrived and a handsome, young, dark haired, 5', 160 lbs fellow dressed in black robes came forward and introduced himself to one of the children playing in the street as Father Cornez Andrico the new priest. The boy smiled and ran quickly to the jailhouse to tell the Sheriff who in turn informed the Mayor.

Father Cornez Andrico was seemingly kind, well spoken and polite as he extended his hand requiring the greeter to go on bended knee while kissing his ring before shaking hands for the first time. He projected an underlying air of superiority and arrogance. This was a silent signal to some that this priest could be bought. Birds of a feather usually flock together and only time would tell.

Cajuns take pride in the well-known fact that they have a reputation for never having met a stranger. Father Andrico thought the rumor of their trusting nature was just an exaggeration but he was experiencing first hand their instant projection of innocence. The warmth of their greeting made him feel that he had genuinely been made a part of their families by a simple handshake and a smile.

Another well-known fact about a Cajun is that he will use any excuse to have a good time and even the eyebrow raising, tight lipped, deep breath taking ladies had to admit this was a good one. Who could frown on a celebration to welcome their Priest? Imagine everyone's surprise at the gathering when Father Andrico asked for a beer. The Sheriff broke the stunned silence by yelling out, " that's my kind of Priest". Everyone laughed and the merriment went on into the night. As they left the ladies invited him to dinner, some offered to wash his clothes and others offered to clean his house. The men on the other hand offered to take him fishing and hunting. He declined their offer to go hunting because secretly only he knew that the sight of blood made him feel faint and he didn't like the troublesome thought that he may appear weak.

At first he slyly ruled these people with kindness, a soft-spoken voice and a smile. He gave of himself, providing help to the parishioner who was building a new barn or a new fence. He often helped repair wagons; helped to finish building the new school and even taught a class when the teacher was sick. He never hesitated to respond to a need whether it was for physical labor or priestly duties or even to help care for the elderly. He always took time to listen, day or night. Some wondered when his other shoe would fall.

Naturally the more time one person spends with another the more they get to know each other. Not just the pleasant, proper, best foot forward person, but the real person. Father Andrico's flock began to notice that he seemed to be two different people and you never knew which one would respond when he was addressed. He didn't guide them any more, he dictated to them in a harsh, stern voice with an angry expression on his face that displayed cold squinted eyes. His word became church law in their little community and no one questioned it because he had put the fear of God into them.

Sunday Mass provided Father Andrico with the opportunity to reach many Cajuns through his sermons, the strong and the weak alike. The message was about the teachings of the faith, which is what people wanted to hear. He stressed the importance of regular confessions because this is where he learned everything he needed to know about everybody, all their dirty little secrets. The church has rules everyone must follow and he told them what would happen if the rules were broken. He always asked for money and made the very poor feel guilty and ashamed about not being able to spare any. The shame they felt was so great that they gave their last penny because father said God told him to tell them that it is more blessed to give than receive. Father Andrico knew that they didn't understand that the true intended meaning was not about money.

Every Monday morning Father Andrico went to the bank to deposit the donations he had received in Sunday's collection plate, minus the amount he secretly decided he deserved for caring for this flock of weak heathens. His weekly share he hid beneath a floorboard under the Holy Water stand in the church.

Maybe the day would come when he would join the elite in a respectable part of the world. He needed any amount he could save to help him in his quest for a better life. After all, he never wanted to live in this swampy marsh with gators, mosquitoes and God knows what else. Let Voodoo keep the secrets and the Cajuns, they deserved each other. He wanted to lead a wealthy flock who were refined and had manners and culture not to mention larger donations.

The President of the Bank, Mr. Batiste, being of the same character as Father Andrico, became suspicious after a time because he noticed church attendance grew but donation deposits remained roughly the same. Mr. Batiste smiled as he decided to let Father Andrico bury himself a little deeper. The evil master trapper was not ready to spring his trap on the unsuspecting novice trapper.

Although Mr. Batiste was older and a pretty good spider at weaving his web as he spoke to the flies who entered the bank, Father Andrico also had something going for him. He had the blind trusting faith of the spiders' flies. The people of the parish listened to everything their priest told them to do, especially if he said, "God told him to tell them something." They endured the extreme penance he imposed after their confession of a minor sin, they married the person of his choosing, they never openly objected at their children's baptism ceremony when he changed the French names they had chosen, and at their death before performing the ritual of the last sacraments he alone would decide if the parishioner had led the life he considered worthy enough to receive the sacraments and a church service.

In the beginning with the arrival of Father Andrico the little church had been filled to capacity but lately attendance had been on the decline. The tension grew amongst the faithful who began to feel like lost sheep. They were devout Catholics, generations who believed in the simple basics of their religion: Baptism, Confession, Holy Communion, Church marriage, and receiving the last sacraments upon their death after which they entered the church head first in a coffin to be placed at the foot of the altar to humbly be received by God as his child with his blessings and to leave the church feet first on the path to heaven in route to the church cemetery for burial because from dust thou art and to dust thou shall return.

Members, old and young alike began to wonder about Father Andrico. Even the most simple minded weak person believed that God was all loving, caring, helpful and forgiving of all sins and would never turn anyone away from his house of worship no matter what they had done in life. It made some long for the olden days when burials were simpler. The dead person was placed in a coffin in the living room then transported by pirogue along the bayou to the community cemetery and buried by the lights of the holy candles with a few prayers from any Priest if he was available, if not a friend stepped forward and said a few words. Maybe it wasn't such a good idea for each community to have their own Priest.

One day Mr. Batiste was at his desk in the bank when he overheard some members of the church talking about the priest. They were thinking about writing to the Bishop informing him of their concerns about Father Andrico's behavior. They felt that most of the time Father Andrico ruled like an evil king. He didn't listen to reason, he didn't ask for an opinion on matters concerning maintenance of the building for example. He's too controlling and no longer interested in the why of any situation. He always knows best about everything no matter what. Some felt he was much too involved in their personal lives He was not at all what they expected. They also believed any person can say anything he feels but it's the way you tell somebody something that matters. There is nothing wrong with a good discussion that brings forth different points of view especially if it affects the whole community. After all, they brought him here and they darn well could send him back where he came from, which by the way they suddenly realized that nobody knew where that was.

Mr. Batiste came forward and tried to steer the conversation in a different direction. He pointed out the good that Father Andrico had done and that maybe he should be given a second chance. Quiet possibly he had become overwhelmed and needed a break or something. Mr. Batiste knew he could appeal to the soft side of these people so he offered to have a talk with the priest before any action was taken. They all agreed and went about their business.

Mr. Batiste returned to his office to think, after all, he was the spider who wanted the priest to become his fly. The bank closed for the day and Mr. Batiste walked over to the church to speak with Father Andrico. As they exchanged pleasantries, they suspiciously looked each other in the eye, something either of them was not use to. People usually lower their heads, eyes gazing down, bodies slightly bent forward uttering "sir or Father" several times as they shake hands with either of these men.

Father Andrico poured the coffee and asked Mr. Batiste to join him. As a small boy Father had observed the amazing powers of a cup of good, hot coffee. He remembered that early in the morning the site and aroma of it brought a smile to his parents' faces. Later during the day ladies visited his mother and were sometimes upset about one thing or another. As they drank the brew they seemed to calm down and by the time they left all was right with their world. When his father came home after work he relaxed by the fireplace and drank coffee while pondering work related problems that sometimes troubled him throughout the night hours, then he drank it to stay awake. This magical, dark water was calming or stimulating. Father Andrico sensed he needed both.

Mr. Batiste began by saying, " No sense in playing games, I'm going to lay all the cards on the table and get right to the point". Father quickly realized this was no simple minded Cajun and he had better not only listen but hear what is not being said in this conversation. Mr. Batiste told how he knew the church deposit was short changed and also that the members of the congregation were fed up with his superiority attitude. There was talk of contacting the Bishop and having him removed. Father said nothing. However, Mr. Batiste continued, there was a way to make all things better for the both of them. Mr. Batiste told him he came on too strong too fast. These Cajuns could be managed but he had to make them feel important, like some things were their ideas and they were in charge. Agree with them in private then slyly turn it around in public where they aren't clear in their own minds what they said or didn't say. This way if it works he takes the credit and if it doesn't they take the blame. Another thing, he must use every means at his disposal to get the upper hand. Hadn't he learned that yet? Mr. Batiste told him to think about everything and get back to him. What a pity he said, that as of now the church bank deposit has been reduced by half, I'm looking forward to your weekly blessings. I don't see myself as being greedy just a good businessman seizing an opportunity as it presents itself.

Father Andrico sat in the dark near the fireplace with a large cup of hot coffee as he heard in his mind the last words the banker spoke. Father knew he was trapped and sharing money did not appeal to him but he would temporarily have to make the best of it. One thing rang true; he did come on too strong too fast and wasn't using everything at his disposal to his advantage. He needed to slow down and think things through. Controlling others was easy but the true challenge was self-control. He had begun to allow his true feelings towards these people and this place to show. This life he felt forced to live had now become a game and he would win. Cajuns would pay and pay dearly for aiding the spider in making him become a fly.

Just as the swamps black water moccasin quietly moves amongst the Cajuns, so would he. The black robes he wore became a symbol of his power. The hot, dark, brew seemed to stimulate the equally dark side of the priest. The slower he drank the better the evil plan came together, after all, evil is as evil does. Tomorrow was Saturday and what better time to go calling on his flock. It took the whole day and part of the night to speak to everyone and extend an invitation to a special Sunday Mass.

He began by announcing there would be no collection plate today and that he asked everyone to remain seated after services because he had received an important message from the devil and he wanted to pass it on. Needless to say this really got their attention. Some town criers left in the middle of the service to tell those who had not attended Mass what was going on. Before you could blink an eye everybody and their dog was there.

Regular services ended. Father Andrico then stood in the pulpit, looked around and began to weep. He openly confessed, "The devil made me do it, yes, he did". When I first came here I was greeted with open arms by loving families. I was made to feel welcome and respected by all of you wonderful people. Overtime I became lonely for my own family. I became weak and the devil jumped into my heart and soul. He filled me with jealousy. I became so jealous of you and yours that I blamed all of you because my own family wasn't here. The more I witnessed your expressions of love and joy the more jealous and outraged I became. Every night when I said my prayers I asked God to help me but the devils grip was strong and getting stronger. Before I knew it I was becoming more like him. I wanted everything my way and didn't care about anybody or anything. All I seemed to want to do was hurt people's feelings and boss them around to make them feel as bad as I felt.

I thank all of you for having the courage to speak to Mr. Batiste on my behalf. God has truly blessed me by sending me here to be cared for by such good people. The message from the devil is," Be careful all of you because if I can get the priest to do my work I can more easily get you". Let's all lower our heads in prayer and ask God's help to fight the evil that may be within each of us, the evil that so quickly comes calling at a moment of human weakness. I ask for your forgiveness and that of Gods.

Women cried, men stood tall, shoulders back and chest out because they felt they had taken the bull by the horns and solved the problem. Everyone stayed over and seemed to welcome the priest back into their good graces. He told them that he was going to ask the Mayor to call a town meeting next Saturday. God had given him a wonderful idea and he wanted to share it with them to see if it met with their approval. They became very excited and told him they would see him Saturday.

Mr. Batiste was the last to leave. When they were finally alone he told Father Andrico," You are good, real good but I still want my money for this week. Half of whatever you collected last week before our bargain will do. Oh, I'll be at the meeting Saturday to watch another performance". They again looked at each other eye to eye but there was no handshake.

The week went by rather quickly and once again the people gathered. Excitement filled the air as they waited. Father entered the room and began the meeting with a simple prayer. He walked amongst them engaging in the usual pleasantries and then told them that no man stands alone. God felt that if they worked as a team they could get any job done. So, with the approval of the ladies he would create a church organization for ladies only. One of their responsibilities would be to keep the church clean and beautifully decorated with flowers; another would be to organize a choir; another would be to provide refreshments for all meetings. They could elect a president and a secretary for the Ladies Cajun Cultural Society. He then turned to the men with a similar proposal. The title for the men only group would be, The Founding Fathers Association. Their responsibilities would be to maintain the church building; maintain the grounds; make it a safe environment for families while on church property. They would also elect a president and a secretary. Father added that he would be honored to accept the duties of treasurer for both organizations if asked. The men could meet on the first Saturday night of each month and the women could stay home with the children. The ladies could meet on the second Saturday night of each month and the men could stay home with the children. Father said he knew it was a bit unusual for men to assume this role but what better way to show their love for their children and to show that a husband and wife are partners while the man maintains his dignity as head of the household. This idea was so well put that the men were afraid to disagree for fear of suffering the silent treatment at home. They knew that a happy wife makes for a very good marriage so they seized the moment to tell their wives how they deserved to have a little fun and spend time away from the children with women friends. Father then said I believe this is enough to think about for now. Let's meet one more time together next Saturday before you begin meeting separately. I will let you know about one more idea I have, this one will bring much happiness to everyone. Hope to see you all at mass tomorrow.

    When the bank opened Monday morning Father Andrico was the first one through the door. He made the usual church deposit and then asked to speak with Mr. Batiste in his office. Father said nothing as he handed Mr. Batiste his weekly payment then turned to leave, no handshake. Mr. Batiste couldn't help himself he just had to taunt Father Andrico by commenting on how they were of one mind, like birds of a feather so to speak.

    Finally it was Saturday. Father was the first to arrive for the scheduled meeting then a few young boys came in. "This is brilliant. I have my disciples Father thought to himself, as the devil kept telling him to get their children, they can suffer if you control their children!" When everyone was seated Father said his usual prayer then asked if anyone had anything to say? The ladies spoke first and said they agreed with everything Father had said last week and they would like to make him an honorary member of their club. He could teach them many things such as how to conduct their meetings and elect officers, including naming him as official treasurer. It would be so wonderful, with his guidance, to learn proper manners, the proper way of speaking, the proper way of walking, the proper everything. If they were going to do this they wanted to do it right. Well then Father smiled and said your first bit of useful club information is that this is called etiquette in polite society. The ladies were so excited because they suddenly felt special, you know better than the rest of the women in town who couldn't join for one reason or another. They never realized that when they started feeling better than the rest the devil was in.

The men played it down a little as men usually do but they were just as excited to belong to an exclusive club and have a night to relax and talk man talk. They too agreed with Father and they too wanted to make him a member and treasurer at their first official meeting. He humbly accepted the offer from both groups.

I now ask for your permission to make some of your boys my assistants, whichever ones are interested that is. They will be called Altar Boys. During each mass they would hold the bible for me, hand me the cup of wine, light the candles before mass, etc. They would also wear black robes and learn Latin. Sometimes when boys are of a troubled mind they tend to feel the need to talk it out and being in a group setting with boys who share the same interest helps. I would always be around and as their priest, I believe I am the person you can trust to give them the best advise. The only thing I ask of them in return is that they show up on time. Anyone interested can see me after mass tomorrow.

Now then, have any of you guessed what my happiness idea is? No, well, I'll tell you. Why don't we have the very first Church Fair in the Parish? In the spirit of brotherly love this is one way we can all help raise money to see to the immediate needs of families who have fallen on hard times. With the mention of families comes the thought of children. Orphans would forever be at the top of our list. A little kindness goes a long way. After all, was it not through your kindness that I was able to triumph over the evil clutches of satin? We can be there for these scared, lonely children and with a little money, time and effort help them become productive citizens of our community.

We know that The Founding Fathers Association is the backbone of our town. Members laid the groundwork for our very foundation. It is with much admiration and respect that we turn to them for guidance and help not only in planning but also in building. At our first meeting we could elect a planning committee who would be in charge of the building and locations of each booth. Labor and building materials would be donated for the first fair but if we make this an annual event our funds would grow and with the guidance of a financial committee headed by me as treasurer, we could deduct the estimated cost of having the next fair before donating the proceeds to the church and the orphans fund.

In large cities it is well known that members of high society groups have a coming out party for their daughters who have come of age. Well, we could have sort of the same thing for our very own Ladies Cajun Cultural Society only your introduction would be more grand because it would be announced at the first church fair and in the presence of everyone in the Parish. At your first meeting you should elect a chairman for different organizational committees. I, as your treasurer should always head your financial committee.

It is my hope that both organizations will consider allowing the Altar Boys, with my guidance, to be in charge of games and contests. For a small fee anyone could compete in any number of things. For example, a game of horseshoes, or pie eating, or spitting the watermelon seed the farthest, or sack racing, or pirogue races, etc. The winner of these contests would receive a red ribbon and a free basket of homemade cookies. There could be pony rides, and many other activities. My Altar Boys will be our one and only committee headed by me, the financial advisor and treasurer.

Everyone, men and women could donate something for sale to get this started in order to raise money for the church and to help the orphans. One person from each both would win a blue ribbon in recognition of being the best; the best baker; the best canner, the best doll maker, the best seamstress, etc. Men would display their fine wood working crafts; their metal works such as knives and tools, and anything else that could possibly earn them a blue ribbon.

Last but not least, let us not forget our lovely young ladies. Each of them could prepare a basket of food such as fried alligator, or fried rabbit, or my personal favorite fried chicken. All of the young men would then have a chance to bid on the basket of their choice and each winner would enjoy the meal on the fair grounds with the lovely cook and her chaperone who remains in the distance. The Ladies of the Cajun Cultural Society know that it is in good form to have an older person present at any social activity of younger people to see that propriety is observed. The ladies giggled as they held their fans up to their faces. They seem to do a lot of that lately, being proper and all.

What say you ladies and gentlemen? Everyone cheered and applauded. Father Andrico reminded them that the more activities and booths they had, the more money they could probably take in for the orphans. Father told them in all of his travels he had never met a more hard working, productive people as the Louisiana Cajuns. Once a Cajun gives his word and shakes hands there is no turning back, right or wrong better or worse, the deed is done until the end. The priest knew that the credit belongs to the man who is already in the arena but thought to himself, " Nothing like appealing to the ego".

This time everyone stayed over after the meeting. They just couldn't stop talking and exchanging ideas. The possibilities were endless. Mr. Batiste moved among them and offered his expertise at money management but Father Andrico quickly responded by openly thanking him and letting him know that both groups could manage on their own, after all, Cajuns are smart enough to have come this far without much help. The men just about burst with pride at overhearing the conversation. Everyone left but nobody got much sleep that night.

Father Andrico decided to back off and let the people lead the way. He had planted the seed and it needed to grow. Grow it did. The ladies grew snooty and uppity and the men became more powerful and boastful. The more power they felt they had the more corrupt they became, the more corrupt they became the more power they had, the devil was in.

Father Andrico's plan was beginning to work. Families had no more quality time for their children. They saw to it that they were fed, clothed and washed but there was no time for a hug; no time to listen. Planning for the fair came first. They were always hurrying to one meeting or another. All the children ever heard was," later, not now, later, I'm busy". The Altar Boys became more friendly and open with the priest. Father Andrico became the best. He was everything they thought their parents weren't. They loved him and did anything he asked of them without question.

Turns out that members of both groups came up with some pretty good ideas of their own. They set May first, as the official date of the church fair, if successful it would hopefully become an annual event. Six month would be just about right for the planning and preparation. The men decided that each Saturday of their scheduled meeting they would have a gumbo cook off during the day and accept donations for every bowl handed out. All proceeds would be deposited by the treasurer in a special account and when the time came the funds would help kick start the fair. Ladies decided they would have a quilting party at their meetings and donate the quilt to the Founding Fathers so that they could auction it at the cook off. They also wanted to set up a table of cakes and pies outside on the church lawn after every

Sunday Mass. The proceeds from their cake sale would likewise be deposited in the special account.

Father Andrico saw the town come alive with excitement and happiness. He began to feel a little guilty because his plan was really an evil one about his own greed for money but he didn't feel guilty enough. All he could envision was having so much money hidden away that it caused the Holy Water stand to rise up, up towards the gates of heaven, which would never open to him because a tiny part of him had become the devil's disciple. He decided to live in the moment and face the music later.

Father Andrico knew that Mr. Batiste was watching his every move so he would exercise a little self-control and not steal any money from the special account. What could the banker say? Nothing, nothing, nothing because to voice any objection would open a very large can of worms. Father had already thought of a story he could use if Batiste suddenly felt a need to feed his own greed from the special account and try to blame Father. Father would act all pitiful and claim he was being blackmailed by Batiste who threatened to tell church members lies about father ravaging a child if he told that Batiste stole from the special account. Father would say that since he was new here and for a time was selfish and not liked, he was afraid the people would believe the honorable banker. There was no way to prove who was telling the truth because nobody knew where Father came from. Little lie, big lie what's the difference. That story would work if push came to shove.

The old fashioned word of mouth proved to be the best and fastest way to spread the news about the fair. Homemade flyers were posted and distributed any way possible, even by pirogue. The success of the event depended on reaching as many people as possible.

After Sunday Mass the Altar Boys were kidding around as they changed from their black robes into their own clothes. They spoke of the fun they always had when they camped out. Father Andrico told them he had never been camping especially not in the swampy bayous. The boys laughed and asked," Wanna come froggin?" Father replied, "What? Froggin." The more the boys laughed, the more appealing it sounded to the priest, after all he was a boy once himself, so very long ago. Father replied, "I'm game." The boys laughed even harder, so hard in fact that Father became a little frightened and wondered what he was in for because everyone shook hands after settling on a day, time and place. These Cajun handshakes are taken seriously and usually mean you are in something or other to the death, but did this apply to deals made by little Cajuns as well? Done is done so next Friday night he was to experience a different type of baptism this one was Cajun style.

   Fear of the unknown had just about exhausted Father Andrico by the time Friday night finally arrived. There was no backing out because of one of those handshakes. They all met at the Banker Ferry near the old oak tree where many Cajuns were hanged for poaching. It was a good thing father wore his long robes because the boys couldn't see his knees knocking together as midnight approached. Why midnight, Father asked himself as he looked around and saw several pirogues docking along the bayou. Apparently his boys had invited others as witnesses to the baptism. One thing he had not counted on was meeting the grand daddy himself, the legendary Cajun Al. He had heard many stories about this survivor of the bayou swamp, mostly good ones, but some bad. None seemed to have been exaggerated. His commanding presence said it all. Finally Father met a Cajun he truly wanted to get to know better. Immediately Father feared him and respected him all at the same time. The boys said he was the best and taught them about surviving out here. The rule was that before the boys could take fresh meat out on a kill they had to meet at the Banker Ferry near the old oak tree so that Cajun Al would know who he was looking for if he didn't come back. They all stood up and gave one of those long Cajun yells then hollered, "let's go!"

   You could have sworn Father was a wooden statue the way he sat so still grasping his seat holding on for dear life. Good thing the boys couldn't read minds because they would have known how hard and fast he was praying for forgiveness. He knew that the lord knew all about him and he wondered if now was the time to face the music. He didn't like being referred to as fresh meat. Suddenly the sounds of bayou life snapped him out of it and he again became aware of his surroundings. He sure could use a cup of good, hot, dark coffee right about now to calm him down. They paddled on as the boys continued to whisper back and forth amongst themselves. Everything was dark, so dark that the moss hanging from the mighty oak trees looked like shadow arms hanging down ready to grab someone and keep them forever. Did the strength of the oak come from dead Cajuns? The noises from the bayou swamp were quiet but at the same time loud. They were creepy, scary sounds and Father didn't know if some kind of animal was warning them to get out and stay away from here or else.

 One of the boys said to pull over, right here was good. Father nervously said, " Good for what? I can't see anything. How do you even know there is land right here? I can't even see the boy sitting in front of me." One of the boys said, "That's because there is no boy sitting in front of you." Father wet his pants but said nothing, he couldn't, he was too scared. They helped Father onto the bank and respectfully told him that priestly robes are not made for froggin. They had borrowed a pants and shirt from one of their parents who was about the same size and it would be a good idea if he changed into them. Father agreed and was grateful for this small miracle saying nothing about his accident.

 It was back in the pirogues for God knows what. They lit a lantern and told Father to keep quiet and hold the lantern high and in front of him as they paddled along. Suddenly they saw a pair of little beady eyes staring back at them, not moving. The pirogue got closer and closer but the beady eyes didn't move. One of the boys told Father to hold steady. All of a sudden the boy in front lunged forward towards the bank grabbing the beady eyes before he could hop away and placed him in a gunnysack. They did this over and over until they felt they had enough frogs to cook for supper. The light seems to cast a spell over the big frog as it shines in his eyes because for a little while he doesn't move. Father feared he had just participated in one of those Voodoo things?

    They paddled back to their good spot to set up camp. Father never could figure out how they knew where the good spot was but they went right to it because there was Fathers robe, right where he had left it. They set up camp then Father watched as they skinned and cooked the frogs. Father didn't know if he was scared or just surprised as the dead frog jumped a little when it was in the frying pan. At last it was time to eat and prayers were said. The boys had made a very good drink from a wild root, and one had brought some homemade bread. Father smacked his lips and commented on how fried frog legs taste much like fried chicken. As they all sat around the campfire relaxing and telling stories Father realized how good these young people were. They got along so well together. Not one time since their adventure began did anyone of them get angry, or bossy, or mean. They worked as a team, the older ones taught and protected the younger ones while all watched out for each other. Their parents were doing an excellent job at raising these children. One of the boys asked if Father Andy had a story to tell. Father suddenly had a lump in his throat. He told them what he had observed on this trip and how they were the product of good parenting and that their parents love them very much and depend on them to try and do the right things in their lives. Right now their parents are setting a good example of the importance of helping others. They are working so hard on the fair project because the orphans have nobody else and that he was very proud of his boys for sharing their parents for a brief time. They all yelled, "For the orphans" and became teary eyed.

    Father Andy began to feel brave, so he asked what's next. They looked at each other, began to laugh and asked Father if he had ever hunted gators. Fathers bravery left his body like a bird in flight and he began to sound like an old owl as he said "who, who me". The boys told Father it was easy and fun. They told him that the alligators are hiding and he should stay here, they would look around and be right back for him and the pirogues. The boys had been gone about half an hour when they began to hear thrashing, sloshing sounds coming towards them. They hid behind the trees on the levee and waited. In the moonlight they watched as Father Andy struggled up and down a couple of small levees and through some marshy swampland pulling the pirogues behind him in search of the boys. He told the boys he did not want to be the bait for any swamp animal so he decided to follow them because Cajun Al had not yet taught him anything. They all had a good laugh, put the pirogues in the water and the hunt began. This time one of the boys held the lantern as they searched the water for eyes attached to a big head with a long mouth. Suddenly Father Andy exclaimed in an excited whisper, "I see one, I see one, hold steady."

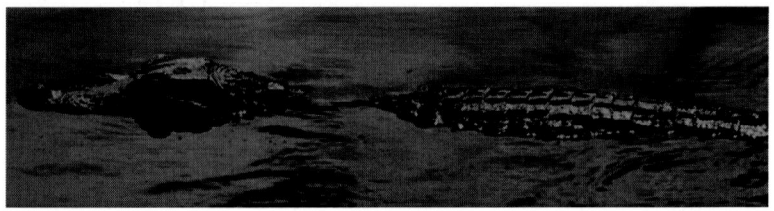

Before anyone could blink an eye Father jumped in the water right on top of the alligator that immediately rolled over and over as father held on for dear life. Finally the gator got tired and the boys did their best to place a rope around his mouth and body. They helped Father into the pirogue then paddled their way back to land dragging the gator behind them. Everyone just lay on the bank staring at the stars. Not only were they worn out but they couldn't believe what had just happened. One of them got up and killed the alligator then looked at Father straight in the eye still in disbelief. All Father could say was, "What? What? We hunted an alligator and I got one. You got the frogs and I got the gator". The boys began to laugh. The more they thought about it the more they laughed until they cried. Finally they explained to Father that the swampy bayous of Louisiana are good hunting grounds. Some things you hunt can hurt you and some can't so Cajuns hunt different things in different ways. You don't hunt a frog and a gator in the same way. The frog doesn't bite but the gator is a man-eater. Cajun Al says you must not fear any animal but you have to protect yourself and know what you're doing. Father Andy fainted and when he came to he almost fainted again. After about half an hour Father was able to talk about the incident and laugh right along with his boys. He even helped skin the gator, forgetting that before his Cajun Baptism he fainted at the sight of blood. Their original plan was to go froggin once more before heading home so they could have a good surprise for their parents but everyone was so tired that they just headed in. This tall tale with the living proof to go with it was good enough.

Father Andrico made it home safe and sound thanks to his boys. He sat by the fireplace, drank a cup of hot coffee and reflected on his adventure. When the boys called him Father Andy it was as though God won this battle with the devil. There was no way that Father Andrico would ever break the trust the parents placed in him. God sure works in mysterious ways. This adventure awakened the good priest and put the bad priest to rest. The shadow arms of the mighty oaks had a purpose after all; they took one and left the other. No longer was he haunted by the thought of Jesus on the cross with blood flowing from his body. Father Andrico was finally a happy, peaceful person who saw everything with fresh eyes. He was the man he use to be, the one who became a priest for all the right reasons. He was a traveling man who came full circle only to meet himself.

Sunday sermon was over and Father Andrico said that he was sure that everyone heard the camping story about how Father Andrico became a true Cajun know as Father Andy, Gator Hunter. Everyone laughed including Father. He said it was an honor to meet Cajun Al, pass the test and be baptized a true Cajun. Father asked the Altar Boys to look under the Holy Water stand and bring him what they found. They told Father there was nothing there. Father said there should be a sack of money. It was yours, every penny of it. It was a little emergency fund I set aside from the collection plate each

Sunday. What could have happened to it? Please forgive me for keeping this secret. I thought it was a good idea at the time. Maybe the Sheriff can find out what happened. Who would have stolen from a church?

Monday morning Father Andy and one of the Founding Fathers went to the bank and made the church deposit. Mr. Batiste was not happy. He asked to speak with Father Andy in private. He told Father he heard what he said at Mass and asked if he had lost his mind. Father told him that he had dealt with his sin and his conscience is clear. They were eye to eye when Father told Mr. Batiste there would be no more weekly blessings. It was up to Mr. Batiste to do what he felt he needed to do and that Father was not in the business of telling tales about anyone so Mr. Batiste would have to wrestle with his own demons.

Cajuns organized their leadership out of necessity when they first settled Erath, but Father Andrico was the one who introduced elections on a lower scale. He had slyly allowed the simple, everyday hard workingman to experience the feeling of being a shepherd who rules the flock. This started a fierce, jealous competition to hold any official position. Education of townspeople created a new breed of trapper, a political animal known as a POLITICIAN. Because of his ability to deal with people and accomplish things for the good of all concerned the politician created an organized system of government for the growing community. Although contemptuous, without principles and always scheming without regard for what is right he became a necessary evil. He used political issues for some gain or advantage in the town's interest but never lost sight of what was in it for him. The utmost thought in his mind was how could he profit and move forward. It didn't bother him a bit to lie, cheat or steal to get what he wanted. Swatting any opposing mosquito was no problem.

Some Cajuns were wise enough to surround themselves with people who excelled at certain tasks thereby making them look good, this way they had all bragging rights and came out ahead of the game. Group meetings began to generate a lot of confidence in one wise Cajun or another. Before the Fair rolled around several people decided they could do a better job at being mayor or sheriff so they decided the people would have to vote and elect the best man for each job. An election of five city councilmen would help assure a fair and balanced system of government in the best interest of the citizens. This Erath Church Fair was turning into a huge event. Not only would there be fun and games but an election as well. There wasn't much time left so the politicians had to work hard at selling themselves to the voting public. It seems that every night there was a free supper, or free drinks at the bar along with free political speeches. Candidates helped ladies across the street, they kissed babies, shook hands, and did everything they could think of to sell themselves and win a vote or buy one. It turned into the dirtiest, mud slinging, lying, and tale telling campaign imaginable. It got so that when anyone saw a candidate coming their way they crossed the street to try and avoid having to listen to him. People just couldn't take it any more.

Finally the weekend of the Fair was here and everything was ready. All the booths were in place and set up for sales. The Grand Stand was in front of the Church and was very impressive. Father Andy had told everyone how it was done in large cities so the Founding Fathers Association really did a good job at putting everything together. There were City Officials, Politicians, a Band, Booths, Games, Contests and an election of the very first Founders Day Queen. Everything was going smoothly but since politics was in the mix anything could happen and it did.

Some sly candidates devised a plan whereby they either paid people to vote or they would kidnap them, bring them to a secret spot in the marsh, put them in a well guarded bull pen, get them drunk then bring them back to town to vote the way the kidnappers wanted them to or in some cases if they could not be convinced to vote accordingly they did not let them vote at all. Just as the best horse doesn't always win the race, well the best qualified doesn't always win in politics.

That weekend Fair would never be forgotten by anybody, young and old alike. It was the talk of the Parish for a very long time. The church made a great deal of money and would donate a sizeable sum to the Orphans Fund. The Ladies Cajun Cultural Society members became more uppity and were trying to forget their humble beginnings. The Founding Fathers Association could pat themselves on the back for the rest of their lives because being first at anything was very important to a Cajun man; it's a pride thing you know. The young queen was proud and happy. All the children couldn't wait for next years fair. The angry politicians who lost remained angry, not much happiness there. The winner soon learned what he had won, and didn't even know what the word happiness meant anymore. The people wasted no time in wanting rules to apply to everyone else and not to them and they constantly reminded him, "You owe me, I put you in office." He remembered how his Mom use to tell him, "Be careful of what you ask for son, because you might get it".

The festivities ended but the political tool was still available, free food and drinks at the local bars. The door was wide open and all Satin's disciples had to do was yell, "come and get it." Satan himself then walked in because politics was too big a game for his disciples. Cajuns had not yet learned that the word, "FREE" was created and used by Satan when he goes fishing. The word is his bait and people are the fish.

The Political Cajun became passionate about his politics. There is just something about the power of it that creates a crazy, greedy, sneaky, liar, womanizing, thief. The political animal is weak but appears strong to supporters. His weakness is what makes him so dangerous because he wants what he wants and will do anything to get it. Gone are the days of the traditional, honorable handshake. No longer will the phrase, "My word is my bond" mean anything.

Crooked politics had encouraged prostitution and many forms of gambling. Too many free drinks had caused some Cajuns to over load their mouths by betting heavily on anything. Their losses and anger helped to awaken more weakness, a false sense that one more bet would put the

Cajun ahead of his game. Naturally it rarely did and heavier losses allowed him to be controlled. Soon you couldn't tell the good guy from the bad guy. Anger made people think differently and thinking is just what a group known as the good old boys did not want people to do. They had gotten use to doing all the thinking for everybody. Politics had created a bigger hungrier dog and they weren't about to let anybody else come in and do any barking. Erath was a comfortable old shoe that would remain just that, comfortable.

    Mr. Batiste was the grand daddy of this group. He was the master trapper before it was politically correct to be a good old boy. Long before the Fair got started he had called a meeting of the good old boy network and together plans were made to assure the election of the candidate they could best control. Mr. Batiste sent a man called Frenchie to the church to steal the savings under the Holy Water stand then use it to buy votes. Frenchie wasn't the man for this job, once a thief always a thief. He stole the money from the church but decided to keep it for himself thinking nobody would find out. Later he would take his pirogue and leave the parish. Frenchie should have remembered that there are no secrets in Erath, everybody finds out everything. Every person in the Parish knows that whatever money is stolen here stays here no matter who is the last one to have it. Some of the good old boys saw to it that Frenchie became a floater, no questions asked.

    After the Fair on Sunday night, Father Andy was left in the church with all of the money. He would meet with the Founding Fathers Association early Monday morning to make bank deposits for the church and the orphans fund. Father Andy was alone and the more he touched, smelled, counted and looked at the money the stronger the temptation to keep it. The devil was back or maybe he had never left. Just think, there was nobody around, not Batiste, not the Association, nobody. He could leave right now and nobody would find him. This money could afford him the luxuries of fine living: good wines, fancy clothes, the best restaurants, etc. He looked around at his living quarters and decided, "I'm out of here." He packed his satchel with clothes and money then went to the bayou to steal a pirogue and paddle towards the Banker Ferry. Father Andy suddenly thought, "Banker Ferry, my adventure, my boys. Father Cornez Andrico could do this but not Father Andy." Father went back to the Church and hid the money under the Altar until the next morning. He prayed and thanked God for being there when he needed him in this moment of great weakness.

Monday afternoon Father Andy and his boys were sitting on the edge of the bayou fishing and relaxing. Father told them that he knew Cajuns have many old sayings and he would like to know a few of them now that he is really one of them. One of the boys said, "Well Father Andy did you know that if a Cajun sits along the bayou long enough he will see the body of his enemy float by." Father was surprised to suddenly see Frenchie the thief floating along as the current pushed him on his way out of the parish. The boy told Father Andy he was wise not to listen when the devil said, " Take the money and leave, go on. Do it!"

A Cajun Miss

Generally when people think of Cajun hardships of the past, they first think of strong men sometimes wearing buckskins maybe a coonskin cap carrying a rifle and forging across an unyielding, swampy, woodsy country enduring much misery and hardship in search of a better life. Women and children would seem to tag along. More often than not they are just an after thought. But think about it. Maybe not all women were happily married. Maybe not all women were lucky enough to have a good, kind, strong person who provided a shoulder to cry on, or arms around them where they could feel safe and secure during a time of crisis. Maybe life itself was the trapper. One such Cajun female was Marlie.

She loved her Father Mr. Batiste, mean or not, and respected his every wish. He was over bearing and would not tolerate any mistakes. He did not accept the fact that youth is about making some mistakes as you find your way in life. Mrs. Batiste tried to help Marlie have good self-esteem and prayed that her spirit would not be broken no matter what life had in store for her.

Marlie was a very friendly and happy person like her mother use to be, not at all like her banker father. She loved life and looked upon it as wonderful. She always looked on the bright side of things and was not easily discouraged. She was tall, slim, had long dark hair, blue eyes, fair skin and a lovely smile. The thing she loved most was dancing because she figured you had to be happy if you were dancing. She would laugh and often ask, " Can you dance when you are angry about something, can you? I don't think so. "

As usual, females are always jealous of the prettiest girl in town. Sometimes this unfounded evil jealousy takes on a life of its own much like a curse and very sad things begin to happen to an undeserving person.

Marlie was very popular with the young men in town. Not just because she was pretty but because she was fun to be with and never wined or complained and never had an unkind word to say about anybody She dressed, spoke and behaved like a lady but she didn't mind getting dirty, going fishing, whitewashing the fence, riding horses in the rain or picking beans in the field. She just loved everything life had to offer and believed that if you did something, do it well. Your best is all you can ask of yourself no matter what anyone else thinks. After all, what is work; it's just the results of living.

One young man in particular caught Marlie's eye. Not only was he tall, dark and handsome but he also loved to dance. They met at one of the house parties families took turns hosting on Saturday nights. They talked and learned a lot about each other. She soon realized she loved him. She loved his eyes, his hair, and the sound of his voice. When they danced he held her close, so close that she could feel his heart beat. As most young girls in love, she couldn't sleep at night just thinking about him. Everything about him was wonderfully exciting.

One Saturday night while they were dancing he told her he joined the army and would not be here next Saturday. Her heart was broken and she began to cry. They became closer than ever that night; they became as one and as they parted

Marlie vowed to write to him every day. Sadly Marlie came to realize that she was the only one who had made that promise.

All too soon Marlie realized that she was pregnant and was more afraid of telling her father than telling the baby's father. She put the news off as long as she could but babies have a way of making their presence known so she finally had to speak up. She spoke with her mother first. They both began to cry. Marlie knew that her mother had no voice in her own home because she was so afraid of Mr. Batiste. Her father became outraged at the news. He would not listen to her and did not want to know who the father was. He threw her out and never wanted to see her again. He felt she ruined his good name and was a disgrace to the family.

Marlie cried for a while then wondered what to do. Finally she remembered this pretty lady with red hair and a kind face that she had seen at her father's bank. She was always nice and well dressed. Other ladies in town were always mean to her and whispered under their breath when she walked by. Maybe this person could help or give her some advice.

Marlie made her way from house to house and knocked on many doors. Finally the same lady she had seen in the bank answered and invited Marlie in because she was crying so much. They went to the kitchen for a glass of lemonade and Marlie explained her problem. The lady said her name was Solitaire and that Marlie was not to worry about anything. She could stay there and they would talk more in the morning. Marlie began to cry again because she felt so relieved.

In the morning Solitaire and Marlie came to an agreement. Marlie could live there as long as she and the baby wanted to. Marlie would clean and cook in exchange for room and board. The plan was a good one but it was a bit of a shock when Marlie learned why so many men were always coming and going from the house at all hours.

Finally the baby was born. It was a boy. He was healthy and had dark hair just like his father. Marlie wrote telling him the good news but he never replied. The truth of the matter was he never did write. Marlie had no choice but to continue living in Solitaire's house. All she did was cook and clean as agreed but men were constantly trying to get her attention for the wrong reasons and she didn't like it. One day she was rejecting an indecent proposal when she saw Mr. Batiste leaving one of the bedrooms with a silly little grin on his face. Marlie never told anyone what she had seen but the painful memory would forever haunt her causing her many sleepless nights.

   A few years went by and she suddenly had an unannounced visitor. The baby's father had returned from the army and was standing on her porch. He looked more handsome than ever and her heart pounded just as it did the first time she saw him. Marlie dared hope he had come to ask her forgiveness for not writing and for her hand in marriage so that they could live happily ever after. She noticed he seemed sheepish and kept his head down gazing at the floor. Finally he told her that her dad had ruined his family farm and his family refused to allow him to marry her. Besides he did not want to start married life with a woman who had a child. He never asked to see his son but did give her his marksman medal to give to him. He walked away and never came back.

   Marlie was very heartbroken and had no dreams left. Her mother had died of worry and loneliness, her dad was unforgiving, selfish and evil and her child had no father. Marlie prayed that her mother never found out that her father was a womanizer on top of everything else. She had managed to save a little money and told Solitaire it was time to move on. Between her disappointment in her love life and the fear of meeting up with her father and having to deal with the embarrassment to him and to herself she felt she just had to leave. She thanked her friend for everything and she and her son moved to the country where she rented a very small two-room shack with an outhouse in the back yard. This was all she hoped to be able to afford. She took in ironing, mended clothes and canned fruits and vegetables for others. Taking in wash was the hardest job of all because she had to haul water from a well, dump it in a tub and use a scrub board to wash away the dirt and grime, rinse the clothes, wring them out by hand and hang them on the line to dry. Hauling water for bathing and washing dishes was also a necessary miserable task but there was no way around it. She took any respectable job she could think of to make ends meet.

One day she decided it was time for a break so she hugged her son and told him tonight they would go out and have some fun. He would have lots of children to play with and there would be music and dancing. They put on their best clothes and walked a couple of miles down the road to Taunt Ness's house. It was her turn to host the dance this weekend. When they arrived Marlie was so happy and excited that she did not notice how many men stared at her. She was still very beautiful so she still got the evil eye from every jealous female in the place who had expected she had turned into a hag by now. Needless to say they were very disappointed.

Her son finally met a few boys he could make friends with and Marlie made a few friends of her own. She danced and laughed all night. There was one short, olive complected, dark haired man who was a little older but a better dancer that the rest and he knew it because he couldn't resist showing off. He asked Marlie to dance but before taking a step he placed a full glass of water on his head and they danced until the music stopped. He then removed the glass and drank the water, he had not spilled a drop, and everyone smiled and clapped. The musicians took a break while the dancers went to the refreshment table.

During a little polite conversation Marlie learned that her dance partners name was Sanchez and he was what was known as a treater, a person who mysteriously possesses a gift for caring for sick people. He specialized in treating people who contracted typhoid fever. Sometimes he made use of the secret herbs he kept in a pouch that hung from his neck and other times he used hands on approach without uttering one single word. Strangely enough he never caught any illness himself. He looked around the room and saw the jealous females still gossiping as they tried to pretend they weren't by using their fans to hide their mouths. He told Marlie they were probably talking about him because he was of Spanish blood and had olive skin. Their mothers would not allow them to dance with him because they thought he was a black runaway slave. Marlie laughed and told him they were probably talking about her because she was an unwed mother and they didn't know who the father was. They both laughed as they walked outside and made those gossiping tongues wag even more. They talked a little longer but it was time to go home so they said goodbye.

A few days later Sanchez came calling on Marlie. He brought her some flowers and sweets for her son. The boy had never tasted cherry striped stick candy before and he was very excited to have a treat. Marlie invited him to supper after which they sat on the porch swing and quietly gazed up at the moon. Soon it was time to leave and they again said goodbye. After Sanchez left her son wanted to know why the man talked funny? Why didn't he open his mouth to talk? Why did he keep his teeth closed so tight? Marlie said she didn't know and it wasn't polite to ask such questions, although she had asked herself the same thing.

Marlie continued to work harder and harder as living seemed to be a never-ending struggle. Sanchez had become a regular visitor almost as though he were a man with a mission. Finally he told Marlie that if she allowed him to move in with her life would be easier, no strings attached. He could keep the place up, help with chores and teach the boy many things a man should know by the time he is full grown. Marlie did not like the idea but said she would think about it. She was a little afraid to be direct and tell him no because she sensed he seemed to have anger management problems. Each time Marlie's reply to any subject was not in complete agreement with his, he resorted to clenching his jaw. Surely if he continued this bad habit one day he would no longer be able to open his mouth to eat. They again said goodbye.

She was over worked and worried all the time. The winter season had begun and washing clothes was a much harder task because she had to chop extra wood for a fire to heat up the wash water. This necessary chore added to the extreme fatigue and she became very sick.

Sanchez heard about her illness from the town gossips that considered themselves good, Christian women but they wouldn't lend a hand. He moved in and cared for her but when she got better he didn't leave. Marlie didn't want him there, she was afraid of him but she couldn't ask him to leave because she felt indebted to him. He stayed and things were a little better at first but he finally demanded sex and when she refused he raped her, mission accomplished. He said he could take what he wanted because there was nobody around who cared enough to stop him. The sad thing was that he was right, there was no one. Sanchez became an added burden rather than any kind of help. Marlie continued to work very hard. Over time they had three children together, two boys and a girl.

As any good mother would, Marlie always managed to set misery aside and give her children her attention. They sang songs and she taught them to find happiness in just being alive. Time and love were all she had to give. The boys liked fishing so most Sunday afternoons she went with them to their favorite spot along the bayou. As they waited for a nibble on their line she would make up stories about fishermen or magic fish and she would educate them as best she could about plants, animals, and nature.

The girl liked to play with the rag doll Marlie had made for her but she mostly liked cloud games. After lunch on Saturday afternoons when the weather was clear the family would lay under a tree, look up towards the sky and say what shape the clouds had. One of the children said that the clouds looked like a soft, white piece of cotton that could maybe take all of them to a place where their mom didn't have to work so hard.

On a clear night they gazed at the stars and asked questions. Marlie told them stories about baby Jesus and the North Star, about how men used the stars to guide them even while they were at sea. She told them that they should each pick a special star, make a secret wish and if they were good, kind and always loved each other their wish would one day come true and they would be so happy they would dance.

  Sanchez continued to care for sick people and when he was called upon to take care of someone, he would move in with the family and stay until the person was well. Sometimes he was gone for two months at a time. Marlie wasn't really sure where he was, what he was doing or who he was with. When he did come home to hang his hat he brought no money or food. All he did was talk about the good times he had for a few days at all of those houses due to the gratitude of the families. They played cards, had gumbo, pork roast, rice dressing, pies etc. Marlie looked at him with disgust saying, " How dare you tell us those stories when your children are starving." He simply looked her in the eye and smiled a little devil doesn't care smirk then went to bed. The next morning before leaving he decided to tell Marlie the whole truth. He said that he was in search of a treasure map he had stolen from some privateers a very long time ago. They had captured a beautiful Spanish woman and kept her as a slave. One night he pretended to be gentleman pirate Jean Lafitte in order to quietly have his way with her. They danced, laughed and romanced slightly but the ship was about to be attacked so he gave her the map to hide in any oak tree along the bayou near the sight of the battle. His plan was to try and find her or the oak tree later if he survived. It became too risky to be a privateer so he had to think of some other means of survival. Knowing that for some unknown reason he never got sick no matter what illness he encountered he decided to use this to his advantage. He flattered many an old Cajun to learn the healing powers of herbs, dog grass, plants, mud and voodoo. He then made himself mysterious by helping the gossipers spread stories as to where he came from. That's how he became a foundling on somebody's doorstep. The only reason he became a treater was to have free food, a place to stay, some fun and maybe through some gossip learn the whereabouts of Sara Fina or the map. He was able to search many an oak tree himself along the way. Now you know. He took a deep breath, turned and walked out the door.

One day while accepting the wash of a new customer who was a real chatterbox Marlie learned that Sanchez was a married man and had a few children. The chatterbox did not know that he lived with Marlie. Much to Marlie's surprise he was married when she first danced with him a lifetime ago and he never told her. It seems that in the past he did his little hit and run act with other unsuspecting, wanting women leaving them to rot or survive, it made no difference to him. All he wanted was a free ride. He didn't care who paid for it.

Marlie's first-born son although not yet full-grown moved out and went to work for a farmer who provided room and board. This helped the family because not only was there one less mouth to feed but the farmer allowed him to milk the cows and bring some of the milk to his family. Marlie learned how to make butter from the cream. The children really enjoyed homemade bread and fresh butter. The farmer also gave him empty flour sacks, which were made of cotton because he knew Marlie could make clothes for her children. How happy and excited they were to have new clothes no matter where they came from.

They were crowded in this two-room house but at least they had a roof over their heads. Marlie had so much to worry about that she forgot that the rent was due. The landlord arrived and gave her another week to come up with the money. All too soon time was up and she didn't have it. The landlord who was married, gazed towards the bedroom and offered to accept payment in trade provided she kept her mouth shut. Marlie looked at her children, began to cry and accepted his offer. This evil trapper would never go away because there would always be rent to pay and never any money to pay it with.

One day while Marlie was trying to haul water to wash the dishes she heard a familiar voice say, "I'm back." Marlie told Sanchez to go away but he didn't, he felt he didn't have to because there was no one to make him leave. Marlie thought how childish he sounded. He told her, "Let's go. I'm in a hurry." Marlie said no and began to cry but this didn't stop him from having his way with her. When the evil deed was done he smiled and told her he would not be coming back. She wasn't pretty enough anymore and smelled like dirty clothes. Marlie was saddened by the remarks but she couldn't cry anymore. She cleaned herself up and went back to washing the dishes as though she were lifeless, just a trapped human who knows the daily routine.

Marlie again became pregnant and gave birth to a baby girl. At this point she didn't know who the father was, Sanchez or the landlord. She never seemed to regain her strength and there after was always in a weakened state.

Her older son came home more often for a visit and would bathe the children and help as best he could. On one of his visits he brought food and canned milk and a little bag of sugar. He said there was a government program that handed out stamps to the poor. The stamps had to be used to buy food and he would try and get his friend to bring her some more. He told Marlie he also had bad news. His boss was loaning him out to another farmer who lived farther away and it was too far to walk so he didn't know when he would be back to help her. She gave him a hug, thanked him for everything and told him she would always love him.

As time went on Marlie felt worse but had no money to see a doctor so she walked to the home of an old woman who sort of practiced voodoo. She didn't cast spells but she did read tealeaves and tarot cards. She told Marlie that the problem lies in her mattress. There are evil, jealous women who are trying to hurt you. Marlie went home and found a live chicken lying in the dirt bleeding but it had no visible wounds. The chicken did not move until Marlie touched it then it walked about the yard as though nothing had ever happened. Marlie frantically prayed hoping to cast out the evil spell if there really was one. She went inside and opened her mattress that was stuffed with tree moss and found a piece of black cloth sewn in the shape of a cat doll and a dried corn cob stuffed with something that looked like crystals. She remembered that the women in town wore black clothes when mourning their dead. They seemed to wear it forever because just when the period of mourning was over somebody else in the family died and it started all over again. She removed the items and sewed her mattress back together. Marlie asked herself why were people being so cruel? She had nothing to be jealous of. Were they trying to make her pay for the sins of her Father? Why didn't someone help her instead of wasting all of this energy to do evil?

After a little rest Marlie went outside to get the wash off the clothesline. She noticed several nails bent in the center, crossing each other and stuck in the dirt at the yard gate as though to warn people to stay away. She removed the nails and thought to herself, "Why try to keep people away? What have my children done to deserve this treatment?"

The two boys moved out and got jobs for room and board with an elderly couple in the next town. They were very young but there was no real choice to be made. They did what they had to do. Things weren't so good there because they were beaten every now and then but at least they weren't hungry and had a warm place to sleep. The older of the two girls went to school every weekday. An elderly farmer used his wagon to transport poor country kids to school and back again because he believed education was so very important. She had at least one good meal thanks to a little school friend of hers who shared her lunch. Marlie added a lot of water to some canned milk before pouring it on some cornbread to feed the younger girl. Marlie added a little sugar in her glass of water for her meal. The children came first and Marlie did anything she could to make any food last.

Sadly, life's misfortunes took a toll on Marlie and she seemed to have suffered a stroke. She became crippled on one side of her body and fell to the floor splitting her head open. The youngest daughter got a cloth and held it on the wound until it stopped bleeding. Finally Marlie was able to get into bed and waited for the other daughter to come home from school. She was also little but maybe she could go for help, which she did but help never came. Marlie got better and had no choice but to approach a field hand working nearby with a proposition. He was to tell the other field hands that they could share her bed any time if they brought food to feed her children. They continued to struggle but just like the rent, food was no longer a problem. All Marlie could do was pray that God's will be done.

A Cajun Barber

Mr. Asa Ifanee was born and lived in Philadelphia. He was a quiet, young, single man that liked to read a lot, partly because he had no friends but mostly because in his mind he could secretly live any adventure he chose. His heroes were strong, rugged men who knew no fear and braved the elements in search of something, anything, they didn't know what but they would know it when they found it. He read many books about the Cajun Man and thought," This is as good as it gets." He was, up until now only a dreamer, a Cajun-wana-be with that Cajun yell playing over and over in his mind. It seemed to warn others that something fun, daring and exciting was about to take place.

Suddenly he decided no more dreaming, he would move to Louisiana, the heart of Cajun land, live among these rough and tough men and hear their stories first hand. Maybe if he walked the same path the trail would lead him to a new life and some of this ruggedness would rub off on him. His only personal strength was gathered by referring to himself as me, myself and I when faced with a major decision, that way he felt he was never alone.

Before embarking on this new life he had to decide how he would earn a living. What service could he provide these people that they really needed and would be willing to pay for, after all, he was nothing like them. He couldn't fight, brave the elements, and live off the land. He wanted to be like that but he didn't know how. While deep in thought he began grooming himself in preparation to go out to dinner. He looked in the mirror as he combed his hair and suddenly exclaimed, "That's it. I am now a barber." How difficult could this be? You simply have a man sit in a chair, grab a pair of scissors and cut. Surely these rugged men need a little grooming when they exit the swampy bayous before they seek a little tenderness. They are suppose to be part human after all.

That very next morning Asa purchased two pairs of scissors, a few combs, shaving equipment and a drape cloth.

He didn't buy a mirror. Suppose he did a bad job on his first customer. The thought of an angry Cajun man giving that yell after seeing his reflection while sporting a bad hair cut was too scary. Oh well, success or failure, either was worth the gamble. He packed his bags and without hesitation off he went with that Cajun yell still ringing in his ears. He was determined to become a Cajun Man, at least in spirit.

The trip was a long, miserable one and Asa was so tired that he made the decision to rest in a little place called Erath. He didn't know that this was just about as far south as he could go. He also didn't know that once the first swarm of mosquitoes bit him the magic spell of Cajun bayou land was cast and he now had the rage. It causes the inner being to take hold. There would no longer be a need to think in terms of me, myself and I.

His intention was to explore the whole area before making up his mind where he would settle, but he figured this was good enough. Asa asked the first man he met where was the nearest hotel. The man laughed and said, "A what?" Asa said, "You know, a place where you rent a room with a bed to sleep in." The man replied," We ant got no hotel. There's a tough, little old woman who runs a room and board just down the street, talk to her." Asa managed to find the place and met the owner, Jo-Jo. By appearance she was just as described but after talking to her a few minutes you knew you might have a friend for life. That rough and tough business was only for self-preservation, a kind of protection from the trappers of the world. She said meals were served on time and if you were late you had to grab what you could from the kitchen if there was any left. The rent was reasonable and due the first of every month. Asa unpacked, freshened up and decided to take a walk around town. The more he walked, the more relaxed he became. By the time he reached the West end of town he felt like maybe he really belonged here. People smiled and greeted him all along the way. He stood around with his hands in his pockets, looking up at the sky then down at the dirt. He turned around now facing East, took a deep breath, raised his head and saw a rundown old shack on the South side of the street. It appeared to be unoccupied. With a little effort it could be fixed up and would suit him just fine. From what he could see the town did not have a barber, he would be the first one and being first just had to mean something around here.

Asa being a city boy had a few lessons to learn. The first one was sleeping late just doesn't happen. A very large rooster crows every morning at sunrise, he is the regulator. He begins his loud unforgiving noise the minute the sun shows over the horizon and no matter how many boots, shoes, frying pans or anything else you throw at him, he does not stop until full sunrise.

There is something to be said about the old saying that the early bird gets the worm. Thanks to the regulator Asa had more daylight time to locate the owners, buy the place and fix it up a little. His barber chair was plain, made of hard wood with a seat covered in cowhide. As he admired his chair he heard the sound of a slight noise come from his throat, not a yell mind you, just a little something. The decision to use the chair inside or outside would be left entirely to the customer. He had a washbasin, towels, a broom to sweep the floor and a big old friendly smile of anticipation. He opened his doors for business but nobody came. A few days went by and still nobody came in. Everyone was very nice no matter where he went in town, but they simply didn't come to his shop and he wasn't about to beg anybody for anything, it was a matter of pride. Unknown to him his inner being, the rage, had taken hold a little more.

One night after supper he and Jo-Jo were doing the dishes and talking a little about things. She told him she believes in dreams and not to give up they'll come. She said that he was so shy that all he ever said to people was a polite greeting, so many figured he was a very private person who wanted to be left alone. This sparked a new bit of life into some of the gossips whose only mission in life is to know everything about everybody. You my friend are an unsolved mystery and are worthy of the secret society of tongue wagers. When your truth is unveiled you will no longer be worthy and their interest will cease for the moment. They laughed and sat at the table for a cup of coffee. Asa said he had to do something but what. Jo-Jo said that maybe he had to put something in front of the shop, you know, like the wooden Indian in front of the General Store. That night Asa couldn't sleep so he went for a walk. He took notice of the post that supported the roof of his building. Suddenly he had a great idea but it would have to wait until morning.

When the General Store opened he was the first customer through the door. He bought three cans of paint and paintbrushes. He went to his shop and painted each roof support post bright red, white and blue using a striped swirl patterns much like stick candy. He cut a large board, nailed it on the outside wall near the door and began painting the letters BAR but suddenly stopped and went home. It wasn't that he had worked so hard but he had begun to worry so much about if he had made the right decision in coming here that he was exhausted and needed some sleep.

The next morning the regulator was out and about crowing ever so loudly but there was also a faint sound of male voices in the distance as though there was a disturbance of some kind nearby. Asa had been longing for some kind of excitement. Being the quiet but curious sort, he finished getting dressed and rushed out to, as the Cajuns would say, " go see what that's about."

Much to his surprise the disturbance was at his own shop. All that Asa could utter along the way was, " Lordy, Lordy." Maybe he would finally meet his idol, the true Cajun Man. It was too bad that the toughies displayed their angry, fearless, rugged side in their first meeting. He took a deep breath as he trembled and prayed, "Oh Lord, Oh Lord, please help me. What could I have done"? Asa drew deep down inside of himself to muster a little courage and invited all of the longhaired men into his shop. The leader seemed to roar like a lion as he said, "What's going on here? The sign says BAR. Where is it?" These very, big men were upset about what they believed to be a lie and that didn't set well in their book.

Asa began shaking like a leaf on a cherry tree during a strong wind and lord knows he didn't want to be chopped down, especially for a lie he never told. Finally one large, 6 ft., dark haired man they called Al said, " OK little buddy let's hear it. What you got to say for yourself?" Asa stuttered out of fear but began from the beginning about how he came to be here and then said that this was not a bar. One of the other big ones grabbed Asa by the collar and the seat of the pants brought him outside and made him read his own sign, BAR. Asa explained the rest of his story and was relieved when those crazy Cajuns began to laugh because the joke was on them. They told Asa he had better finish that sign! They would find a real watering hole and come back later to see what he could do. Asa did as he was told. The first letters BAR were nice and neat but the last letters, BER had been written by a very unsteady hand.

Asa sat and waited and waited, afraid to stay but more afraid to go. He had so hoped that his first customers would be children so that he could practice a little before taking on men who said something only once. Asa suddenly thought about swamps, gators, bears and snake pits and how maybe these BIG men would take him on a sight seeing trip, never to be heard from again if they didn't like the job he did.

    True to their word the men returned all liquored up. The first man seated in the barber chair, outdoors of course, was Cajun Al. He decided to start over and introduced himself. Cut my hair, but just a little bit because I like it long. My lady friends like to grab it and pet me like a good old dog. Al winked and all the men laughed. Al told Asa to have at it. Asa said a silent prayer, " Please Lord, I know that if it is to be, it's up to me, but your guidance is appreciated." After a few deep breaths, Asa began. A snip here and a snip there, maybe just a little more near the ears. Asa took a brave step back to evaluate his work. Much to his surprise the scissors had not touched one hair on Cajun Al's head, not one. Cajun Al was growing impatient and asked if Asa was done yet, remember there was no mirror. Asa said, not quiet but understood that it was now or never so he told himself, "Here goes." Finally after what seemed to be a lifetime Cajun Al rose from the chair paid Asa for the job and left without saying a word. His friends followed him laughing all the way down the street. Good thing Cajun Al was Asa's first customer because any other one of those big men in from the swamp would probably have hanged Asa in front of his own barbershop, especially since they had been drinking. Asa was bewildered and for the first time he felt the need for a beer, or maybe three or four beers. He dared not go to the nearest watering hole for fear of meeting you know who, so he went home and had a few with Jo-Jo. She was so proud of Asa as she said, " I told you they would come, I told you." Asa wondered if he would ever see them again. Jo-Jo told him to stop it and drink his beer.

Cajun Al had peaked the curiosity of the people yesterday with all the shouting so today some of the not so brave men decided they would pay Asa a visit at his shop. They liked Asa's friendly nature and decided they too would get a haircut because their wives didn't do a very good job of it. Asa figured that this was just about the bravest thing any of them had ever done but he didn't say anything. Asa wasn't as nervous around this bunch because they seemed meek like him, so he was able to focus as he calmly tried to do a much better job. The left side was shorter than the right and the top had not been cut but no gashes anywhere. There was no reaction, not even one complaint.

One afternoon a shy, young man walked past the barbershop several times. He was tall and could easily see above the divider curtain in the window. Asa noticed how nervous he seemed so he stepped out side and introduced himself. The young man said his name was Eli and he could use a job. Asa said that maybe he could clean up once a week. It was only part time work because he was just starting his business and didn't have many customers. Eli asked if he could start tomorrow. Sounds good to me, tomorrow it is. Well, the next morning Asa found Eli asleep right in front of the shop door. He told Asa that he didn't want to be late for his first job so he slept over. Asa smiled and invited him in for coffee. I tell you what, you go to the boarding house and tell Miss Jo-Jo that Asa sent you to get some biscuits and I'll start the coffee, by the time you get back the coffee will be done. Jo-Jo asked Eli if she could join them. He just smiled and nodded. The three of them sat around the barbershop and had one of those good old times as they got acquainted. Eli said, " Fun's over, time to go to work." They all laughed and told him he was right. At the end of the day Asa paid Eli and Eli gave Asa a red stone. Asa asked what it was but Eli said nothing as he walked away. The next morning Asa showed his red stone to a few customers and asked what it meant. Each one of them said it symbolizes courage and confidence, that's Eli's wish for you.

Asa began to have a few steady customers so he decided to go to the bank and start a savings account. Mr. Batiste, the Bank President greeted him at the door and trapper that he was, made Asa feel special, you know, one businessman to another. Mr. Batiste immediately saw Asa as another means of finding out even more information about the people in town, so he told Asa he would go by for a haircut later in the day. Asa was happy to have him as a customer because he wanted to hear any story the banker had to tell. Surely his past was interesting but in a different way because he was more gentlemanly, not so ruff and tough.

It seems that the only people who walked around with haircuts that looked like the mark of the beast were Cajun Al and his friends. Asa made himself believe that the haircut didn't make them look any different, not really, because when they came in from the swamp they already looked wild and when they were ready to go back out they simply looked more wild, as though they loss patches of their hair in a fight or something. The big men never complained because they liked little Asa. They knew that they made him nervous and sooner or later that would change.

Eli stuck his head in the doorway and asked if Asa had any work for him today. Asa said he sure did and to come on in. Eli smiled and gladly did anything Asa asked of him without complaining. He was so innocent that you liked having him around. Asa heard Eli's stomach growl. He looked at the clock then told Eli it's lunchtime. Let's eat with Jo-Jo at the boarding house. Eli was so happy to be with his friends that he couldn't stop talking. Asa learned that Eli's family made wine from just about anything. They liked muscadine wine the best, but other people, especially the ladies, have their own favorites, like blackberry, pear, strawberry, or would you believe, carrot. You know what the men like most Mr. Asa? No, what? They like homemade beer, sugarcane rum and corn whiskey. Asa wanted to know how the family learned to do all this. Eli simply said that when you need it you make it, end of story. Jo-Jo- said, " fun's over, time to go to work."

   At about two o'clock Asa paid Eli for another job well done and Eli gave him a green stone. Eli told him to keep it with him always because it will help him overcome. Asa asked, overcome what? Eli didn't answer. He went outside for a few minutes then came back and asked Asa if he could give him a haircut in exchange for a gris-gris. Asa said yes, have a seat. While Asa was very slowly cutting, he thought, " I remember hearing about a con-jo, a mo-jo, a taunt-jo and a beau-beau but never a gris-gris. What could it be? It couldn't be too bad because Eli is not an evil person. I guess I'll have to wait and see because right now Eli is as quiet as a church mouse." At last the best haircut Asa ever gave anyone was finished. I do a pretty good job when they don't talk and I don't listen! Eli admired himself in the window glass then said, come on Mr. Asa time for the gris-gris. Several people were walking by and noticed a string tied to a chicken's leg and to a post. Curiosity had gotten the better of them when they saw Eli and others walking toward Eli's chicken. First he drew a circle on the ground and marked an X in the center, then he untied the chicken, placed it's head under the left wing, held it tight and quickly swung it North, East, South, West. He did this circular motion three times before placing it on it's back right on the X. Eli said, now Mr. Asa, leave it here until you close up your shop, it won't move, then take it home. You have to make a chicken and egg gumbo, but you have to cook the feet too. Invite only your friends to eat with you. All of you will have what you seek because the dream can't walk away. Asa smiled, thanked Eli and invited him to the gumbo that he hoped Jo-Jo and Eli would teach him how to make. Eli brought wine; Jo-Jo made biscuits and Asa was in charge of the main dish. It turned out pretty good because a good listener follows instructions. Every time they scooped up one of those chicken feet, Asa gagged, but since he had the rage, that inner strength, he was man enough to at least share one leg with Jo-Jo.

    Asa figured this gris-gris was a wish of good will to help a dream come true. He closed his eyes, and envisioned himself quietly moving along in a pirogue among the water lilies. Mighty oak trees, their limbs covered with moss, were stationed all along the bayou and beyond. Unique sounds of the creatures of the marshy swamp added to the unsolved mysteries. The white flowered herbs dubbed the "Enchanter's Nightshades" blanketed the shady woods. Everything, both real and imagined, enhanced his dream. Asa crossed his fingers behind his back and softly, childishly chanted three times, I want to be a Cajun Man, I want to be a Cajun Man, I want to be a Cajun Man. Asa took one deep breath and returned to real time.

    Asa was so grateful to still be alive after giving Cajun Al's friends some of those awful, nervous, haircuts that he decided to attend mass at the little church up the street. Father Cornez Andrico always shook hands with all of the people in attendance as they left the church after services. Asa was the last to exit and asked Father if he had a minute. Father said, "anytime" and invited Asa to share a pot of coffee in his quarters. Asa began by saying that he knew Father Andrico was not a Cajun. Father interrupted and said, "Oh yes I am." Asa was puzzled but listened as Father shared his story. Asa said excitedly, "That's what I want. I want to be a Cajun Man. I want to be accepted by these people especially the tough ones, like Cajun Al. I loved everything about them even before I came here." Father told Asa that the only advise he could give him for now was to listen, just listen. Most of these people like to talk about themselves and others but few listen. Asa thanked Father Andrico and left thinking to himself, " Wow. This is what I do best, LISTEN".

  Asa opened his shop bright and early every morning hoping for new customers. While sweeping the floor and stirring up dust he suddenly had an idea. Some of these tough men come in from the swamp for only one day to get supplies and a haircut. Maybe he could buy one of those #3 tubs some Cajuns use for bathing, some extra soap and a few bath towels. The supply room could easily become a bathroom. For a small fee they could clean up before getting a few beers. It's just a plain common sense idea that's profitable and almost fool proof, besides maybe he could really hear some good stories while they relaxed. Lord knows they talk loud enough.

  Suddenly the shop door opened and in walked a lady holding the hand of a cute, little boy. Asa thought finally, a child. Mr. Asa, can you cut my sons hair she asked. Yes I can. Well, the boy was too short so Asa placed a bucket he called "the butt bucket" upside down on the chair. He had wisely anticipated that children would need to rise to the occasion. Jump up here sonny, so far so good. Asa was not nervous or tense or worried and completely unaware that the devil had just walked in. The minute little Blondie saw the scissors he went nuts. He screamed, jumped down, ran around like an Indian and just about gave Asa a heart attack. The mother paid no attention, sat quietly in a corner darning socks and waited for Asa to catch him and cut his hair. Asa wondered what kind of Cajun is this? It's much more scary than the big ones. It's little, has long hair, squeals, runs and bites. It seems to be more animal than human. This is nothing like a city child. When he finally grabbed Blondie in the supply room, he tied him up, sat him on the floor, stuffed a rag in his mouth, gently of course, placed a bowl on his head and cut the visible hair hanging all around. Asa calmed down a minute and remembered he had a piece of stick candy in his pocket that he was saving for a snack later. Before he released "it" from bondage he told "it" the rules. You will always behave when you come here and I will always give you candy. If you ever act this way again I will feed you to the river witch that I have locked up in the trunk over there in the corner. Be sure you never tell anybody what I said or else. Asa released Blondie and brought him to his mother, who, by the way, loved his haircut. Asa shook hands with her and commented on how quiet and well mannered her son was after he became less frightened. Asa thought to himself, "Lady you just shook hands with a sinner." Surely Father Andrico will go easy on a confessed liar when he hears the circumstances. The mother told the boy to thank Mr. Asa. The boy was scared and couldn't pronounce Asa's last name so he said, " Thank you Mr. As-if." Asa thought maybe he should reconsider his original plan for the supply room because there are more of these little Cajuns out there. Then he thought that since there are no secrets around here, surely Blondie told the other little ones about what happens if you misbehave. That's good because this means there will be no need for the river witch and the big ones will have their bathroom.

Asa decided to talk to Jo - Jo about his new idea for his storeroom. When they put their heads together things usually worked out pretty good. After supper they did the dishes, got some hot coffee and sat near the fireplace. After discussing the ups and downs of their day Jo-Jo asked Asa what was on his mind. She always knew when he needed to pick her brain. Asa smiled and didn't hesitate to spill the beans. Jo-Jo told him he would do anything for a story, but the bathroom really was a great idea. She suggested that he hire a nice, pretty girl with a bit of an attitude to help out, nothing else, no hanky-panky. The men could look but they couldn't touch. Asa agreed but wondered where he would find this person because he hardly knew anybody in town. Jo-Jo laughed and said, " You know me". Asa gave her a big hug and said that maybe he could pay Eli a little extra to help her. They shook hands and that was that, no further discussion necessary.

Asa was a little late the next morning and found a young boy sitting outside his shop. Asa said good morning and asked if he could help him. The boy asked if he was Mr. As-if the barber. Asa said, "what". The boy again asked if he was Mr. As-if the barber. At first Asa was puzzled but remembered Blondie called him that in a moment of fear. Not wanting to belittle the young lad Asa simply said, " I guess I am, why do you ask?" The boy said because I like my friend's haircut and my Mom says I can get one just like it. Asa told him to come right in, sat him on the butt bucket, placed the bowl on his head and cut the hair hanging down all around it. The boy paid, and asked if he could have his candy now. Asa told him he sure could. The boy said, thank you Mr. As-if, see you next month.

   The next day Jo-Jo was busy at the boarding house, so Asa started the storeroom project alone. He had noticed that Cajuns want people to do less for them, not more. They like to do things for themselves and he wanted to be just like them. He pretty much had it set up like he wanted and decided to sit in the empty #3 tub to try it out. Everything looked pretty good until he looked up at the ceiling in the corner of the room. He almost died of fright when he saw a few very large roaches crawling around. They had to be at least two inches long if not longer, some real monsters. Never in his life had he seen anything like it, big Cajuns, big alligators, big roaches, what else? Asa started to get out of the tub when one of the roaches flew into the tub with him, right on his lap. It was a real shocking, awful, moment. The things have wings, Asa thought, what next, " BIG TEETH". Asa suddenly gave a shrill, not a Cajun yell, a shrill as he ran out of the room. There would be no haircuts today for fear of maybe cutting an ear off or something. Asa took the day off and would have a serious talk with Jo-Jo tonight about how she solves this problem at her boarding house. Probably she uses a voodoo spell on those big devils! One thing Asa did know, a cold beer was not going to cut it tonight, Jo-Jo had better have some of the hard stuff hidden somewhere! He really, really felt the need for a sip or two of Eli's strong whiskey.

There was no rest for the weary, headache or not Asa couldn't close shop for two days in a row, the people would talk. He thought, what am I saying. Judging by the way people laughed as they passed him on the street this morning they already knew all about his only day off. The more he thought about it the more he realized it was pretty funny. Suddenly Mr. Batiste, the banker walks through the door. He apologized for not coming by the other day but something came up. Asa told him not to worry about it because he was pretty busy that day anyhow. So, Mr. Batiste, how are things with you today? Before he knew it, Batiste was telling Asa many things he had never told anybody in his life, especially about the frequent trip to Solitaires house. The barber chair was better than a confessional because he said things he would have been embarrassed to tell a priest. By the time he got his shave, haircut and conscience cleansing he felt like a new man and promised to return next week, providing Asa was not a talker. Asa simply replied, not to worry sir, not to worry. Asa's ears were burning and his hair stood straight on his head by the time Mr. Batiste left. Asa wanted to hear Cajun stories but hoped there were no more like this one. Calm water sometimes runs deep, right into a cesspool. Who would have thought?
    Asa was cleaning his shop as well as his mind, of the things he had been told by the banker when who walked in but Cajun Al. Asa was so happy to see him that he almost gave one of those yells. So, little buddy, how's everything? What's the latest and the straightest? Asa laughed and said about the only new thing was that his name is now As-if and told him the cute little story about Blondie. As-if was so very proud to bring the barber chair outside so that everyone could see that he was cutting the hair of his friend, Cajun Al. As-if asked Al how would he like his haircut? Al said, " Oh, about the same as the other time. You know, a gash here, a bigger gash on the other side and one side shorter than the other in the back. They both laughed. Al told As-if that his nervousness has got to go. This barber chair probably has a birth control curse on it. As-if said, " a what? " Al said yeah,

that's right! After me, and my friends leave the barbershop, no self-respecting woman wants to be seen with any of us! I don't care what people think, I do what I want to do, always have, but let's face it, I like women, I miss being petted like a good old dog, you know what I mean? We have no choice but to hide in the swamps until our hair grows back! Good thing trapping is seasonal! Al was serious for a minute then let it go, but not before gruffly telling As-if, " and another thing, get a mirror!" As-if became very, very nervous and Al ended up with his usual haircut. Since Cajun Al strongly believes in taking it like it comes, he had no choice but to suck it up and head for the swamps hoping for better luck next time.

  Poor As-if, he was filled with mixed emotions, excitement at seeing his friend and drained from getting so nervous again. He brought the barber chair inside and went to the backroom to lie on the floor and take a nap. Although he fell asleep, his mind wasn't at rest. He thought, why a Cajun-wana-be? Why a mocking bird deluding myself into thinking I can be someone else? Why not a humming bird full of energy, all strong and vigorous? I know who I am! I know! As-if woke up and felt that he no longer had a nervous bone in his body and from now on he would have more discussions with his customers, nothing invasive, just let them know he cares and will help them if he can. Listening and a little interaction will be the key to his success.

  Hey Mr. As-if, do you still give candy if I let you cut my hair? As-if looked up and saw a little red haired boy standing in the doorway. As-if smiled and said, you mean one of those bowl cuts? The boy smiled letting As-if know that he had twice been visited by the Tooth Fairy lately. As-if said come on in son let's have at it. Red sat on the butt bucket then asked As-if if he wanted to know something? As-if smiled and said yes, he sure would like to know something. Well, I have been watching people read a newspaper and they talk about a lot of stuff afterwards. They sure are smart. I wish I could be smart like them. As-if asked if he had ever looked closely at a newspaper? No sir, I never have. Why not?

Because Mr. As-if, I told you, you have to be smart. As-if finished the haircut then reached for his newspaper and handed it to Red. Here son, take your time and look at this for a few minutes. Wow! I can read this. Mr. As-if, I'm smart! I'm smart! Oh, thank you Mr. As-if, thank you. Red tried to pay for the haircut but As-if said this one was on the house. Thank you kindly. Give my candy to the next kid.

It was a beautiful day and As-if was feeling good about himself, almost like he belonged here. His favorite pass time, between customers, was people watching. He relaxed on his porch with his hands clasped together resting them against his lap. He leaned back in his chair and crossed his legs as he raised his feet, propping them up against one of the post. Most men had not yet come to his shop, but he knew of them because people talk and he listens. He looked across the street and saw Mr. Boudreaux and Mr. Thibodeaux walking towards the saloon laughing about something or other. Those two were always laughing. Mr. Babineaux and Mr. Arceneaux shook hands as they passed each other on the street. They were courteous to everyone, a couple of real gentlemen. The simple gesture of tipping their hats to Mrs. Desormeaux and Mrs. Gayneaux as they entered the bank was a result of their proper, southern, education. Mr. Reaux was at the feed store getting feed for his chickens. He never took time to socialize. He was always in a hurry to get his farm work done. Miss Meaux, our schoolteacher, called her students to class by ringing the school bell. Helping children see the world through her eyes and her books was very gratifying to her. Mr. Badeaux was riding his horse around town to show off a little because the horse was bigger and better than Mr. Brasseaux's horse and he wanted to make sure everyone knew who owned the best. Poor old Mr. Comeaux just sat in front of the saloon waiting for a handout so that he could enjoy another cold one. Mrs. Godchaux, was on her way to church to pray for our sinners, especially Mr. Comeaux. As-if smiled as he thought, let's see, I cut hair for Mr.Gautreaux, our Mayor, Mr. Guilbeaux, our deputy sheriff, Mr. Malveaux, owner of the general store, the one with the

Wooden Indian in front and Mr. Manceaux, Mr. Marceaux, Mr. Neveaux, members of our Founding Fathers Association, as well as citizen Primeaux, citizen Quibodeaux, citizen Robicheaux, oh, and I can't forget Mr.Vigneaux because he tells good jokes. As-if began to laugh because he had just realized how unbelievable this was. It almost sounded like a chant. Mr. Smith was walking by and asked As-if what was so funny. As-if said how odd it was that so many people who live here, have a last name that ends in aux. why is that? Smith said he didn't know but asked if he had met Mr. Bernard, Mr. Bessard, Mr. Blanchard, Mr. Broussard, Mr. Edward. As-if yelled stop! Please stop, I get it. There was no stopping this man. Looks like he planned to finish what he started. As-if had no choice but to do what he always does, listen, and hope that the chant ends soon. Smith continued, Mr. Mayard, Mr. Menard, Mr. Picard, Mr. Richard, Mr.Ward, Mr. Gaspard, or Mr. Leonard. Finally Smith paused, caught his breath and asked if there was anything else he could help him with. As-if quickly said no, thank you. That was quiet enough. His question was never answered and he dared not ask it again, not of anyone, not even Jo-Jo.

 As-if's went back inside and was followed by a man who fished crabs along the bayous for a living and wanted a haircut. He didn't seem to need one but he was the paying customer and maybe he just needed to talk. He asked if As-if had heard the news? What news? Mr. Batiste is dead! What? Yep! A farmer went crazy after loosing everything he had. Seems that Batiste had drawn up one of his crooked contracts and the desperate farmer signed it without understanding the fine print. When the bank foreclosed the farmer had one too many drinks then went hunting for Batiste, found him in Solitaire's bed and shot him dead before he could finish his business. Then to make matters worse, the farmer shot himself. As-if asked," What about poor Marlie? Do you think she knows by now?" I sure hope so. There's so much unfounded jealousy towards that poor girl that you never know if some will tell abruptly to cause her quick pain like sticking a knife in her gut or try to tell the whole ugly story first then say that he's dead. The fisherman went on to say that Batiste was a hard nose trapper of men. He cheated people and showed no love or kindness to his own family. Probably the only one at the grave sight was the gravedigger! As-if finished the haircut, closed shop and went home. He had heard enough.

   The regulator woke As-if up the next morning, not a minute sooner, nor a minute later than usual. That's pretty much all he did but As-if had to admit he did it well and he would miss the old bird if anything happened to him. As-if felt that there was something different in the air this day. It was chilly but hot, it smelled of rain but it wasn't raining, it was dark like early night but it was early morning. He looked out the window and became a little tense. This was becoming a bad storm. He saw people scrambling up and down the street carrying their children and belongings as though they were afraid and were leaving town. Business owners locked windows, closed shutters, brought goods inside placing everything as high off the floors as possible. Lastly, they boarded up the doors. Animals ran for higher ground as they were quickly released from their pens and stalls. As-if couldn't figure out why these brave people were in such a panic because of a storm, surely in their travels they had been through bad weather before. Tree branches, chairs, paper and anything that wasn't tied down was blown away. More people began to leave as the streets began to flood a little. As-if paced back and forth across his room wondering if he should leave or not. Finally everything stopped. No more rain, no wind, the sky was a little clear and everything was quiet. As-if went outside to look around and try to find Jo-Jo. He looked all over town for a very long time and didn't find anyone, not alive or dead. Suddenly he heard someone calling his name. When he looked up he saw Jo-Jo and Father Andrico hanging out of the window from the attic of the boarding house. She motioned for him to go up there and yelled at him to hurry up. He asked why? She commanded him to do as she said, so he did. Just as he made his way to the attic window the stormy weather began again, only with much more force. Buildings were knocked down, roofs were blown off of homes, and large trees were uprooted and lay across the street. Water began to rise very fast. Jo-Jo explained that they were riding out a hurricane. There was nothing they could do but wait and hope that it would be over soon. Father Andrico suggested they pray for the safety of their friends and neighbors. As-if had never seen anything like this and asked if there were two storms. Jo-Jo explained that there was just one bad one and that people call the quiet time the eye of the storm. They think it's like stirring water in a glass with a spoon, the middle is open and clear but the outer circle is quickly spinning as the whole thing travels. Understand? When it's over and things gets calm again, the water goes down, the sun shines bright in the sky, the birds sing, people rebuild and clean up, hoping no lives were lost. As-if prayed that Cajun Al and the rest of the wild men were safe. If they survived this, they were truly the best!

    As-if was in his shop making sure that everything was ready for business when he heard a faint rustling sound and out of the corner of his eye he saw a black shadow like figure float across the room. He turned and looked around but there was nothing there. His heart fluttered a little and he didn't know if he was scared or ill. Had death come calling? He took a few deep breaths and went about his business. Jo-Jo came by later that morning to see if he needed anything and asked if he was sick, he looked a little pale. He told her what happened and she told him not to worry because that was probably Old Veuve {OLD WIDOW}. She married a sickly man who died a few days after the ceremony. Eli had placed a black stone in her husband's coffin symbolizing the end, but she removed it and displays it on a black ribbon hanging from her neck. She wears a black veil, a black dress, and black shoes as she tries to scare people into believing she is now a voodoo priestess, keeper of secrets. She'll probably be in mourning for the rest of her life. She's so nosy that she sneaks around like an old witch trying to find out stuff. For a time she was considered the Queen Bee around here because she was the first to find out something. If you were curious about anybody or anything, you went to her for answers. Now she's known as The Gue`pe {THE WASP} because she has become mean and vicious with that stinging tongue of hers. She always did gossip, but it was always the truth of any matter, now she makes up lies and doesn't care who she hurts or how much trouble she causes. Stay away from her if you can. Before you know it, she will have you in her secret society of liars, and you won't even know you are a member. Bye for now, call if you need. As-if felt sorry for the poor lady, and decided that he would be very kind to her if she came around. What harm could kindness do? It seems that some people have to learn the hard way. Hopefully, As-if won't be one of them.

    As-if had not realized that his barbershop had become the best place in town for some henpecked men to hangout. Hell had not frozen over yet so they didn't dare go to the saloon during the day. Wives knew that As-if found out all the latest gossip but wouldn't talk, so they sent their extra pairs of ears over there under the guise of getting haircuts or just a little coffee visit among men. Afterwards the men went home and were forced to repeat everything they had heard. One customer was having his haircut and three others were waiting their turn when they heard a steady thump, thump, thump. It got louder as it seemed to get closer. Ever since that hurricane As-if couldn't shake his fear of the unknown. He hoped that the wild bunch would come to town for a bath and a hair cut, hang around for a few days, and tell a few stories about bravery or something. Maybe that would help. Being nervous didn't seem to be as bad as being scared. Suddenly the thumping stopped and who appeared at the door but a real live pirate. Everyone was scared speechless. Finally one uttered in fear, "SON OF L'EAU NOIR come to life!" This longhaired man looked as mean as they come. He had a gold tooth, a gold ring in is ear, a black beard, a tattered skull and bones flag tied around his neck and was wearing some very dirty, smelly clothes. He was strong, and had a deep, hardy laugh. He knew he scared everybody in the place and he loved it. How would you like to cut the hair of a one legged man? I'll bet I would be the first peg leg to ever sit in that chair! As-if told him yes, he would be. The regular customer got up from the chair and stood near the door in case he had to make a fast getaway. Not even the meanest wife in town could have made any of them leave the shop right now. Not only did they want to hear what he had to say, but they also wanted to see if he killed As-if after getting one of those nervous haircuts. As-if began to cut and asked him what his name was, as five pairs of ears listened. The pirate said his name is Henry-Henry. He told of his many adventures including how his ship attacked the SOUTH WEST PASS and won the battle. He said he loss his leg because the fight took place too near the swampy, marshy, bayou of Beau Chene. The unwritten rule of the swamp is to take only what you need and leave the rest. Us Pirates, we have no rules. I helped take everything I could from that ship as she sank! So, an alligator took one of my legs for his supper and left me the other one. He took only what he needed. Maybe the swamp wanted to teach me a lesson and make sure I remembered it. As-if asked if he weighs more with or without his leg. The owners of four pairs of ears gasped and asked As-if why he was so nosy? Because, I want to know! God gave me a tongue so that I can talk! The pirate laughed. He looked in the mirror and noticed his hair was shorter on the left side of his head than it was on the right side, but said nothing about it as he paid his bill with a gold coin. As-if told him that there was a bathroom in the back but he said he preferred to jump in the bayou and return the dirt to the sea. As-if asked, " what about the alligators". The pirate said, " I won't take anything this time, little buddy." As-if walked Henry-Henry to the door and watched as he thumped along. He though to himself, " I like Henry-Henry, the bold, brazen man, but not the thieving, pirate".

    It was getting late. He was about to close up and wondered what they would have for supper tonight when he heard Jo-Jo yelling. He saw her in the middle of the street, right between two men who were having an argument. They were about to come to blows but she managed to take control of the situation. She sure is a tough little woman, just like they say. As-if hoped he could at least be like her if he couldn't be like Cajun Al. Afterwards he told Jo-Jo he saw the whole thing, and was just about to run over there and help her when it all ended. He knew she didn't believe him, but because she was his friend, she simply thanked him and gave him a hug. The four pairs of ears heard what he had said and as they left, one of the men remarked how poor old As-if is still just a Cajun-wana-be.

   After supper As-if felt kind of depressed and went for a walk. He met up with a tiny little woman who was sitting on a bench crying. He introduced himself and asked if she needed help. She said, " I know who you are Mr. As-if, you're the listener. He smiled and said, " I'm listening." Please don't laugh, but I want a back porch. I feel that having one is a right of passage for any Cajun. I'm a very hard working homemaker just like the other ladies. I'm tired of them being mean and nagging me about when my husband will get around to building ours. It may not be important to a man and I can understand that. He can plop himself down anywhere for some quiet time. I want a beautiful, peaceful place to enjoy my morning coffee and my private thoughts, or have friends over, or snuggle with the man I love with all my heart and soul. I would never bad mouth him to anyone, but sometimes I feel like getting Miss FAYDOE to cast some kind of spell over him to make him understand. Do you understand Mr. As-if? Yes, I do. I know how it feels to want something that's very important to you. Does your husband come to my shop? Yes he does. His name is Zed. You go home now. Everything will work out for the best. A week later Zed came in for a haircut. As-if cut, listened, cut, listened, and cut some more before he began to talk. You know Zed, I've heard many things from many married men since I've been here. I think that in the beginning couples put each other first in their hearts and minds, but as they take each other for granted, they begin to feel a certain entitlement. They forget that all the things they do for each other are out of love and respect, nothing else. As-if continued to cut. You're so right Mr. As-if. It's easy to get too comfortable, too selfish and sometimes too mean for no good reason. Zed paid for his lopsided haircut and left but forgot his work gloves. A few days later As-if went by Zed's house to return them. The two happy lovebirds were sitting on their back porch holding hands, just smiling, and swinging.

 When this little woman was so emotional she reminded As-if of Jo-Jo, the real Jo-Jo, not the tough little woman she wants everybody to think she is. They are good friends, help each other and lift each other's spirits when they are down. Every Sunday after church, Jo-Jo rides her horse out into the woods and along the bayou. Sometimes she visits with old friends and usually comes home around suppertime. As-if decided he and Eli would try and find out what girlie thing she would secretly like to have and surprise her with it. It took a lot of paying attention and listening to what was not being said, but finally they knew what it was and bought it, then planned a surprise supper party for the following Sunday. Only the three of them would be there because they knew she would cry and that should be a private moment. The happy day was here and after they were sure she had left town they cooked a very good gumbo, very terrible biscuits, baked what they hoped would be a delicious syrup cake and made sure there was a bottle of her favorite wine so that they could make a toast. Eli was so excited that he couldn't wait any longer. As soon as he saw her coming down the road he rushed out to meet her yelling, " Hurry up, hurry up!" She was very confused as he dragged her by the arm and insisted she come inside and sit in her favorite chair by the fireplace. As-if just stood there with the same silly grin on his face that Eli had on his. As-if kept taking a deep breath and motioned for her to look towards the kitchen. She smiled and said, " Something sure smells good. Somebody's been cooking my favorite food." Eli seemed as though he was just about to burst. He jumped up and down clapping his hands then ran out the room, but quickly returned with a beautifully wrapped present and gave it to Jo-Jo. She was speechless. Eli kept telling her to open it. She had suddenly become just as excited as Eli and tore the package open. Inside was the most beautiful, light blue dress she had ever seen in her life. She began to cry softly and asked, " How did you know? " They simply told her that they listen. She laughed and immediately went into her room to dress for the supper party. When she came out, both men had tears in their eyes because they realized how much they had taken her for granted and they were sorry. Eli gave her a pink stone to wear around her neck. He had cleverly fastened it to a very thinly braided locket chain he had made from his own hair. He told her pink means beauty. As-if escorted her to a candle lit table with a beautiful arrangement of wild flowers as the centerpiece. Some how the mismatched plates, glasses and utensils were suddenly transformed into things of beauty by the eyes of the beholders. There was no doubt that on this wonderful, beautiful night these three were a family of friends.

 Cajun Al was back in town. As-if could recognize that yell anywhere. He wanted some hot coffee so he went to the boarding house and banged on the door. It was so early in the morning that the regulator wasn't even up. As-if didn't mind one bit because he just loved that man! Jo-Jo made biscuits and a big pot of coffee. As-if told him that he thought he was dead. Al told him that you can't kill bad marsh grass. I'm a survivor, that's what I do best! Al told a few stories, Jo-Jo told the story about As-if meeting the Wasp, and As-if told about meeting Henry-Henry the pirate, the one customer who really wanted As-if to repeat every word he said, and Eli told the story about the blue dress and the pink stone. Al asked if As-if gave better haircuts yet. Eli answered, " Yes he does, look at me." Al could hardly believe his eyes and said, hurry up, let's go before he gets nervous. This time Al got a very good haircut, and a much needed bath, before his ladies ran their fingers through his hair and petted him like the good old dog that he was.

Stones

After Cajun Al left, As-if asked Eli to tell him more about his stones and how he found them. Eli said that one day when he was a little boy he was walking all over in the woods. Nobody ever cared where he went or what he did, just so he came home every night so that the family knew he was still alive. As-if said surely he got thirsty and hungry if he was gone all day. Eli said that sometimes he drank rainwater that he found in wagon tracks and he ate wild berries. When he was a little older he killed a squirrel with a rock, cleaned it up a little then cooked it over a small campfire. He had learned how to start one by watching some men once. He laughed because he remembered his first bite was mostly fur. Good thing he had brought some drinking water with him that time. He climbed trees, swung on vines and even tried to fish in the bayou that ran through the woods. One day he came across a big hill. Maybe it wasn't so big, but it looked big to me because I was so little, anyhow, I thought something might be buried there so I scratched at the dirt with a stick and found some real arrowheads, lots of them, scattered all over the place. I buried all of them in one secret spot I marked by taking thirteen big steps towards the bayou and away from a big oak tree with one branch that touched the ground. I didn't tell anybody what I found. Every time I went back I found more stuff and buried it in a new place but close together. I started to think that maybe some Indians lived here a long time ago. The more time I spent there the more I wanted it to be a secret place, I didn't know why, I just did. One day while resting in the shade, I found some human bones sticking up through the dirt at the foot of the old oak tree I was leaning on. I moved some of the dirt a little and saw some stuff buried with the bones, a feathered thing around the head, some beads around the neck and a very big bow with some arrows. It made me so sad that I cried and I told this Indian how sorry I was that he was dead as I covered him up with lots of fresh dirt. Afterwards I was so tired that I lay right next to the grave and fell asleep. I dreamed of Indians sitting around a small campfire making sad music. A big Indian Chief sat in the same spot that I found the bones. He died, the music stopped, and he was buried. Many gifts were buried all around the oak tree in his honor. After a time, smugglers came around to hide stolen stuff. They planned to use the same oak tree as a marker. When they dug up an Indian grave they got mad because Indians had been there first. They threw arrowheads and other gifts all over the place. I woke up and sadly went home. The next day I went back to the woods to make sure that I buried all the Indian stuff I could find close to the Chief's grave, but all around the oak tree, just like in my dream. To me, this was a holy place, so I never told anybody where it was. The trees are mostly evergreens, the branches hang low; natural sounds of nature help make it very peaceful as animals quietly move about the woods and along the bayou. I sometimes go and sit under the oak tree and talk to the old Chief. I'm always happy when I'm out there and I find the most beautiful stones anybody ever saw in their whole life. As-if asked Eli how does he know what they mean. Eli smiled and said, "My Chief says it's a secret and the spirit of the oak doesn't want me to tell.

As-if told Jo-Jo that he was tired of just hearing about this great place and it's people. He liked the stories, but he wanted his own, sort of like Father Andrico when his boys took him camping. I want to be part of a story. Live it, feel it, see it, even taste it, you know what I mean? Ok. Ok. Let's think a minute. You know it by now and lord knows you feel it, now go get it! As-if suddenly felt a slight rage that threatened to destroy his common sense as he yelled, " I'll do it!" Jo-Jo said that she and Eli would help him gather everything he needed for his daring adventure.

As-if decided that a good place for him to start is by having a cup of good, hot coffee with Father Andrico. The conversation brought back many memories, some good and some not so good, as Father recalled his own story. He encouraged As-if to follow his heart, do no wrong and always watch his back because evil does not exist only in the bayous. Now, let's call my boys together for a little parley. The boys decided to gather at the Banker Ferry around midnight to have this parley, whatever that word meant. This time Father wasn't the one who was afraid! By the time Father Andrico and As-if arrived at the roundup the boys had already built the campfire and were cooking their usual, fried frog legs. Father told the boys that since As-if was one of Cajun Al's best friends, he was sure that he would want the boys to help him if they could. The food was ready so Father said his usual before meals blessing while everyone bowed their heads. As-if said a very special, silent, prayer of thanks to his little friend, Eli, just in case he played a special part in helping this dream come true. As-if had never tasted root beer, fried frog legs or homemade bread. Jo-Jo always served biscuits. He really enjoyed the meal at the Banker Ferry roundup because he knew his dream had begun, right here at the foot of this mighty oak tree, right on the edge of the Cajun bayou.

The boys proudly shared everything they could. They told him that when he was ready he should put in here, at Banker Ferry and paddle along until he comes to the red bucket. It might take an hour or more depending on how strong the current was. Paddle as little as possible so that he doesn't get too tired, the current can do most of the work if you let it. The red bucket is at a fork in the bayou. Take a right and continue on. After each bend in the bayou yell out, " Is any body there" and move your lantern from side to side. With any kind of luck they will find you. As-if asked, " Who will find me? " Father Andrico laughed and said that As-if sounded like him when he went camping. The boys said, one more thing Mr. As-if, keep your hands and feet in the pirogue, right, Father. Father laughed and said, " You got that right. Keep your whole body inside!" They laughed, gave one of those yells and wished him good luck as they cleared the camp sight and went home.

 As-if returned to the boarding house where Eli and Jo-Jo were waiting. They loaded everything in a wagon and headed for the Banker Ferry. It's now or never. Eli's pirogue was in the water, supplies were loaded, and the lantern was in place. Eli asked As-if if he wanted him to tag along to be his guide but As-if said he really had to do this alone because it might be his dream come true, after all he did eat a chicken foot. The three friends hugged, and said goodbye. As-if shoved the pirogue into the strong current as he jumped in. Eli and Jo-Jo watched from the bank, as the dark of night seemed to swallow their friend without a sound. Eli said, "Listen!" Jo-Jo said that she didn't hear anything. Eli said, " I know. I hope he has his green stone."

 The current steadily moved As-if along. Every now and then he would put his paddle in the water and go through the motions, just for fun, but didn't really paddle because he remembered what the boys told him about saving his energy. There was no moon, no sounds, no visible anything. He was slightly disappointed, but he thought that maybe the swamp was watching him just as he was watching it. Soon they would both be at ease. He was about to let his fear get the best of him when he ran into something. It seemed solid because no matter how hard he paddled he didn't go forward. He raised his lantern and saw the red bucket. It was hanging upside down on a tall tree stump along a small levy. As-if was very relieved to realize that he was not lost. He maneuvered his way to the right, away from the bank, and with the help of the current continued his journey. He used his lantern as a signal each time he yelled out, " Is anybody there?" Finally he noticed a return signal and heard somebody yell, "Here". As-if quickly paddled forward as though his life depended on it. He docked his pirogue and even in the dark of night, recognized the very large, strong, helping hand that was extended to him. He stepped onto land, grabbed the big Cajun and held on for dear life as his eyes watered a little. His friend said, " Well, if I'm not the most surprised coon-ass that ever lived. As-if, it's really you!" Yes, it's me. I made the trip all by myself. They laughed and hugged in disbelief. Finally Cajun Al told As-if to go inside and relax while he got the stuff from the pirogue. As-if turned around but couldn't believe his eyes. He knew his friend was a real rough and tough wild man, a survivor, but he never dreamed he lived inside of a giant oak tree. As-if thought about it a little, and realized how smart Al was. It provided protection from every thing. It had a lot of living space, a good lookout if you climbed up and it didn't need repairs. When they unpacked they found several bottles of wine, and sugarcane rum with a note from Eli saying, "This wine is so good". Jo-Jo sent a large batch of biscuits. Her note said, "I love you guys, have fun". Al said you know what they are telling us? We should have a party. Cajun Al climbed high up into his oak tree with a lantern in hand. He swayed it left to right several times, hollered out his Cajun yell, then climbed down. As-if wanted to know what that was all about. Al said that when Cajun trappers want company they signal each other to come over. You'll see, just wait a little while. We have to kill something to eat, come on, let's go. We have to get something small because we don't have much time. They walked a pretty good way before finally coming across a few marsh hens. Al shot them and As-if carried them home. Al smiled all the way because he knew As-if was in for a little surprise. They made it back, and had a drink before Al told his little buddy the hunting code. If you go on a hunt and don't kill anything, you have to clean and cook whatever is brought back, that is the rule. Now, hurry up, company's coming. Poor As-if didn't know where to start. Al laughed but gladly told his friend what to do until he got back, he was going to catch a few crabs. It wouldn't take him long. When the moon is full, so are the crabs. When Al returned he was speechless and couldn't tell what kind of birds As-if had fought with. When he saw how proud As-if was, he laughed and told his friend he did a good job but thought to himself, what a mess, as he began plucking the feathers from As-if's whole body even his hair. Al decided he would clean the crabs himself then see what he could salvage from the hens. They had a few more drinks and cooked a very good gumbo. As-if soon learned that when he has a few drinks he talks too much. This time Al was the listener. As-if said that he closed shop for a few days to spend a little time with the wild men. Who better to bond with? Real men are direct and can solve a personal problem. They know how to sift through it, help you keep the good, and encourage you to let the bad go. Little Jo-Jo wouldn't admit it but sometimes she is too emotional and lets friendship get in the way, just like most females do. As-if drank a little more and began to feel no pain of any kind, not anxiety, not nervousness, not even fear of the wild men or their homeland. The carefree, tipsy, barber asked his friend if he wanted a haircut. Al told him, "Your shop is closed, remember." He asked Al if he thought he was too much in a hurry to be a Cajun man. Al simply said, "nope".

   Pirogue after pirogue arrived bringing food, drinks, music and happy go lucky Cajuns, wild and otherwise. They left their troubles behind for a few hours and didn't worry about anything. Short notice didn't matter, they came prepared to make the good time last. As-if learned to dance and sang along even if he didn't know what he was saying. He was even brave enough to play Al's harmonica while Al played his fiddle. Two wine-o's sure make for a fun party. Tonight As-if had better be ready to eat what he sees no matter how strange it looks. It is better not to refuse and insult any wife's cooking, especially if the Cajun has been drinking. If he wants to be a Cajun Man he has to eat like one. He was called to the serving table and got the shock of his life. A fish head was floating in a pot of red gravy. As-if swore that he saw the mouth pucker up! The eyes stared up at him as he stared back. Some lady insisted he try her fresh fish court bouillon. He smiled politely expecting the worse but got the best. It was delicious. He tasted squirrel, armadillo, deer sausage, and asked what no alligator? Somebody yelled out, that's over here on this end. It's all fried and ready to eat. As-if asked some older man what they did with all the marsh hen feathers Al had made him put aside. Our ladies stuff mattresses and pillows with all feathers. Nothing is ever wasted out here. Have you tried our de`bris yet? It's really good with rice. As-if asked if he was talking about the brown sauce with all kinds of stuff in it. Yes, that's it. As-if said he had tried it and thought it was very good. He knew what the word meant in English and didn't dare ask what was in the dish because he wasn't sure if he was ready for the answer. Finally everybody had enough of everything and said their good nights and went home. Both Al and As-if thought they heard the spirit of the old oak tree tell them to go to bed.

    Early the next morning Al cooked breakfast outside over a nice little campfire. Fried eggs and bacon fat smelled so good to Al this bright, beautiful morning, but As-if had a very different opinion. He promised himself that he would never eat or drink anything ever again, not even water. Al laughed and told As-if that he knows he feels like he's in hell, but he's above ground, and should be grateful to be alive. He only has to fight the devil just a little longer. Good, hot, black coffee is just what he needed and plenty of it. When you finish, go for a swim in the bayou, then, we'll talk. As-if jumped in the water, swam around and relaxed. They say that once you swim in the bayous you never leave Cajun country. Could this be true? If it was, As-if made sure he got a good soaking, all the way to his bones. By the time he got out, his skin looked like the wrinkled bark of an old tree. He wondered, had he and the swampy marshy bayou become one and the same? Had the roots of the might oaks soaked in the same water? After all, they looked wrinkled too. He decided it was time to find out what Al had to say, and returned to the mighty oak for a parley, As-if liked that word, it sounded so Cajunish.

    Al asked if he was feeling any better and As-if said yes, he really was and that he was glad he took this trip. Al told his friend that this last hurricane made him think about his own life. It's a good life but it's too lonely. Maybe one day I'll go on a special hunt. As-if was puzzled, and asked what he planned to hunt. Al said, "Come on As-if, use your head! A woman! One who will belong only to me". What about you, what's your plan? As-if said that if Al could tell him a little more about how to travel the bayous and what markers he has to watch for, he would go it alone for a few days and take his chances. He loves this place and he wants to see more of it before going home. You got it little buddy. In your case, a lantern is especially important. If it is wide open, it means send help, somebody is hurt, if it is halfway opened, like we had it, it means come to your camp site for a party, and if it is as low as possible it means trouble, danger, come over but be careful! If you are about to be attacked, try to appear calm. It's not easy but you have to do it because your life could depend on any survival plan you can come up with. After a few instructions about healing herbs and their uses the two friends enjoyed some hot coffee and shared a few laughs, mostly about who got the worse haircuts.

    There was a full moon tonight, so As-if decided to pack his herb pouch and other belongings and move on. This was too beautiful to pass up. The vision he had when he made his wish was exactly like this. Even the Enchanter's Nightshades were all about. As-if paddled along and eventually reached the Intracoastal Canal. The more As-if paddled the more Al's stories came to life. As he crossed the canal he saw a few Cabins scattered along a nice little bayou. He thought how strange it was to think of a bayou as being something nice, but that's what he thought it was, nice and quiet. These homes weren't fancy by any means, but to him they were beautiful. The people seemed poor by city standards but of royal blood in what really mattered in life. As-if wasn't being nosy, just observing how at peace these dwellers seemed to be. One man sat in a large chair, a child observing as he repaired a crab net by candlelight. He drifted along and noticed a very old woman sitting in a rocking chair. A lantern gave a soft glow to the whole room, much like a fire place would, but there was no heat, only a facial expression of warm and tender feelings, as she seemed to be telling a story to little children who sat on the floor, at her feet. On the other side of the bayou some men were standing over a large table sorting shrimp and crabs while swatting mosquitoes by the light of the moon. Suddenly one of them reached in his shirt pocket and removed a pouch containing tobacco and rolling paper. He made a few cigarettes passed them around, lit each one and as the men puffed and puffed the smoke kept the mosquitoes away. No matter how miserable the task, they enjoyed what they were doing. Maybe they were thinking that in the end, they would eat the delicious food from the sea and the mosquitoes wouldn't have any. Maybe not, it was just a silly thought. They waved to As-if and As-if waved back as he paddled on, looking from side to side, admiring everything; large boats with trawl nets attached on each side, pirogues for inland hunting, the vastness of the marshlands and its wildlife. When he finally faced forward, there it was, the Vermilion Bay! He secured his pirogue to a wharf that reminded him very much of a back porch and let out the biggest, loudest, best CAJUN YELL ever! He could not contain his great enthusiasm, his passionate rage. He couldn't explain his sense of freedom. He had heard the word many times and always thought he was a free man. He never realized that during his whole lifetime, he had trapped himself in his own body, by his self imposed worries and concerns.

 He wanted to stretch his legs and decided that the beach seemed like a pleasant place to take a walk. Many thoughts of the past ran through his mind. Had Henry-Henry passed this way before him? What about slave ships, or maybe soldiers? There was no doubt that Cajun Al had left his footprints in the sand. He walked back to the wharf, sat with his feet dangling just above the water and waited for daylight. Too bad the regulator wasn't around for this sunrise, because it was sure to be the best one ever. After a while, As-if stood up, stretched his arms and took a deep breath. He put his hands in his pockets and felt the green stone. He suddenly understood what Eli meant when he said, "Overcome". As-if had not given up in his long effort to toughen himself, win control over his feelings and realize his inner strength. The innocence of Eli and his belief in the power of his stones sure is a good thing. As-if grasped the stone tightly as though to say, thank you, and watched as the golden sun rose from the far side if the waters edge. It seemed to push small white caps along while a slight breeze carried the hypnotic, scent of the sea across the bay and towards land for the enjoyment all who dare to dream. It was beautiful and added to the magical, mystery of Cajun Country. Vermilion Bay indeed belongs to the Cajuns. Each one can lay claim to it, no matter how or why they enter it. Lessons have been learned all along the way. Once there, it invites you to rest. Some relax and fish from their boats, some lye on the beach, but As-if chose to sit on the wharf. It was his back porch. He was enjoying the moment when he heard a slight noise in the water and a voice calling out. He turned and saw a young man paddling a pirogue towards the bay as he loudly yelled out, "Hey, Mr. Cajun Man."

Miss Mary Irlanda

    Eventually Al realized he was becoming lonelier and day dreamed of how perfect his life would be if he had a wife and family. The old oak served him well but was not large enough for a family. He decided to build a better camp near by along the bayou in the marsh and so he did. At the end of this season he again headed for ERATH, which was the nearest town. This time the hunt was for live, human game, Mrs. Al. The trapper was determined to bring the prey to the marsh alive and kicking if necessary. One of the things he learned over the years is the human is easier caught with honey than vinegar so his plan was to come across as the strong, silent type who didn't know he needed the loving care of a woman's touch. He had noticed that marrying women seem to be attracted to that needy type.

    No sooner had he arrived in town when, he heard of a dancing party at Taunt Ness's house. Cajuns work hard all week and on Saturday nights families would take turns having a dance in their home. Anyone who could play a musical instrument and sing a song was invited. The ladies would bring a covered dish and everyone enjoyed the food. Al figured out that since families would attend, there should be single women to dance with so he set his plan in motion. He bought a new set of clothes, greased his boots with gator fat, got As-if the barber to give him a hair cut and hoped for a good one. The memory of the first haircut still haunted him. He took a bath, splashed As-ifs good smelling stuff all over his body and the hunt began.

    Al had a commanding presence about him as he appeared at the door of Taunt Ness's house. He created a buzz amongst the young, single ladies. Al had dark hair, a pleasant smile, and green eyes. He was over 6 ft., well built and portrayed a man of great strength. Each young lady managed to be standing nearby when the music began. These seemingly desperate females became bold enough to ask Al for a dance. He politely accepted but all the time thinking this hunt was going to be harder than he thought because he was determined not to leave town with a female that resembled a dog or a big nose gator or even worse a bear. Finally the musicians took a break and so did Al.

    Feeling smothered and wanting a little freedom he moved about the yard breathing in some much needed fresh air. He was thankful for the cool breeze that kept the mosquitoes away. Suddenly a soft, gentle voice said, " Isn't it a beautiful night? The moon is so clear." Well, the trap was sprung but guess who became the trapper, none other than Miss Mary Irlanda. Al suddenly became Crazy Al. His knees were weak, he was speechless and could not move. The pounding of his heart deafened him. This creature had to be his and he was going to bring her to his nest. As they talked they became friends. She listened with interest to everything he had to say. Yep! Al was indeed trapped but very willingly and hoped to be happily ever after.

When things are meant to be they are meant to be. As was the custom at the time, the wedding ceremony was held in someone's yard. The scent of honeysuckle filled the air on this beautiful day. Mother Nature provided the warmth of the sun and the cool breeze of the wind that swayed the moss hanging from the mighty oak trees that seemed to have been purposefully arranged as an aisle for the brides' walk. Jo-Jo, the maid of honor, sure was getting a lot of use from that beautiful blue dress. Eli was so proud to escort her and be a part of it all. Al appeared more handsome than ever, a real cock of the walk as he impatiently awaited his bride. She was beautiful as she walked down nature's aisle smiling shyly, gazing downwardly but eyes up and focused on the love of her life. Over the years Father Andrico, As-if, the barber and Al had become true friends so it was not surprising that Father Andrico performed the ceremony and As-if was the best man. Eli and As-if knew Al very well. He was a hard, tough, direct man with a heart of gold but he would never think about getting a ring for his bride. All he knew was that he loved Mary and that's all that mattered to him. So, As-if had the blacksmith make a ring from an old, Spanish coin and Eli provided a yellow stone for it because that one meant joy and happiness. Cajun Al had a big lump in his throat when his friend handed him the ring. He then smiled at Eli because he knew where the stone came from. The official words were spoken as Al placed a very beautiful wedding ring on Mary's finger. The couple held hands, turned and faced their guest for the first time as Mr. and Mrs.. This little introduction was as binding as a hand shake and meant they belonged to each other as long as roosters crow. The couple cut the wedding cake, toasted each other first with glasses of blackberry wine then, toasted their guest, welcoming them to the party. Al played his fiddle to show off a little, and to get the dancing started. As usual everyone ate too much, drank too much, and didn't want the good time to end, but the sun was lowering in the sky and it was time to say goodbye. The bride stood in the pirogue as she threw her bouquet. After a few more pleasantries the couple embarked on their new life by pirogue in route to their peaceful camp on the bayou. Well, at this time love is in the air and newly weds, young or old forget that they are not in heaven. Friends of the groom feel that heaven can wait. Quietly they hide in the bushes all around the home of the couple until the kerosene lamps are out, then, they spring into action. They yell, laugh, sing and bang on pots with spoons while dancing around the home all night long. As dawn approaches they all go home for a much needed rest.

    The couple was so very happy. The bayous were great. Gators were great. Everything was great, especially life itself! Odd how when you're young and in love you see no misery or hardship. You find a way to work things out thereby becoming stronger together and separately.

Miss Faydoe

After a time Mary realized she was pregnant. She and Al had prayed for this with all their heart and soul. Mary decided she would go down the bayou and speak with the old voodoo woman, Madam FAYDOE. All her life Mary had heard of the powers of FAYDOE and she hoped to find out if her child would be a boy or a girl. She figured Al might want to know. As Mary approached the old cabin by pirogue, she thought to herself how scary this place was, even in the daytime. There were holes in the roof, floor and walls. It was badly in need of a white wash and the porch supported only by cypress knees was sinking in the bayou. Full-grown cypress trees were all around with moss hanging from them. Just hanging, all gray and thick like a cushion as though death itself was hiding in wait. Mary wondered if they protected the cabin or possessed it. Mary's heart pounded in fear but she wanted to have good news for Al so she yelled out, "Is anyone here?" Mary noticed the door on the front porch opened slightly and a thin, frail, worn out looking elderly female with long gray hair came out asking, " What you want?" Mary asked if she was Miss Faydoe and the female grumpily said, "So" Mary told her the reason she was there. Then Miss Faydoe's old, tired face softened and she smiled. "Come in, come in child and be careful of your step." Miss Faydoe told Mary to give her the wedding band she was wearing and lie down flat on the floor. Mary did as she was told because she was never confrontational. Miss Faydoe then tied an old dirty piece of twine to the wedding band and held it over Mary's stomach. If the band began to sway North and South she was having a boy and if it swayed East and West she was having a girl. Mary began to cry learning she was having a boy and knowing how excited Al would be because he could teach his son so many things. Mary and Miss Faydoe happily chatted a little before Mary thanked her and left.

As Mary arrived home Al was beside himself with worry. Where have you been? Where were you? Mary smiled, took his hands in hers and asked him to sit down. She then gave him the good news. Tears came to his eyes and he held Mary close but gently so as not to break anything. He thought to himself, "What a rich man I am. Why has God been so good to me? Thank you God, Thank you." Mary then told Al of her new friend, Miss Faydoe. They both decided they would help her as much as they could. It seemed that God led them to her because she needed help, voodoo queen or not. Mary brought food and Al brought tools to repair the cabin as best he could.

Magic Jack Callahan

Maybe Miss Faydoe and her husband Jack had fallen in love much the same as Mary and Al. Mary asked her to tell their story if she didn't mind, and start from the beginning while Al did some repairs. Please Miss Faydoe. Faydoe smiled as she sat in her rocking chair near the window, looking out as though she saw Jack paddling his pirogue down the bayou on his way home. Once, there was a very beautiful young girl from Haiti who came from a very good home. Her loving family protected her all her life. They always feared the worse possibilities and never trusted her to use her own good judgment. Every minute of every day she felt that she was controlled. She felt trapped to the point that she could no longer breathe. Dreamers, especially young ones, always think life is better somewhere else. She heard many romantic stories of southern Louisiana and the secrets of the bayous. Secrets kept by the moss covered oak trees as many drifters bared their souls. The beholder seldom leaves and never understands why. As a dreamer, she had her own ideas about life in that part of the world. Ladies wore beautiful dresses to many balls and were always treated politely by many rich, well dressed, gentlemen who wanted to gain their favor by granting their every wish. She became so obsessed by her fantasy that she dared to steal money from her parents, left a note telling them that she loved them and that she was sorry. She ran away and traveled all the way to New Orleans on a very big ship. The journey was long but very pleasant. Ladies always seemed to be busy entertaining each other in a different part of the ship when men paid attention to her and made her feel like a queen. She thought that she must be very beautiful, why else would they like to be seen with her? It was almost as though there was a silent competition amongst them. At this point she didn't know that she might have a long, bumpy road to travel by sea or by land. It's a give and take thing in the south and you had better be able to handle it. Right when she set foot on the dock, her dream became a nightmare. This was a very large, loud, crowded, scary, place. She just stood there, right on the dock of the mighty Mississippi River, alone and feeling like the helpless little girl she was. She noticed a sign that said FRENCH MARKET. Since she spoke French she felt a slight glimmer of hope. She began to walk around because she didn't want any undesirables to approach her with questions she couldn't answer. Everywhere she turned people were trying to sell something; fruits, vegetables, fish, breads even human beings. Some ladies stood in doorways, half dressed and laughing; other ladies passed by, fully dressed and looked as though they were lemon tasters. There were more men than women walking around; happy sailors, strong looking dockhands, even praying priests. Some who dressed like gentlemen didn't behave like gentlemen at all. There were people of all different skin colors, all shapes and sizes and all dressed differently. Excitement and music filled the streets but she was filled with fear. It was sad to see how many children were begging for money. They wanted to carry bags, or lead people to a restaurant or hotel, or shine shoes, just about any small job for a very little amount of money. She wondered if she would ever be like them or worse. She made her way to a hotel and rented a room for the night. It was charming, clean and had a beautiful courtyard filled with flowers, plants and various statues that seemed to filter the noises of the streets. The faint sound of music was constantly in the background like an evil spirit daring some to come out and play. Because she had to make her money last, she decided to wait until she was starving before going downstairs for a bite of food. Much to her surprise gumbo was listed on the menu. She couldn't believe it. It made her so homesick for her mom's cooking that she began to cry. She tried to be quiet and lady like as she bowed her head using her napkin to soak her tears, but it was obvious that she had a problem. Soon, a very handsome young gentleman seated across the room came to her table and introduced himself as Jack Callahan. He asked if he could be of any assistance. She asked if she could trust him and he said what a strange question to ask somebody you don't know. Suppose

I lie to you, then what. She began to cry again in desperation and said that he may be seated. He said he was only teasing and would try and help her if she told him everything, so she did. It was a very short everything. She ran away from home. He laughed then quickly apologized. I'll tell you what, go to your room, have a good night sleep and I'll come by in the morning to take you out to eat. Then, we will decide what you should do. She stopped crying and felt very relieved, maybe even safe. He rose from the table, bowed, kissed her hand and left. She ate two bowls of comfort food, hot gumbo, before going upstairs to bed. She couldn't stop thinking about this stranger she had just met. He was tall, green eyes, dark red hair, trimmed moustache, beautiful white teeth, wore expensive clothes of the latest fashion. His hands were as soft as a woman's with manners to match. How in the world had she observed so many details about him when she was so troubled? The wonderful scent of his cologne lingered on her person as she fell asleep hoping for pleasant dreams. She was up early the next morning, waiting for her date. She waited and waited not knowing that in New Orleans they had brunch around ten o'clock. In order to pass the time and avoid negative thoughts about Jack, she decided to read her tarot cards and see what her future held. For many generations they had been handed down to the firstborn female of the family. She couldn't bring herself to part with them even if she had abandoned her family. They would belong to her daughter one day! Leaving home was a big mistake she would have to live with for now, but hopefully not forever. Just as she finished dealing them there was a knock at the door. In her excitement some of the cards fell to the floor. She quickly gathered and put them away for safe keeping. What a pity she didn't read the sad story of her future before answering the door. Jack tipped his hat and asked her name. Oh, I'm sorry. My name is Faye Dore` of Haiti. Well Miss Faye Dore` let's eat. She laughed and took his arm. They strolled through the French Quarter, had coffee, powered doughnuts and pleasant conversation about the magic of New Orleans. She quickly became aware that during the day light hours everything is about following rules of behavior in polite society but during the bewitching after hours of the night, on these very same streets, anything goes. It seems that the more wild, daring, lawless, scary and sensually exciting the better. Finally, she and Jack began to address the problem at hand. She said that she never had a job because she was so young and her family would never have approved of the idea. The only thing she knows how to do is read tarot cards to tell fortunes. His eyes lit up and just as quick as lightning the trapper knew she was his. "Perfect"! He grabbed her by the hand and quickly led her to a beautiful place on Bourbon St. As they stood in the middle of the street, Jack told her to choose, her past or her future, which was it to be? The sign above the door said, " Magic Jack Callahan's". Is this yours? Yes it is and I will give you a job. Doing what? Reading your cards, that's what. We will dress you like the mysterious beauty from Haiti that you are, Madame Dore`. You will remain a mystery as long as possible, answer no questions about yourself, past or present. Mine is a house of magic. I practice slight of hand at the card table, my ladies of the night make men's problems disappear for a little while and you will tell of the unknown. But, know this about me Madame Dore`, I am all about making somebody else's money disappear, anybody's money. Do you understand? By this time she was already in love with Jack and didn't care what he was saying. He wanted her to say yes so she did and that made him happy. Jack took her shopping and personally chose what she was to wear at work. He had excellent taste, because as a free spirited man of the south, he knew what clothes made a woman appear charming, but sensual, sophisticated but desirous. Each time Faye wore his clothes she was suddenly, as though by some magic spell, transformed into another person. She became what the clothes represented and had the confidence to read the tarot cards with total conviction. Men were captivated by her charm and stunning beauty; women were mystified by her tarot readings, either way Jack won. Word spread quickly and Magic Jack Callahan's became the best place in all of New Orleans to enjoy the bewitching midnight hour.

His instincts were good and he seized any opportunity to apply them without the slightest bit of hesitation. He believed his love of money gave him an edge. A moment lost, was money lost. Jack secretly figured that it was a good move on his part to keep Madame Faye Dore` happy as long as possible. Jack was so pleased about the money Faye brought in that he had a pet name for her. He called her Faydoe. Because Faye would forever be a dreamer, she was very happy and believed this term of endearment was a pre-marriage proposal, next she would have a ring, then a wedding. Never mind about the fancy dress or the celebration, she wanted Jack for now and forever, forsaking all others, until death do they part. One day she would come to realize the truth about his feelings for women, he loved them, all of them. He seemed to work his magic very well because they always wanted to make him happy no matter what he asked of them. During their time together, none realized that he never said he was in love. There was, however, one good thing about Jack. He was true to one woman at a time and never lied to her. Jack went to the waterfront to make some kind of deal with some shady characters and would be gone a long time so she decided to read the Tarot cards on her own behalf. She hoped to read her happily ever after future, but instead saw mighty oak trees, bayous and pain. She was stunned. Surely there could be no pain from her relationship with Jack. Not the Jack she loved completely and would give her life for! He always treated her with love, kindness and respect, but the tarot cards had never lied to her. Jack always told her, "don't believe what you see, believe what I tell you". She shuffled them and put them away, not having the courage to have another look, not now! She sat on the balcony over looking the quarters and the riverfront. A cup of good, hot coffee with a shot of whiskey added was just what she needed right about now. Dreamers see only with happy eyes and loving hearts, they simply try to erase some truths from their minds but inch by inch, year by year the truth slowly works its way to the forefront and one day even a dreamer has to painfully see what is. After a few cups of the Cajun style brew, she admitted to herself that Jack was her man as long as he would have her. She had come to love New Orleans, this garden of saints and sinners. There was no doubt in her mind by now that Jack was a sinner and by loving him on his terms so was she. Sadly, theirs was an unhappy destiny that probably could not be avoided in the end. She began to wonder why Jack was taking so long. Time was never of concern to him because he was such a free spirit, but something was wrong. Since he was all about making and taking money he could be in trouble. She felt it in her bones, in her soul, in her whole being! All she could do was wait, maybe even say a prayer.

Jack's meeting was taking place on Capitano Philipe`s riverboat. The working lower deck transported any cargo for pay but the upper deck was reserved for the exclusive use of the aristocracy. Jack was a silent partner who insisted that no expense was spared in making this the most beautiful restaurant, hotel and gambling hall on the Mississippi River. The staff dressed as Privateers to add to the excitement, and was well trained in making anyone who visited the upper deck feel like nobility. It always began with, "Compliments of the management, sir". Some had no intentions of gambling, only to have dinner in the restaurant then a stroll around the deck, but a few drinks always worked like magic. The trap door was wide open, anything and everything for a price. Most were easy pickings for the Privateers who were pretending to be the staff. Although Jack was a thief, he didn't see himself in that light. He played the game of spreading the wealth. He was a firm believer that the few who have too much should share with the many who have too little. Naturally they will never give it up, so Jack simply has to quietly take it from them. It's not his fault if they freely come to the gambling table and allow his magical hands to take their money. Patrons were too ashamed to complain, after all, they were rich and smart; they were the elite. Those who did had no proof of being robbed or cheated because they couldn't identify anyone after enjoying too many of those aristocratic drinks.

    After a late dinner in Capitano's cabin, it was time to clear the air. Jack said that things were getting out of hand. Privateers had become too bold and began stealing too often. Capitano may as well fly the skull and bones flag because rumors of the riverboat's reputation were that of a pirate ship. Jack went on and on about how he was like champagne and Capitano was too much like rum. He wanted to climb up the social ladder and Capitano was going down the ladder, straight to hell. Finally, Capitano had heard enough and simply told Jack that he may leave now. You run Magic Jack Callahan's and I'll run the Riverboat; we will see who has the last dance with the devil. Capitano was a very arrogant Spaniard who always did as he pleased. He was a very short man, had very little hair so he always wore a Panama thinking it made him unique. He had dark eyes, a round face, a gold tooth, skinny arms and legs but unfortunately, a very large stomach. His clothes were always too small because he never tasted a plate of food he didn't like. His laughter could clearly be heard on the lower deck as he shut the door behind Jack, drank his rum and continued to count his profits, never giving Jack another thought. As Jack reached the gangplank a dockworker called out to him. Be careful Mr. Jack. Watch your back! Don't you know by now that Capitano is not your friend? He sold his wife last week, what you think he wouldn't do to you? Your share is getting smaller, not his. Go see for yourself, he's counting the money now. Jack was stunned but knew it was a strong possibility. Maybe Capitano spread the rumors himself. Jack gave the dockworker $500.00 in cash and thanked him for the information. Never mind watching your back Mr. Jack, I'll watch it for you! Jack quickly but quietly went back to the upper deck. He looked through the louvers on the cabin door and watched Capitano divide the profits into one very large pile and one small one. Jack entered the room just as Capitano opened his safe. Well Jack, cooled off yet Capitano arrogantly asked. Oh, I see, you came back for your cut. No, replied Jack, I came back for the whole thing. Didn't you hear the rumor, there's a thief on board. I think this would just about make us even, hand it over. I'll clean out the safe too! What, uttered Capitano. He couldn't let that happen so the two men fought furiously with great passion because both had one great love, her name was, "MONEY". Suddenly Capitano went limp and fell to the floor. The $500.00 man had kept his word and knocked Capitano out cold. Jack thanked him again, gave him the smaller pile of money and told him he had better leave New Orleans now and maybe he should change his name from whatever it is to what he would like it to be. I think Sanchez is a good name; I will keep it. Nobody had seen him talking to Jack but they couldn't take any chances. They shook hands and parted company. Jack took all of the money and the deed to the riverboat. Maybe he should follow his own advice and change his name because Capitano was a Pirate, a Privateer and a Smuggler all rolled into one. He would never quit looking for Jack. There would be no place to hide.

    Jack returned and for the first time since Faydoe had known him he was scared, just plain scared. She asked what was wrong but he didn't answer. He sat down; he stood up; he kept pacing the floor back and forth, back and forth, while wringing his hands the whole time. This was a real panic attack, the first of many to come. She waited for a while hoping he would calm down, then asked what had happened. We have to leave Faydoe, pack your things. I'm going to the bank, be ready when I return. Jack met with Mr. Oswald who was President of the Bank Of New Orleans. They had become good business friends over the years and Jack knew there was not one crooked bone in his body. Actually, he was crooked in appearance and had to walk with a cane for balance. He was a very handsome man with blue eyes and blonde hair but most women never bothered to look past the bone deformity which resulted in a large hump in his back. It was their loss because he had good character, much kindness, embraced all life had to offer and never pitied himself. He was a professional who never knowingly allowed himself to be part of any dishonest deed, financial or otherwise. Some people didn't like him because he was brutally honest and thought nothing could be gained by giving a polite answer rather than a truthful one. Men knew where he stood on any issue. Women carefully avoided asking his opinion about their hair, their new dress or anything else of a sensitive nature. Jack explained that due to a sudden emergency he had to leave town for an undetermined length of time. He signed the deeds to Magic Jack Callahan's and the Riverboat officially granting power of attorney to Mr. Oswald over all of his business affairs during his absence. He was to quietly sell both places for a fair price and deposit the money into a new secret account under the name of Argent {MONEY}. Jack handed him $500,000.00 in cash to open the Argent account immediately. Jack would have access to the account at any time from any city bank. He also wrote a will, in simple terms, directing Mr. Oswald to follow the instructions without hesitation should he learn of Jack's death. These arrangements were to remain confidential and he was to tell no one that Jack had left New Orleans.

   It was hard to believe but Jack once again came home in worse shape than when he left. Had he robbed the bank or what! No, he was too shaken to have done a foolish thing like that, but he sure looked guilty about something. They hurried to the waterfront and boarded the first old, run down, freight steamboat leaving the dock. Jack paid his friend, Captain Woody, to regard them as cargo and say nothing if anybody questioned him about Jack and a beautiful woman. Nobody in his right mind would ever question Woody about a beautiful woman. Nobody! You see, Woody is a little strange and believes that soap is a man made poison and should never be used. He lives with his little pet flees, ticks, roaches and bugs and they don't like soap either so, he figures he must be right! After all, a lot of good stuff comes from dirt and when you die where do you go, in the dirt! Thank God Woody doesn't have strange ideas about clothes. What a frightful thought, Woody without clothes! Nobody knows where he comes from, only that years ago this very tall man with wild bushy, dirty blonde or dirty brown, maybe black hair, dark leathery skin, bad teeth, large shabby, dirty clothes that seemed to have belonged to a three hundred pound man not a one hundred fifty pounder, using a rope for a belt and animal hide for shoes simply walked out of the woods one day asking if anybody wanted him to haul freight up river on his old boat. He had been alone so long that he didn't remember his name so people simply called him Woody. Even back then Magic Jack knew that there would come a time when he would need to disappear so he made sure his associates sent a little freight business Woody's way in Jack's name. When they finally did meet Jack shook his hand and called him Captain Woody. Woody smiled and was happy to have a human as a friend even if he did use soap and smelled like a flower.

    Faydoe was pleased that the cargo was cotton and not animals but wondered why travel by freight; why be on the run, hiding like criminals? Now was not the time for answers, now was the time for a shot of bourbon. Faydoe opened her purse and surprise, surprise there it was; the cutest, little, silver flask Jack had ever seen! There was nothing funny about Jack's old flask but the tension had become so great that the slightest reason to smile sparked an explosion of uncontrollable laughter. They hugged each other and sat on a bale of cotton as they sipped their whiskey. Any boat ride exposes the beautiful Cajun wilderness of the bayous and while sippin or sittin you simply hold your lovers hand, forget your troubles and become at peace with yourself.

    As they floated along Faydoe took notice that the swamp seemed alive! With a steady gaze of awe and respect she decided to appeal to it for help and protection. Her heritage was one of religious beliefs made up of mysterious rites and practices. Surely with a little conjuration it could accept her as one of it's own. Gradually she seemed to be in a state, somewhat like a deep sleep with little will to control any spiritual suggestion. Her body remained active and wandered about the deck. Suddenly she stopped, knelt down, reached into the bayou and vigorously splashed water with her hand, as though communicating with swamp life. She said nothing, smiled and nodded her head. Her appeal had been granted. She was now a CHARMER. The scent of Enchanter's Nightshades filled the air as Faydoe took a deep breath, became aware of the beautiful, bright, sunny day and her path of pleasure. She looked around and realized that she was alone and soaking wet from her face, down towards the upper part of her dress. She seemed to be all right but was very puzzled. She found Jack asleep on the opposite end of the boat and decided it was best not to disturb him because he would ask questions and she had no real answers. A good nap was probably just what he needed while her clothes dried.

Finally they arrived at Cheniere Au Tigre. Jack had chosen this settlement along the gulf coast because it was accessible only by water, had many good places to hide and very few inhabitants. Less people, less questions giving Jack more time to calm down and think things through. They came upon an old hut or shack or cabin whatever you chose to call it and settled in. Faye preferred to think of it as their first home and began to make it so. Tree stumps for tables and chairs, moss for bedding, seashells for dishes. Being from Haiti she knew how to use natural, earthy things to bring comfort and warmth to a room so that all who enter, relax and feel at home. Leaves and wild herbs were wrapped around fish and placed in an earth pit with hot rocks for cooking. Wildflowers were in abundance and added a very nice feminine touch through out the cabin. Even Magic Jack began to have warm, fuzzy feelings although he wouldn't admit it.

One day when Faydoe was walking along the beach she began to wonder about their life. Would they stay, would they go, would they have children? She decided that she would deal the tarot cards. Maybe they would reveal what Jack was not telling her. She had always promised herself she would never nag him about anything but how do you comfort your man if he doesn't share his troubles. When she got home Jack had packed their belongings and was ready to leave. Once again he was in a nervous panic, so off they went nothing asked, nothing said. This time they would travel by pirogue with the help of a Part-Indian guide. A pirogue moved quickly and quietly like a snake. It could hide anybody anywhere in the bayous, maybe never to be seen again, maybe not, but that was a chance Jack was willing to take. Jack hired this particular guide because he knew the ins and outs of the bayous and had better instincts than any Indian born to man. But the main reason was he had a reputation for keeping his mouth shut about where he went and who went with him. Try as they may, nosy people couldn't find out anything. When questioned, his answer always began with, "I'll be honest with you" or "to tell you the truth ". Each and every time people found out he was lying. Finally, they came to realize that his business was nobody's business so he moved about somewhat unnoticed. He had long white hair, a long body, short legs, brown skin with dark, age spots and was so quiet he seemed lazy. White men called him Beagle but Indians called him Quiet Tongue. Beagle insisted on being paid thirty pieces of silver before leaving shore. Jack thought why not paper or gold but decided not to waste time asking questions that would not be answered. Beagle said they were moving along the Vermilion Bay and would soon enter the Boston Canal. Those were the last words Beagle spoke. Jack wondered if Faydoe had become Mrs. Quiet Tongue in some kind of secret, Indian spiritual ritual because she hadn't said a word since they left the shore. Jack made a mental chart of certain landmarks as they traveled many bayous deeper and deeper into the woods, moving in one direction then suddenly in another. Jack knew he was lost but worse than that, so was Beagle because many times they paddled right past a red bucket hanging upside down on a broken tree. It was one of Jack's unforgettable landmarks but where was it exactly and where did it lead? The bayous became narrower and the woody, marshland became denser and scarier much like Voodoo New Orleans. By now Jack began to feel fearful and hopeless as he gazed at the full moon and listened to the sounds of the bayou filled marshlands as his pirogue slithered around quietly. Suddenly Faydoe noticed a small cabin straight ahead in the distance and yelled out with excitement. She startled Jack so much that he had to check the seat of his pants for fear that he may find a little deposit. Beagle paddled swiftly towards the shack and docked along side of the old wooden porch. The three of them looked around and found a few candles, lanterns, fishhooks, canned goods, etc. The bunks were crudely made but it was a good resting spot if nothing else. It was abandoned and had been for a very long time. Suddenly Faydoe realized Beagle was gone. The pirogue was still there, thank God but what happened to Beagle. Now Jack knew who was really lost. Faydoe began to laugh and said, " Well Jack, you got what you paid for. We are really hiding this time. If anyone is trying to follow you they are out of luck because we can't even find us." Jack was in no mood to kid around. After the initial shock of their situation they had no choice but to make the best of it. Jack was no hunter but he managed to put food on the table. Faydoe was happy because after all, she had Jack. She began making their home as pleasant as possible. But this time there were no warm, fuzzy feelings inside Jack. They were replaced with a growing silent but apparent anger that was always there just below the surface feeding on evil thoughts. Day after day he thought of his bank account, of Capitano and of Beagle, yes Beagle with his thirty pieces of silver. Where was he? Had Capitano paid him to get rid of them? Did he plan to scalp the red head and keep the woman for himself? What? One night Jack couldn't sleep, just as so many other nights and went for a walk in the woods. Suddenly he saw a leather pouch hanging from a large branch of a mighty oak tree. Jack reached for it and found thirty pieces of silver inside. Beagle, what are you trying to tell me? Jack built a small campfire and sat there, thinking and thinking. His funds were low and he could use the silver to make his way back to New Orleans and his bank account, then become known as Monsieur Argent {Mr. Money}. He would change his appearance perhaps grow a beard. Once again he would enjoy the finer things in life. Maybe open a fancy restaurant complete with entertainment consisting of various plays, maybe even operas. Capitano would be searching for Jack in every corner of the South for the rest of his life never suspecting Jack would be foolish enough to return to New Orleans. The next morning Jack told Faydoe that he was leaving to try and find a way out of these swampy bayous. He convinced her that she would be safer at the cabin than with him. He, the pirogue and the silver disappeared as he slithered away like the snake that he was, not knowing he was bound for hell! Jack chose thirty pieces of silver over true love. Turns out that Beagle was really a swamper who quietly watched over Charmers. Jack failed his test. He deceived, he misled, he betrayed and sadly he deserted. Worse of all, he broke Faydoe's heart and the pain was so great that she never allowed herself to feel it preferring to dream a dream that would never be. Faydoe loved Jack completely and was never true to herself. Year after year she waited for his return, after all he had never lied to her. He may not have lied but he never said he was coming back. Since becoming a Charmer she learned all of the healing secrets of the swampy bayous. Being a Haitian born, tarot dealing, Bayou Charmer soon earned her the legendary status of Faydoe, voodoo witch of the bayous. She could prepare a mixture guaranteed to make anything right in your troubled world. Her spells varied and so did the price you paid. If you had a medical problem you crossed her palm with a silver coin, if it was a matter of romance the debt was settled by sharing a glass of blackberry wine. Faydoe never cast an evil spell no matter what anybody offered her. Those who persisted were given a table spoon of simple syrup flavored with fish oil to give it an evil taste, then she displayed the tarot cards and let the determined mind of the cold heart fantasize uncontrollably. They were so consumed by evil that they saw what they wanted to see and didn't realize Faydoe had not said a word. There was no reading! No spell! People tend to forget that evil is as evil does. For those filled with hate and an overwhelming desire to do harm in any fashion their payment would be as it always has been, an eye for an eye. There would be no changing your mind after the deed was done and your temper cooled. During Faydoe's lonely lifetime many privateers found her. Some were grateful for her healing hands and gave her food and clothes. Realizing how lonely she was waiting for Jack, they stayed a few extra days and had a little fun drinking rum, playing music and dancing with her. These big, fighting men were teary eyed as they said their goodbyes wishing they had a woman who loved them that much. They knew that Jack would probably never return. Sadly, all men are not the same. Other pirates came along and did God awful things to her. Quiet Tongue made sure they slowly, painfully suffered the wrath of the swamp never to be seen again. In his search for Jack, Capitano heard of the witch of the bayous and eventually found Faydoe. She told him the truth, she didn't know where Jack was and that he had not yet returned. He didn't believe her but she was too frail to man handle so he left vowing to continue his search even if it meant to the death, his or Jack's, it made no difference. Quiet Tongue was watching and listening. He smiled as he thought to himself how lucky Capitano was that he had not harmed Faydoe because there would have been a difference for him just as there was for Jack, a long lasting, miserable, painful, difference. Faydoe remains in that very same cabin, dreaming of the day Magic Jack Callahan will rescue her just as he did so very long ago.

 Mary was teary eyed and thanked Miss Faydoe for sharing her story and vowed that if she ever had a baby girl she would tell her the beautiful, romantic, love story of her good friend. Mary and Al reminded her of herself and Jack and she was thankful for their kindness and friendship so she cast a good spell over them but would not say what it was for fear that the spell would be broken. Shortly afterward Miss Faydoe died. How sad it was that for a very long time creatures of the swamp, and Quiet Tongue were her only friends. Legends of the spirits of the mighty oaks seemed true, secrets shared are secrets kept. She was a beholder who never left. Al believes she died of a broken heart because she missed Jack so.

Mary's pregnancy went well but it seemed to last forever. These days Al rarely left Mary's side. While pregnant he made her get in the pirogue and go frogging with him down the bayou because he wanted to make sure he was there when the baby was born. Mary was tired and didn't think this was such a good idea but did as he asked trying to ease his mind.

Just when Al couldn't take it any longer Mary began to go into labor. Well, Mr. Al became so frightened he began to yell, "not now, not now". Too late, exit Mr. Roland. Al fainted dead away at witnessing this miracle. However he came to as quickly as he went out because he came to his senses realizing Mary and the baby needed him. The baby was such fun, loud, strong and smart as could be. Wanting to be the center of attention he learned quickly and liked to play hide and seek and other games. In fact he was too playful causing his parents, especially his mother to worry, after all, they lived near water and gators, etc. But, the little creature was lucky and escaped the jaws of death several times.

Five years had passed and Mary once again came to Al with the good news. Yep, she was pregnant. This time their good friend was not around so they would have to wait with even more excitement for this birth. Was it a boy or a girl? Al often said it was a girl, yep, a girl. After a few weeks he was convinced it was a boy. Al saw the not knowing as some kind of torture for something he had done but he did not know what and that thought became stressful in itself. Thank God Mary finally went into labor but Al did not faint. Exit Mr. Steven. Al yelled and yelled at the sight of his new son. Baby Steven, as he became known for a time, was strong and healthy but quiet and kept to himself. He too was smart and learned quickly.

The first of the boys to sustain an injury was Steven. He fell from a tree and broke his leg. Mary cried and cried. Al set the leg and made a small crutch from a window shade rod. Steven who hated to be held back by anything whether it be human, animal or circumstances was very, very excited to be able to move about thanks to the man he loved most in the world. He noticed the good things his dad took time to do for the comfort of the family. Like the time one ever so cold winter that his dad killed a deer and hung the hide on the outside wall of the cabin until it dried. Then he brought it in, placed it on the floor near the bed so that they could have something warm to walk on when they got up in the morning. The main heart felt thing Steven learned by example from Al is the love of family.

Al was very happy with his wife and two sons, after all he was living his dream even if it was a struggle. Life was still hard. One thing that often made him smile was the thought of having a beautiful baby girl. She would have blonde hair like the morning sun, blue eyes like the sky and fair skin like the clear, soft, glow of the moon.

Five years after the birth of his second son, the lord answered Al's prayers and a baby girl was born. Exit Miss Lois. She was just as he had wished and God threw in a little bonus because she had a happy, friendly personality and never met a stranger. Could she be the product of Miss FAYDOE's good spell? Al told Mary that he would run the traps a couple of extra times so that they could afford to buy a proper christening gown to present their daughter in church and have Father Andrico baptize her.

Lois' brothers were very protective of her but at the same time as she got older they gave her a hard time by playfully teasing her, a lot. She on the other hand was spoiled and could sometimes take a joke but if she was in a bad mood she would throw herself down on the floor, pretend to cry very loudly as though in great pain until Mary came to her rescue and scolded the boys even if they were innocent which mostly they weren't. Lois walked away all smug and satisfied until the next round. But life has a way of helping the under dog. One day Lois was sitting along the bayou opening a napkin that held a fig tart her mom had made for her because it was her favorite treat. She removed it from the napkin but accidentally threw the tart into the strong current of the bayou and kept the napkin. Her brothers were fishing near by and saw the stunned look of disbelief on her face. They began to laugh and asked her how she planned to blame them for it. Needless to say she cried every time her stomach growled calling for that fig tart. Life isn't always fair or is it?

With the growth of the family, life became too hard on the bayou! Al could endure but he and Mary thought it wasn't fair to the children. They needed friends, better clothes, a better home and schooling. Although they had knowledge of the land and survival skills they also needed to learn how to read and write properly in order to survive in civilization. So Al went to Erath in search of the means of a better life for his family and hopefully would return with good news.

While in Town Al spoke with Mousier Talle`. He was a wealthy man who owned several houses, land and a general store. Mousier Talle` offered Al a deal that seemed too good to be true; you know what that means. Al could become a sharecropper. Mousier Talle` explained that Al and his family could live in the house rent free for now, work the land for a share of the crops and at the end of crop season the rent would be deducted from Al's share. This seemed fair to Al. Mousier Talle` sweetened the pot by telling Al he could also trap on his land and keep 50% for himself. This also seemed fair to Al but he began to be suspicious. Finally Al said "what else". Well, your 50% has to be sold to me at my store in exchange for certificates to purchase flour, clothes, and other supplies. Al felt sort of trapped but his family was in need so he agreed and brought the family to the marshlands on the outskirts of Erath. Al had not thought to look at the house before striking a deal. The disappointment showed in Mary's face but she didn't say a word; after all they were a team and always had been no matter what although she had secretly hoped for a more modern place to live.

The house was nothing but a run down camp that was falling apart. There was no running water, only well water that they had to haul inside from an outside pump. There was an outhouse for a toilet, a # 3 tub for bathing, a scrub board and washtub for washing clothes. The potbelly stove was used for cooking and warming the house in the winter but it was sometimes so cold you slept with all your clothes on, including a hat. Once the children stayed in bed the whole day and night. There were two irons for pressing clothes. They were made of cast iron and were heated on the potbelly stove. As one was used the other was kept hot. There were no screens on the windows. In the summer the shutters had to be closed at night so the mosquitoes would not eat you. It then became unbearably hot and sinking into a feather mattress didn't help. The one thing it did have was electricity. There was a light hanging from the ceiling in the center of the room on a long electrical cord. This became part of the children's amusement. They would swing the cord from side to side causing shadows on the walls. Through some fancy hand gestures each child had to guess what the shadow represented. Steven became very good at this. However the games ended when the dive-bomber mosquitoes found them. The light was turned off to make the search harder for the enemy.

One good thing about the move was that the family had a social life, especially on Saturday nights. There was always a dance and an adult card game at someone's house. Men drank, women gossiped and children became friends. They played, fought, cried and played some more with toys they had made themselves. They ate watermelon, home made fig tarts and other good treats. Other times there were all day events such as making boudin and cracklin. This was the most fun. Everyone was always excited and happy. The boudin was made by cooking odd parts of the hog, removing the meat from the bone, mixing it with rice, salt, pepper, onion tops, garlic and onions and stuffing the mixture in a casing which happened to be the intestines of the pig. The cracklin was made from the fat and skin of the pig. This was chopped in large pieces, fried, drained and seasoned. No part of the hog was wasted. The head was used in the boudin or hog head cheese, the skin was fried, the feet were pickled and the lard was saved for use as cooking oil. The choice cuts of meat were shared by all and brought home for family use. Children rode horses, went swimming in the bayou, hunted and even did a little crabbing and fishing. By the end of the day everyone was exhausted.

Sanchez

    It was at one of these gatherings that the family heard about a man who lived in the area. He was what was called a guardian of the sick or a treater. There weren't many doctors around and the few in existence were so far away that a person had time to die before one could arrive. He was gifted in the knowledge of the use of herbs, roots, leaves, and etc. much like Indians or believers in voodoo. There was a mystery about him because nobody knew where he came from, only that he supposedly was found on somebody's doorsteps and raised by the founders as their own.

    He was short, had dark eyes, dark hair, olive skin and had a strange way of talking. He kept his jaw tightly closed when he spoke. He never uttered a word with his mouth fully open.

Another odd thing was that he was a fighter. It wasn't really the fact that he was a fighter that was odd but the method he used. He never started trouble but never ran from it. Many a man was fooled by his short, small stature and thought he was easy pickings for a bully who wanted to show off in some public place. When the game was afoot it really was afoot because this Spanish looking person was a Zapatieur who expertly practiced the little known art of "ZAPATO". He always fought with his feet, never his fist. The bully never knew what hit him. Just like lightening, fierce, fast and powerful this little man kicked the bully in the face and knocked him out cold and never lost his upright stance or his balance. He would then walk away and go about his business as though nothing had happened.

Unfortunately there came a time when Al needed the help of this man. Mary became very ill and had a high fever. Al desperately went from farm to farm trying to find this man. Finally the little man had gotten the word and he went to Al's home. He knocked at the door several times and was about to leave when Al answered. Mr. Sanchez introduced himself and said that he had gotten word that his help was needed. Sanchez explained that he had just left from Dr. Henry's house where he had cared for the Dr's brothers. Dr. Henry had tried his best to cure his brothers but nothing seemed to work and in desperation he had called on Mr. Sanchez. They were fine now and no longer needed him so he came here. Al began to tell him that Mary had a high fever for several days and Al didn't know what was causing it. Sanchez then told Al that he could help her and that his specialty was caring for victims of typhoid fever. Sanchez made it clear that he moves in with the family and does not leave until the sick person is cured He accepts cash or barters for payment of his services. Al said he understood. After a few days Mary slowly began to show signs of improvement.

During the time of treatment Al and Sanchez became a little better acquainted. Al suddenly missed his Mom very much and began to tell the story about how she came here from Spain and how a privateer treated her so kindly when she was captured. Al laughed as he said that the privateer called himself Jean Lafitte but Al's Mom knew he wasn't. Sanchez began to sweat and became anxious as he urged Al to continue. The privateer gave her a treasure map but she didn't remember where she hid it. Sanchez asked Al where his Mom was and Al said he didn't know. He didn't even know if she was still alive because she was so sick when he left home as a child. Sanchez then told Al a little about himself. He had been married and had children but the marriage didn't work out. He then met and sometimes lived with this beautiful young woman. She was tall, slim, blue eyes, long black hair, and wonderful smile. She was fun to be with and was a good dancer. She had one son but was never married. Sanchez thought to himself, "Why do I terrorize the one I love? How can I be so mean and so kind? I trouble myself to no end." Suddenly he had an odd look, one of remorse. That's enough about me. Let's check on your wife. They were pleasantly surprised to find Mary sitting up in bed asking them what had happened. It was now time for Sanchez to leave. His job was done.

Daniel

    Over all life was better for Al and his family. Farming was harder than he thought it would be and picking cotton was no easy task either. It was while in the cotton fields that Al looked around and noticed that many people were poor, black and white alike. A black man named Daniel picked along side of Al and as they became acquainted he told Al that he owned a little farm but in order to make ends meet he hired out from time to time as a cotton picker. Al liked him and thought he seemed to be a good man. Time went on as time does with little change. Things were somewhat harder for the black man than for the white man in similar circumstances because skin color was still an issue. Overall everyone got along, at least for now.

   Daniel often hired himself out to work Mr. Talle` 's fields but Daniel knew his reputation for being a sly fox when making working arrangements so Daniel was always clear about working strictly for cash, no side arrangements. Mr. Talle' also knew Daniel's reputation for giving an honest days work so they never haggled. This particular field was very large and would take a long time to clear. It just so happened that Daniel worked along side of the same white man every day so they became acquainted. When Daniel went home he often talked about this man and said how much he liked him. As he described him to Lucille she said, "Why Daniel, sounds to me that he's much like you except for the color of his skin." Daniel thought a minute than said, "You're right, but if he spends any more time in the field without a hat he will get darker just like me." They laughed and laughed at the thought of two Daniels. Lucille wanted to meet this man so she suggested that since they would be working so close to home the next day that Daniel should invite him to dinner. Daniel happily agreed.

   Daniel was secretly very excited to invite this white man to his home. Turns out the man was just as excited to accept the invitation. They shook hands and continued to pick cotton until lunchtime. Finally they got in Daniel's wagon and on the way to his place they talked and talked. When they arrived the white man said, " My name is Al. They sometimes call me Cajun Al but I like plain old Al better." Lucille introduced herself and so did Daniel. All three began to laugh because they suddenly realized that in all this time of working together the men had not known each other's names. They washed up then sat down to a good chicken and sausage gumbo. Al wouldn't want Mary to know but Lucille was a better cook. Afterwards the men sat on the back porch and rested while they got to know each other better. Lucille listened to their conversation while she washed the dishes and thought that they sounded more like brothers than friends. They liked horses, hunting, trapping, and working the land, earning their own way, and above all else family life. No wonder they never ran out of things to talk about. Lunch break was over, time to go back to work so Al thanked both of them for their kindness and for the meal which happened to be his favorite thing to eat. Finally the fields in this area were cleared and all workers went their separate ways in search of another job. Daniel thought about Al often and hoped they would meet again, perhaps in another field while harvesting another crop.

Uncle Bud's prayers were finally answered. Daniel and Lucille were going to have a baby. Gabriele and Lucille cried and Uncle Bud and Daniel had a beer while quietly wiping away tears of joy. Uncle Bud quickly took Daniel to CRABBYS where they shared the good news with the OLD CRABS. This new baby was going to have more loving aunts, uncles and cousins than anyone could imagine because they suddenly had a very large extended family. Everyone attended Mass Sunday to thank God for this wonderful blessing.

As time went by Lucille was smothered by the family's well-meaning attention. She felt she just had to get away by herself just to take a deep breath of fresh air without everyone around her jumping to his or her feet thinking something was wrong. She took a slow walk to the old fishing hole where Daniel taught her how to fish. She admitted to herself that she was afraid to deliver their first baby and didn't really know what to expect. She had never witnessed any birthing before not human or animal. She sat and prayed that her baby would be healthy and that God would help Daniel and Uncle Bud when the time came.

This was a quiet, pleasant spot with happy memories and it was a beautiful sunny day with a soft, gentle breeze flowing the scent of honeysuckle in the air while the moss hanging form the oak trees swayed back and forth. The sounds of the bayou were so calming and relaxing that Lucille seemed to be in a trance as she heard a whisper. She looked around and nobody was there. Again she heard the same whispering so this time she listened as it told her she would have a strong, healthy baby and not to worry because everything would be fine. She suddenly felt calm, no longer troubled and returned home.

    Lucille was so happy that she began to feel guilty because most of her friends and relatives weren't. She remembered that as young children they all played make believe with their dolls. They pretended to have a nice home and a few beautiful children but for some the pretending ended there. Never did they talk of a male figure in these games. The evil whoremaster, the evil overseer and sometimes their own evil family members had brought the pain that ended their dreams with the loss of their innocence. It was as though the devil had stolen their cries because although they were sad most of the time there were no tears.

    In the past most marriages, white or black, produced ten or more offspring as an advantage to free labor and if the wife died the husband, who happened to be a poor farmer, would seek out a very young child like girl to become his new wife because he needed a housekeeper and someone to care for his children. The younger the better because she was more likely to live longer, less likely to refuse his sexual needs and more easily trained like a good, obedient dog. Unfortunately some larger, poor families readily agreed when the farmer came calling to explain his need for a wife because it meant there was one less mouth to feed in their own household. A monetary token of appreciation was offered and accepted to seal the deal. It never entered the minds of the families, white or black, that they became slave traders. The child bride had no say in the matter the trap was sprung. After a time she said secret prayers for a merciful death to finally have heavenly peace.

    Some of Lucille's other friends and relatives married because that's what you did, you got married to whoever asked you first hoping for a better life but since there was no love there was no happiness. They soon realized that they had trapped themselves. The sad thing is that very few female children escaped this pattern of helpless existence.

Generation after generation of Mothers were under so much constant stress trying to cope with life that children rarely received a smile, a hug or a kiss on the cheek; they were always to be seen and not heard therefore the pattern was rarely broken. The why of anything was never asked and answered. They dare not voice an opinion about anything because to do so often meant punishment of some kind; maybe a slap across the face; maybe kneeling in a corner for a long time on top of a few grains of raw rice all the while with arms extended. In most cases the crime was simply being in the wrong place at the wrong time.

Sometimes when people are destroying themselves you feel helpless to intervene. Unlike Lucille they never had a Daniel. A kind, loving hero never came along and rescued them from their burdensome life of pain and sorrow. All Lucille felt she could do was lend an ear, encourage them to show loving kindness towards children and never let them underestimate the power of prayers. But for today, Lucille's quick fix to make some of her friends forget their troubles is to surprise them with a good pecan pie, a blackberry cobbler and fig tarts. Lucille figures that God made her a good baker so that she could be the Sweet Tooth Fairy who spreads a little happiness

Jacquee

Mary and the boys helped as much as they could while Al did some trapping to supplement the family's income. Finally the crops were harvested and the traps were cleared. It was time to tally up at the general store.

Much to Al's surprise he was left owing Mousier Talle`. It was then that Al realized he was trapped. He also learned why people called the man Mousier Talle`. It was because he was always ready to tally up, but always very much in his favor. In order to plant a new crop Al had to add charges on his existing account leaving him further in debt.

That night he and Mary sat down and had a long talk trying to figure a way out of this. Would they ever be able to own their own place like the man from the cotton fields? Just then they heard a noise outside so Al grabbed his gun and went out asking,"Who's there. Who? Tell me now or I'll shoot." There was no reply so Al walked around and found a somewhat elderly black man crouched down in the long grass shivering and looking helpless. Al couldn't decide if he was cold or scared, probably a bit of both. He and Mary brought him inside and gave him a cup of hot coffee, which he was reluctant to accept, but did so eventually. Al asked who he was and how did he come to be in their yard.

He began by telling them that his name was Jacquee and he was wandering around for a long time with no place to go and his mind was a blank when he tried to think of where he came from. He knew he had been a slave for many years but now seems to be free. The strange thing was that he did not know how to be free. For a whole lifetime he had been told when to get up in the morning, what to do all day and when to go to bed at night. He had been told to go here, go there, eat this, don't eat that; here, you can have these old clothes. He was taught to be submissive at all times and was not to learn to read and write. He was never paid any money and would not know how to use it if he had some now. Freedom must be a wonderful thing but how does a person survive? Al told him that God sent him to the right place because survival was one thing Al had become an expert at. Mary and Al laughed and invited him to eat supper, sleep near the warm stove and they would talk more in the morning. Jacquee said, " Thank you sir" Al said, "Let's get one thing straight right now, there is no sir around here. We are friends and we will help each other. Agree?" Jacquee smiled, they shook hands and all retired for the night. Al figured Jacquee must be one of those runaway blacks he had heard about who was abused to the breaking point and thought to be possessed by the voodoo spirit prince L'eau Noir. If there had been an evil spell it was broken now and this black man needed help. There was no need to speak of what might have been in Jacquee's past only the good that lies ahead.

The next day everyone said their good mornings and the children, as Mary always called them, were surprised to see a black man in their house. After they were introduced they had a hundred questions for him. They liked the idea of having a new friend that could tell them so many good stories. After breakfast Mary told them to go out and tend to their chores, they could talk later.

Al told Jacquee how Al was supposed to be a free man but was trapped and sort of a slave himself. He asked Jacquee if he had any ideas. Jacquee began to tell him how the slave owners maintained their vast wealth and that he figured maybe they could use some of those ideas. So Jacquee became a member of their team and they shared each other's knowledge.

They decided they would grow vegetables and fruit for their own use. Some they ate fresh and some they canned. They would make Tasso, which was alligator garfish that was salted and sun dried for preservation. Al and Jacquee would hunt and fish along the bayous away from Monsieur. Talle`'s land that way he did not have to give up 50%. Beef was too expensive so they ate deer, geese, ducks, etc. They had no refrigeration so they would partially cook the meat by browning it in a black iron pot then putting the meat in a six gallon crock pot filled with hog lard thereby preserving the meat. Al also tried to use his 22 bullets sparingly and with as much accuracy as possible when shooting a deer. The same logic was used in shooting geese with his shotgun. When hunting rabbits Al was an expert at killing them with a stick.

One night while Al and Jacquee were sitting under an old oak tree in the back yard having coffee and waiting for the boys to come back from catching frogs Al suddenly remembered seeing a very old abandoned boat on the edge of Tiger Bayou. Al told Jacquee about it. Just as he sprung to his feet, Al said, "I'm thinking," Jacquee said, "I'm thinking too," let's go. They wanted it so bad that they managed to find it in the dead of night. Half of it was under water but that didn't matter to them because after all a boat belongs in the water. All these two grown up little Cajun – Mulatto boys saw were the good parts not the rotten boards etc.. They threw some tree branches and moss across the bow to try and hide their newly found treasure so nobody would steal it before they could return. Early the next morning they walked to Mr. Neotis's farm and asked if he could lend a hand. They explained that their boat took on water and maybe his plow mule could pull it on shore so they could check out the damages. Poor old Mr. Neotis was so very happy that somebody needed him in his old age that he was more than happy to help. Once the boat was on dry land all three Cajuns had a very strong opinion as to what and how to do the rest of the job. Cajun men never have a problem speaking up. They say what they feel needs saying, take it or leave it. Mr. Neotis said that he had some aged cypress wood in his old barn that they could have because he probably would never use it. They shook hands and thanked each other for everything. After all repairs were done Roland and Steven wanted to paint the boat. Al said they could but they had to get the paint themselves because he didn't have any money or paint. They did one of those Cajun handshakes and said it was a deal but nobody could see it until the job was done. The boys took off running straight to As-if the barber. They figured he was bound to have some paint left after painting the post in front of his shop every few months. Sure enough Mr. As-if had some and was happy to help them out, after all, they were his favorite customers. The job was done and it was time to show off. The team gathered together to see THE DEVIL for the first time. They had painted the boat red and the name white. At first all anybody could say was Wow. They all laughed and said how it was a good job and probably it would be the fastest boat in the bay. The next thing was to get an inboard engine. By the use of bartering Al had an old engine installed in it. The boys really had fun helping Al and Jacquee troll for shrimp, fish and crabs. Jacquee thought this was the best time he had with the family. There was just something about the sea and the real sense of freedom a person feels when the wind blows fresh air in your face and you feel the warmth of the sun on your body especially when your boat is the fastest, you know, the best. There was nothing like it. Finally by the family, including Jacquee, pulling together they were able to clear their debt with Monsieur Talle` and move away from the evil trapper.

   Jacquee wanted a life and family of his own; he figured it wasn't too late, so he decided to move in a different direction. He thanked the family for all they had taught him and for their friendship. He would miss them, especially the children. Jacquee said he now knew why people fought so hard for this thing they call freedom, it is a wonderful thing and should be cherished by everybody no matter what. Al quietly slipped a little starter money in Jacquee's pocket. He knew his friend wouldn't take it outright.

   Al was smart and quickly landed a job at the sugar refinery in Erath. It did not pay much but this time there was no sharecropper lying in wait with his well-planned trap for the poor man. They had rented a house on LeBlanc St. and life was better but Al was not happy. This job was not self-satisfying. Somehow he felt less of a man even though it was good honest work. Mary thought that if Al learned to read and write he might cheer up. After much coaxing she went with him to enroll in an adult night class offered at the Erath School. They attended each class together. Things went well at first but the instructor was attracted to Mary and began openly belittling Al. The more he talked down the angrier Al became. Finally Al rose from his seat, walked up to the instructor, knocked him out, grabbed Mary by the hand and left. Members of the class-applauded saying, " Good. There's a long time he was asking for it" It wasn't until his temper cooled down that Al realized he had learned to write his name. He and Mary began to laugh but Al never returned to school.

Al quit the refinery job and was unable to find another right away so in order to pay the bills he had to return to the bayous. In a way it was a blessing in disguise because it allowed him time to think about his future while in familiar surroundings. He hunted, trapped, fished and trawled for shrimp. He never told Mary how he was almost caught one night poaching gators. He had an iron bar about eight feet long that was pointed on one end and had a strong hook on the other end. He had just hooked a very large alligator when some wardens happened by. Al saw them but they didn't see him. He quickly went under water dragging the alligator with him below the marsh grass. The alligator fought hard for freedom and Al fought even harder for air and to maintain his grip. There was a mighty struggle. The Wardens saw the alligator thrashing about in the marsh grass but never saw Al. They probably figured it was eating an animal of some kind and moved on. When Al thought it was safe he returned to land, carefully skinned the alligator and preserved the hide and meat with salt. He would return home for a couple of days to sell his catch, give Mary the money and go back out again. Al felt he was back to surviving in a place he knew best and for now it had to be by any means necessary. Each time he returned to the bayous he searched for the pirate treasure his mom told him about but he never found it. Somehow it didn't matter because his real treasure was the memory of his Mom and Dad and their loving family.

The Boxing Ring

One night Roland and Steven had overheard their parents talking in the kitchen about their financial struggles. Steven was very troubled and asked Roland what he thought they could do to help. Roland told him not to worry that he would take care of it. The next day while walking around town the boys noticed a boxing ring behind the old grocery store. Some men from up north went from town to town making money by fighting. There was a sign saying that the fights begin at six o'clock on Friday night and winner takes all. Roland got all excited and told Steven he would do it. Steven said do what? Fight, that's what. Steven said, look brother I know nobody can beat you when you're mad but this is different. How, a fight is a fight but don't tell Mom. Friday night was finally here and sure enough Roland and Steven were ringside watching everything. One big man kept winning but Roland noticed he cheated. After a few rounds Roland yelled out, cheater. The man looked around and saw that Roland was a very young, skinny fellow and began to laugh. Roland again yelled out, cheater. By now the crowd was getting a little excited because they knew the north and the south would again do battle. Roland yelled out if you want to fight a man, fight me. The big man noticed nobody was laughing. They knew the little stick of dynamite and they also knew that he was ready to explode. The big one was secretly a bit afraid but he had no choice, he had to invite the skinny thing into the ring. Steven held his breath but didn't try and hold Roland back because he saw what happened to a friend of his who tried to stop Roland from doing something he wanted to do. It was not a pretty sight. The fight went on for a few rounds but whether the people bet or not they sure got their money's worth. Roland won by a knockout but suffered a slight cut to the face, just enough to help with his bragging rights. The big man left town in the middle of the night and never fought again after losing to a skinny little Cajun bayou kid from the Deep South. The boys went home and proudly gave the money to their Mom who began to cry.

The boys told her the whole family was a team and they wanted to help. When Al came home the only thing he wanted to know was the whole story blow by blow minute by minute and said how he was very sorry to have missed all the excitement. Al and the boys laughed but Mary just cried again.

While Al was home he would search for a new job but they continued to be hard to come by. One day he learned about a new industry called the oil field. It was his understanding that the company hired a crew of men who worked as a team in different positions to drill for oil with heavy equipment. They each received money for the work they did and were paid different amounts; depending on what job they had to do. Any regular amount of money provided more and better security for the family. This was appealing to Al because in his mind it was rugged enough to allow him to keep his dignity as a Cajun outdoorsman; he did not like what he thought were sissy jobs.

Al got the job and the crew agreed to provide transportation until Al could afford to buy a better vehicle. He could have borrowed money from the bank but Al heard stories about Mr. Batiste, the bank president who had a bad reputation of going so far as to remove gold teeth from a dead man before burial in order to clear a debt, that's how evil a legal trapper he had become. Al would have none of it. Saving up was the best and safest way. That day finally arrived. Al was so proud to park his brand new car in the yard for all the neighbors to see. Life was so much easier now. There were more extended family dinners and a better life style. They had a refrigerator instead of an icebox like some people and the first television on the block. The neighborhood children spent more time at Mary's house than their own.

While at the post office one day Mary heard about this unwed young woman about forty years old who was very sick and had small children. She went home, gathered a food basket and went over. She knocked at the door but there was no answer so she went in and found a little girl standing on a stool trying to wash on a washboard. She told Mary that her mommy was sick and she was trying to help her. They went into the bedroom where Mary propped Marlie up on a pillow and fed her some chicken soup. She managed to eat a little but fell asleep. Mary fed the child, cleaned the house and picked a few wild flowers from the yard to put in Marlie's room to cheer her up. Marlie slept for a few hours and when she woke up Mary gave her a bath and some more soup.

They talked and Marlie told her all about how she came to be in this condition, and how she recently learned that her father had been shot and killed. Her Father was Mr. Batiste, the banker who treated people so unfairly. The piper had finally come calling.

She had always hoped to make him understand that babies are a gift from God to grandparents; their second chance to correct all the mistakes they made with their own children; the chance to say they are sorry. She wanted to make him understand that she had not ruined the family name; he had done that all by himself. Most of all she wanted to tell him that she loved him. All of these mixed emotions distressed her.

She smiled faintly and said tell Nathaniel, the father of my first born that he was my first and only true love and that I will always love him. You know Miss Mary there is just something everlasting in ones memory about a first love. No matter how old you live to be, you never forget the first exact moment you met and everything about it. The pounding of your heart, how he looked, what he said, what you said no matter how silly it seems now. How you smiled when you thought of him no matter where you were or who was around. Your first innocent kiss, no matter how awkward, was meaningful. You don't think about when you broke up or why. That doesn't seem to matter much. I do know that you keep a little special spot in your heart for the innocent memory of that person.

She knew she was going to die soon and asked Mary to please see to it that her girls go to live with good people who would be kind to them, they had suffered enough. She wanted her children to know that she loved them very much and she was sorry. Most importantly Miss Mary, please be sure and tell my children to never lose sight of their dreams and to remember me when they dance.

Luckily Mary had left a note for Al telling him where she was if he came home from work early. Al arrived and wanted to know what was going on and why Mary was crying. She told him the whole sad story and that she would never understand why this little person's life turned out the way it did. Mary regretted not knowing this woman. Al told Mary he believed the man who saved her when she was sick was the same Sanchez in this girl's life. How could he be so kind but yet so cruel and selfish? Al remembered briefly seeing remorse in Sanchez's eyes that day he spoke of a beautiful young woman he lived with for a time.

The doctor and Father Andrico did the necessary paper work to properly record the passing. Sadly Mary, Al and her children were the only ones at the gravesite. Afterwards they all went to Al's house where they rested for a few days while deciding what to do. Finally Marlie's boys went back to work. Al's brother, Whitney and his wife took the smaller girl. They had several children of their own but this little girl touched their hearts and they just had to do something to help her. Whitney thought of his own baby sister and regretted that he was not able to be there for her when she needed him. The older little girl was placed with a distant relative who lived in another town but wanted to help.

The girls were so very afraid. They were little and could not fully understand why somebody put their mommy in a hole in the ground and threw dirt on her. Why did they have to live with other people? They were loved and comforted as their healing progressed.

The children and grand children planned a family reunion on Marlie's birth date. They invited Al and Mary and at the end of the day they sat outside, looked up at the stars and said, " Granny, we just want you to know that we are all happy and will love you forever. "

Al's new profession meant that in order to keep his job and steady paycheck he had become accustom to getting over the years, he had to follow the job site with the rest of the crew. When one job for rig 153 was completed there was another some place else, usually in Louisiana or Texas. The rig, equipment, and crew would move to the new location for the duration of the job. This meant uprooting the family, renting a house, and having the children attend a new school. Sometimes this move lasted a few months, sometimes a couple of years. Al decided to maintain his rent house in Erath in order to have a home base when the rig operated in an area close by. The children were not excited about moving from place to place but they survived. It reminded them of the covered wagon stories they saw on television. However, they made friends easily and were happy enough.

Al was working in Louisiana, very close to his home base when he was asked to go to Texas and fill in for a fellow worker who had been injured on the job. The job would last two weeks and the boss offered to let Al take a much-earned two-week vacation with pay afterwards if he helped him out now. The boss was no fool and knew it was to his advantage to sweeten the pot with the offer of a paid vacation. He realized how valuable a worker Al was. Al had learned to work any position on the rig including the responsibilities of the company man He was never late and never asked for time off. He admired and respected Al and could not understand how Al managed to accomplish these tasks without knowing how to read and write.

Vacation

This time Al went alone and the family stayed home in Erath. When he returned he announced to the family they were taking a vacation, the first one in Al's whole entire life. For two weeks they were going some place where they could have fun. Mary asked if they could go to the bayous and visit their old campsite where they first lived as a family. The children were mostly grown but were very excited about riding in a boat again. Al felt an odd feeling come over him as that of a bad omen. He thought no more of it and began getting things ready for their morning trip. Everyone was so happy and excited.

They all enjoyed the fresh air, sunshine and cool breeze. Nature was at its best, almost as though all the birds, animals and other creatures were welcoming them home. A small wooden bayou side dock was all that remained of their first home. The land was over grown with trees and brush. They set about clearing an area to pitch a tent. The children began to explore, Mary cooked and Al just sat on the dock looking around and thinking how much he loved Mary. She was the best thing that ever happened to him. He felt that through her his life had really begun. After supper the children went to sleep and Al and Mary snuggled on the dock. He told her that she was the only woman he ever loved and he would love her with all his heart and soul for the rest of his life. She smiled and gently held his face in her hands while she kissed him softly and said, "Isn't it a beautiful night? The moon is so clear." They gazed at the moon as they had done so many years ago when they had first met and she said those exact words to him. After a while he got up and went to the tent to get his tobacco pouch and roll paper so that he could have a relaxing smoke. He was only gone a short time and was not far from the dock when he heard a fierce splashing of water and a faint, small, voice in the distance. He ran as fast as he could while calling to Mary but he could not find her. She had fallen through the rotten boards on the end of the dock into the strong water current and had been swept out from the bayou to the sea. He dove in but could not find her body. She had never told Al she was afraid of water and could not swim. The happy family vacation had turned into the saddest, most miserable time of his life and he would never forget, never! It was at this time that Al lost some of his character and dignity. He became a little more like the evil trapper.

The children as Mary always called them were adults now. Roland married, Steven joined the service and Lois lived with relatives for a short time before she too married. Al tried to move on but was never the same. He had lost the real joy of life. Naturally he would breathe, eat, sleep, get up in the morning, keep clean, get a hair cut from As-if the barber every now and then. It was as though the desire to be a good honest man that a wife could be proud of had been chipped away a little allowing another slightly evil, sneaky conman side of him to enter and fill the gap. He left the oilfields in search of a new way of life.

Although a man of many skills Al always had a love of animals, especially horses. He was in awe of their strength, muscular build and speed. There seemed to be such beauty and sense of freedom in the way their mane moved as they raced the wind. There's just something about horses.

Al began to think about horses day and night. Each night he had the same dream. In this dream his Indian ancestor, Chief Spirit of the Oak would appear. Al was a youngster full of life and eager to learn anything the Chief had to teach. There was a strong spiritual connection between the two of them and Al knew that the Chief would be with him the rest of his life and beyond. The horse was important to the Indians. It was sacred and should be treated with respect. The dream continued and Al bonded with the horses. They whispered to him in the wind. He learned of their journey, their pain, and their playfulness. He learned of herbs and oils for their healing and most of all what gave them strength and speed. Each time Al reached the point in his dream where he was taking a breath of fresh air on a beautiful sunny day, sitting along the bayou feeling free as the wind he would wake up but not before he saw a strong, beautiful, blue stud on the horizon running towards him.

Al being a poor man could not afford to buy a horse with a good bloodline so he decided to go to the sale barn to look around. Farmers in the area brought their stock to the auction barn hoping to get a good price. Mostly the stock was healthy but sometimes the goods were considered damaged so to speak and this allowed the buyer to practically steal the animal at a very low price. Al overheard the sheriff and his brother Joe talking about Joe's horse and how Joe was going to sell it at auction because he was lame. Al observed the horse and knew right away that the horse had a slight sprain, nothing major. He worked his way into the conversation and told Joe his horse was so messed up that it was not worth the trouble preparing paper work for auction. Al offered $100.00 to Joe, who replied, "deal" and they shook hands. Al then made arrangements to take the horse home for a little tender loving care.

When the time was right Al brought him to Cajun Country Race Track where he portrayed Joe's old horse in a negative light and had the jockey hold a tight reign to make the horse lose the race. After losing two weekends in a row, Al knew that the bets would again be against him, so Al bet all the money he could beg, borrow or steal on his horse and told the jockey, "cut him loose". The horse won by several lengths and Al was temporarily off the poor mans list. The sheriff was not amused about how his brother had been conned and poor old Joe could not show his face at the race track for a long time because people continued to tease him about his $100.00 deal and how old Joe's horse was really a runner.

Now, funds were low and Al needed money. Naturally, these days he came by it by hook or crook and the racetrack was the best place for either. So Al came up with a sure win plan for his second race, after all he had made a statement by winning the other race. Being first at anything meant you were the best and he aimed to be just that.

The country track was a form of entertainment on weekends and who's who in Cajun country was there. There was money to be made and if you were lucky enough you won. This was truly a game of chance. You took a chance by betting because the best horse did not win. The winner was trained by the shrewdest, sneakiest, most under handed, slight of hand trainer who could set a cheating plan in motion for the winning horse and get away with it. Al saw these tactics as a fun game of wit. One trainer used a shocking battery concealed in his whip, one used drugs, one out right beat the horse excessively with his whip and one made the horse drink several cold beers then put a rooster on the horses back in place of a jockey, after all the rules said the horse had to have a live, light weight mount, it said nothing about the rider being human or the horse being sober.

    Al pranced his horse around patiently and waited until all other horses were in the gate. He then secretly rubbed gator grease on the rump of his horse before placing him in the stall. Al knew that the scent scared the other horses into thinking a gator was around and they went crazy. The jockeys could not understand why and they had a hard time controlling their mounts. Naturally Al's horse was calm because the breeze blew the scent away from him and towards the horses slightly behind. Al then began yelling, "Let's go, let's go. I'm ready." The gates sprung open and Al's horse ran the track with ease while the other jockeys struggled to force their horses to try and catch up. After the race Al could not stop himself from telling the joke of the day while counting the cash from the large purse he had won. He laughed and laughed. SOME WERE NOT AMUSED.

    One thing Al realized along the way was that he was practically an expert on judging horseflesh. He could easily spot a runner, a cutter, or a show horse from a mile away so he began honing his skills.

Al's Chat

Al was always appealing to women young and old alike. He had certain magnetism. Women loved him and men loved to hate him while at the same time wanting to associate with him. One day he met Miss Lilly who was a lonely widow. They immediately made eye contact, the kind that said, "I'm here for the taking." Well, trapper that he was and having learned that she owned a few horses Al seized the moment. They spoke often and upon one of his visits to her ranch he spotted a beautiful, blue, muscular stud in the pasture. Miss Lilly said he was used for breeding purposes and could no longer race. Al knew better and quickly set his plan in motion. He offered to board the horse, train it and use his healing techniques to restore him to full racing form. A monthly fee was agreed upon and the deal was struck.

Al used his charm and made emotional progress with Miss Lilly. She was so enchanted that she did not pay attention to the business end of the deal." Miss Lilly went to Al's place every now and then to check on the progress of her horse. Al had taught the horse to take a bow, count to four by tapping his hoof, even lie down and roll over on command. Miss Lilly was so amused she forgot to question the physical fitness of the horse. All the while the horse was getting stronger, faster and more magnificent than any horse in Vermilion Parish. Each time she tried to pay his monthly fee he would say, "Don't worry about that, you can do that later."

Al thought that the less people that knew about this horse the better. If some big mouth trainer with half an eye for good horseflesh would come around his plan may go sour or worse yet something may mysteriously happen to the horse. So Al decided to get a guard dog but not just any old guard dog. This one had to be Al Jr. He had to be big, strong, silent, smart and patient just like Al. Al found a beautiful German shepherd with the right temperament. Trainer Al taught him exactly what to do and he learned quickly.

Sure enough, here comes the unsuspecting, snooping, loud mouth trainer crowing like a rooster making negative comments about Al. Suddenly out of nowhere Jr. attacked He bit the loud mouth on the rear and stood steady until Al gave the silent command to release. The victim said, "Are you crazy!" While cleaning his fingernails with his pocketknife, all calm and unconcerned, Al replied, "Nope."

Soon the story with its half-truths was out and all the nobodies knew. Horse trainers became fearful that this horse could indeed be the best, after all Al was the trainer. So one brain surgeon of a trainer decided to visit Al's training camp and take a hand full of small, red potatoes with him. He doped up the potatoes hoping to feed them to the blue in order to make him groggy and sluggish. Before he could execute his plan Jr. attacked and grabbed him by the crouch sending a strong message, "don't move". Al slowly walked towards the commotion asking, "What's going on?" The victim said, "Nothing." Al replied, "Oh no my friend, tell me the truth." Jr. held steady. The victim in fear of a fate worse than death confessed. Al said, "Ok" and gave the silent command to release. The victim staggered off, wet pants and all. Al wanted this story to get around and it did. If you were to bad mouth Al at his camp you got it from the back, but if you tried to hurt the blue, you got it from the front and you had better hope that Al was around to give the silent command to release.

    Finally the time came for a show of hands. Al had deliberately allowed his fee to amount to $25,000.00 owing. He suddenly told Miss Lilly he wanted his money, all of it. She was in shock and began gasping for breath when struck by reality all the while wondering how could she have been so stupid? She explained that she did not have that amount of money. Al counted on this reaction and calmly stated that she would have to sign the necessary papers making Al the sole owner of the horse in payment for the debt. Miss Lilly shouted, "Never" and threatened to sue, which she did but to no avail. The papers were signed and the horse became known as Al's Chat, because of the chatter about Al's blue horse. He was the best racehorse around, thereby making Al also the best. The best horse trainer, the best snake oil man, the best charmer and did I mention the best trapper?

Uncle Bud

    Uncle Bud and Gabriele were sitting on the back porch taking it easy. Gabriele was snapping beans for supper and Uncle Bud was smoking his corncob pipe. After a bit of small talk Uncle Bud said, " Gabby." Gabriele instantly knew that they were going to have a long, serious conversation because each time he calls her Gabby he wants to lovingly discuss a matter about which they have a difference of opinion. Gabriele said, " Go ahead. What is it?" Have you given any thought about telling Daniel who you are, or where you come from, or about your first love and the good and bad of your journey leading to our wonderful life? It's a good interesting story and should be passed on. Don't sell yourself short Gabby; you come from a proud people. You and I are getting on and shouldn't take anything for granted. Gabriele said nothing and continued to snap the beans all the while listening as she rocked back and forth gathering speed as though she would fly away. Uncle Bud decided to finish what he had to say once and for all. He would never bring it up again so he continued. There is always an easy way out of anything and that would be to not tell Daniel the truth about his poppa. If you take it for granted that Daniel will outlive you but he dies first, you will forever thereafter look back and ask yourself why didn't you tell him, why didn't you see that it was the right thing to do. We have a new baby coming, our first grandchild, if the truth comes out during its lifetime, what will you say to Daniel when he asks you why didn't you tell him first. Well Gabby, that's all I have to say. I promise to stand by you as always whatever you decide to do. Uncle Bud got up and walked to CRABBYS for a beer.

   Gabriele began to rock slower as she snapped the remainder of her beans and prayed to the Lord for peace of mind. She loved Daniel and didn't want to cause him any kind of pain but would she hurt him more by revealing the truth or by continuing to lie. Everyone has a God given right to know about how they came to be. Gabriele suddenly noticed a small oak tree growing in the yard and she thought, God planted the acorn from which the mighty oak grows with branches extending every which way, taking their own path but always connected to its roots; all the while making it bigger and stronger. Gabriele decided the oak tree was a sign from God and that she would find a way to tell her family everything.

   The next morning Uncle Bud came to the kitchen for his usual kick start cup of hot coffee expecting to find Gabriele in a sad, thought filled mood but much to his surprise she was just as pleasant and beautiful as the day they met in the dress shop so many years ago. It touched his heart to the point of causing him to be teary eyed as she said the same words today that she said then, " Would you like to sit and have coffee with me?" All Uncle Bud could say was, " Yes dear lady, I most certainly would. Thank you kindly." They snuggled on the back porch as they enjoyed the beautiful sunrise. The morning sounds of the marshy bayou, the morning dew and the scent of honeysuckle that filled the air was Cajun country's way of adding a brand new day to old style living. Uncle Bud asked Gabriele if he had told her today that he loved her and she said not today. Well, I love you with all my heart and Gabriele said I do too. They both laughed when she made it clear that she meant she loves him with all her heart not herself with all her heart. Gabriele told him that she thought he was right and it was time to tell Daniel the best story he would ever hear, one that would never end. It was a long time coming but hopefully their son would understand the reason and forgive her. She had decided to have a family dinner next Sunday. She wanted it to be special so she asked that Uncle Bud deliver a hand written invitation to Daniel and Lucille. The note would simply say, " Children please meet us under the big, old oak tree in the back yard after Church Service Sunday for a family dinner and story time." Uncle Bud said he would be honored to run this errand and took off. Gabriele had to call him back and remind him that she had not yet written the note. They laughed and enjoyed another cup of coffee. This was the second best sit down they had ever shared since they met.

    Daniel and Lucille welcomed an unexpected visit from Uncle Bud. He looked like a child that knew a secret and was anxious to tell it. They figured if there were a serious problem he would be very sad but he was filled with joy, dancing around and kicking up his heels, so everything must be all right. They were puzzled by the odd behavior but graciously accepted their very first written invitation. Lucille said she would keep it always. Uncle Bud smiled as he walked away knowing that the invitation was more important than little Lucille realized. Kind, loving Lucille was and still is a blessing to this family.

    The day was finally here. It seemed like it was a long time coming but today was the day. Uncle Bud and Gabriele had gotten up just after midnight to begin preparing the wonderful meal the family would share and long remember. Gabriele wanted to make family members feel special so she served their favorite dishes. Uncle Bud enjoyed pork roast and candied yams, Daniel enjoyed chicken and sausage gumbo, Lucille simply loved rice and gravy, mustard greens with ham hocks and sliced cucumber- tomatoes salad,

Gabriele liked fresh homemade bread and butter and corn on the cob. The drink of the day would be root beer, Armade'ous's favorite and what better way to complete the meal then to have pecan pie, syrup cake and homemade vanilla custard. Gabriele was not the Sweet Tooth Fairy of the family, but she came in a close second.

The food was cooked just in time. Uncle Bud and Gabriele cleaned up and went to Sunday Mass. They met the children outside, exchanged hugs and kisses and entered the church. They sat in the same pew and each said their own silent prayers. Uncle Bud was very thankful and prayed that God would help Gabriele and give her the courage she needs this day, he prayed for his family's health and well-being especially his grandchild. Daniel was thankful for the blessing of having a good, growing family, but especially for his mother who always put others before herself. Daniel asked God to help him to help himself to be a better man. Lucille thanked God for her new family especially her baby. She asked God to help her be a good mother and a better person who tries hard to find good in any bad because she believes things happen for a reason. Gabriele believed that Uncle Bud was God's messenger of peace. She thanked God for giving her the courage to be free of the past by bringing it forward and releasing it to the future. The church service was especially beautiful this day. Oddly Father John spoke of the importance of family, of how doing the right thing takes courage and how people should never remain bitter because things happen for a reason, of how we should remember to be kind and do onto others as we would have them do onto us. The service was over and the family met on the church lawn. Uncle Bud said, "Let's go, I'm hungry."

Everyone went in the house for a minute while the ladies removed their hats and gloves. They chattered away like youngsters as they brought the food to the table under the old oak tree. Daniel was stunned at the sight of so much food for four people, or should he say five people. He wanted to know what was going on. Gabriele said, "Later. Right now we are starving, let's eat." Daniel said grace and the family thanked

Gabriele for the thoughtfulness of preparing their favorite dishes. Uncle Bud tapped a glass with his fork and said, "I would personally like to thank me, Uncle Bud, for getting up so early to help my wife cook this good food." Everyone laughed and Gabriele gave him a little kiss on the cheek. The conversation at the dinner table was light and you couldn't help but notice everyone had one thing on his or her minds. The family decided to have dessert later, much later because they had over indulged in their favorites. The ladies cleared the table and everyone gathered in the shade and sat comfortably in rocking chairs.

As head of the family Uncle Bud decided he should speak first. Daniel, your mother and I have called our first official family meeting to discuss our past. Don't worry it's not as scary as it sounds. It's really about our lives and telling our stories openly and honestly. By doing so we hope to bring strength to our family and instill pride in generations to come. Let me begin by saying there are many races of people in this great country. Some were born here, some came of their own free will and others were forced to come. The reasons we are all here don't seem to matter much any more. All endured hardship while always hoping in the end to have a better life. As these proud people worked side-by-side nature sometimes took its course thereby producing biracial children, some married some didn't. Other bi-racial children were brought into the world under different circumstances. Over time everyone becomes related to everyone else, not necessarily by name but by blood. Mother Nature's melting pot created a great blend and united us forever and we are one: The United States of America. We my family, are part of the mix. This great country had a rough start and many kinks have to be ironed out but I feel we are on the right road, it may be a long sometimes-rocky road but it leads somewhere. I'm very proud of the fact that history will show Africans were among the first to shed their blood.

My name is and always has been Uncle Bud, why I don't know. Seems like a strange name to call a child but that's me, Uncle Bud. I was told that my Poppa was a black slave who worked on a plantation some place in Louisiana. He couldn't read and write. He was a rather large man, well built, dark skinned, nice looking. The Master was married to a very wild, young, Irish woman who liked to take chances and do any and everything she shouldn't. The Master was a very old German who was secretly aware that he could not have children. He, like everyone else, knew that his wife slept with any man within arms length but he didn't care because he was desperate to have a child, hopefully a boy. He counted on the fact that his wife would claim the child was his and he would have the heir he wanted. Putting up with gossip was a small price to pay for his legacy. Finally the wife was pregnant. She told her husband they were going to have a child. He was very excited but she hated the idea. She was very mean and hateful to everyone around her during the whole pregnancy. After a long, miserable nine months she gave birth with the help of a black midwife. I was born big, healthy, and black. The only person who was not shocked was my mother. The midwife thought to herself, "No wonder she was so mean, she knew this day would come and what could she say." The mistress had skin white like snow and so did the master. Everyone was deathly afraid of the Master so the midwife simply answered his question when asked if it was a boy or a girl and let him be shocked just like the rest of them. He was happy and excited at the news but when he laid eyes on me he exploded, gave me to the midwife to dispose of and started to beat his wife with a bullwhip, demanding to know who the father was. Love, hate, hate, love these are very powerful emotions to suddenly feel all at the same time. The poor man suffered a heart attack and died on the spot. The mistress never told him who my Poppa was but she did tell the midwife. I was given to a black family who couldn't have any children. They knew my Poppa and that he died before I was born. The nice, loving couple that raised me told me my story before they died but never mentioned my Poppa by name only that he was a good, kind, quiet man. I sometimes wonder if his name was the same as mine. They left me this little place and here I am light skinned Uncle

Bud, a free man who met Daniel, met and married Gabriele, met Lucille who married my son Daniel and we are all having a baby.

Lucille wiped her teary eyes and asked if she might be next because she feared she would be too emotional to speak if she waited any longer. She thought this was such a wonderful idea.

Maybe as a child I had a last name I don't know. For as long as I can remember I've been called Lucille. I don't know much about my parents or grandparents, only what I was told. My grandparents were both light skinned black people who were married to each other and like most black people they were slaves but were lucky enough to be sold as a young couple to a plantation owner somewhere in Louisiana. After many years my grandmother got pregnant with my mom. By the time mom was born my grandparents were allowed to go to the general store in town twice a month by wagon to place a dry goods order for the master who felt he could trust them to return without incident. There they befriended a couple of white people who were against slavery and claimed to be part of an old movement called the Underground Railroad. Members secretly helped runaway slaves to travel north to freedom. Because they desperately wanted mom to be free they were brave enough to eventually trust these strangers. Mom was still a baby when my parents handed her to them knowing they would never see their child again. My grandparents were able to keep secret the fact that mom was no longer on the plantation but eventually the Master noticed and because they wouldn't tell where mom was he hanged them from the nearest tree in plain view of all of his slaves as a warning of what would happen to them if they crossed him. The Master was trying to hold onto the past ways of life. He knew slavery had ended but kept this news from his workers as long as he could. My grandparents didn't know at the time that there was no longer a need for the Underground Railroad when they handed mom to these people. So over the years she was lost in a shuffle from one family to the next but for the grace of God she was mostly safe. Finally, as an adult, she somehow ended up along the bayous on a gambling boat working as a dishwasher. Her skin color was the shade of a white person who had too much sun so people assumed she was white. One day Captain Capitano heard her singing and asked her if she wanted a job singing and dancing in the gambling hall. He said she was too pretty and talented to waste away washing dishes. She deserved better. She accepted the offer and became very famous up and down the bayou. She met and married a wealthy white Cajun landowner but never told him she was black. Soon she became pregnant but convinced her husband she should go away to have the baby, someplace where there were better doctors. Her husband loved her very much and wanted what was best for her and the baby so he agreed. She didn't go far away as planned, she went to a nearby town and had the baby at the home of a friend who had no children of her own. She made a deal with the couple. They could keep me if they agreed never to tell anyone who my real mother was. They couldn't even tell me. She would tell her husband that the baby died in childbirth. The couple was getting on in age and had mixed feelings. They were happy to be blessed with this child but were saddened at how easily this mother gave her own flesh and blood away. She never held me in her arms, never even kissed me goodbye. The couple decided to move to Vermilion Parish to raise their daughter hoping nobody would question their parenthood. They named me Lucille and gave me all the love and attention any human being could wish for. When I was old enough they told me everything. They encouraged me to be nice and kind and always try and help someone if I could because being bitter was not God's way; it served no good purpose and in the end would lead to self-destruction. They always believed that things happen for a reason. My real grandparents were light skinned slaves, my mom was lighter and my dad was white. When I got a little older I met Gabriele, worked in her store, met Uncle Bud, fell in love with Daniel the first time I ever saw him even if I was too young for him. He didn't notice me then but I caught up and here we are married and having a baby. I want you to know something else. The other day I took a walk to the old fishing spot and while I was resting a whispering breeze told me I would have a strong, healthy baby and not to worry because everything would be fine. I don't know if I was dreaming but I suddenly felt safe and calm.

    Gabriele with a loving memory of her mistress in mind gathered strength right here, right now, this minute because she was no longer at war with herself, after all had she not become an eagle who walked with a lion.

    My children, maybe you don't know that I am really from the great land of Africa. My African name is Shebo, daughter of a tribal spiritual leader. One day the villagers were tending to their daily chores when suddenly white men wearing strange looking clothing raided our village with the help of a neighboring enemy tribe. They shouted loudly and seemed angry as they captured as many villagers as they could, including me. We were chained and forced onto a large ship that sailed out to the open sea, never again would we see Africa. We were frightened and made to suffer many indignities but we survived. After a very long voyage we landed and were placed on an auction block to be sold like trapped animals. We never saw each other again. The rich, white landowners who bought us were called master and their wives were called mistress. Most were mean and evil but some were kind. Men worked as hard as mules and were beaten, starved and in some cases hanged for little or no reason. Women were the sole property of the whoremaster to do with as he pleased. Some he kept, some he sold and some who had the misfortune of bearing his children, he practically gave away. All slaves had to learn English by word of mouth. They were not allowed to learn how to read and write; however some secretly did. I eventually became the property of a gentle, kind mistress who gave me the American name of Gabriele. We became friends in misery like frightened chickens and later in strength like eagles. She gave me a letter granting my freedom and we both left the plantation to follow our dreams. This journey taught me much about life and along the way I met a tall, strong, handsome, kind, white Cajun man of French and Indian descent who reminded me of a great African Lion, a protector of the young, of the helpless, of the weak, always ready to right a wrong and never knowing fear. He came along when I was wandering from settlement to settlement along the bayous like a lost soul. He listened to my story and said, "Well dear lady, where I go you go until you tell me different." One day I heard the faint whisper of an African prayer song telling me it was time to move on. I told my Lion, Armade`ous Peltier goodbye. We loved each other enough to let go. When I arrived here I opened a little shop and later learned I was pregnant. I decided not to return to Armade`ous because I did not want to be the one to break his spirit. I told everyone my husband died of a fever and no questions were asked. Daniel you were born and you were such a Lion Cub. The spitting image of Armade`ous, mind, body and soul, the joy of my life. My shop became successful so I hired Lucille to help me. Uncle Bud became a customer, a friend and finally my husband but not before I told him my story. He felt I should tell you Daniel about Armade`ous but I didn't. One day a customer came in with a story about a good, Cajun man named Armade`ous who died suddenly. His wife and two little children were left alone so the wife had to marry an evil man who threw her boy named Al out but kept the girl child. I told Uncle Bud the story but again I decided not to tell you Daniel. Uncle Bud convinced me that there should be no secrets among family. Gabriele began to cry and asked Daniel to forgive her.

    Daniel was speechless and teary eyed as he took a deep breath. Everyone was quiet and hoped for the best outcome to what up until now had been a wonderful day. The quality of their family life depended on Daniel's reaction. Would he be bitter, would he chose never to speak to Gabriele again, what? Uncle Bud was confident that his son would be true to himself. Daniel got up, walked towards the picket fence, bowed his head in silence then returned and began to speak.

We all know about me but I would like to say this anyhow. I am the son of Armade'ous a strong Cajun white man, son of Shebo a proud African American woman known to many as Gabriele. I am also the son of Uncle Bud a wise Cajun Mulatto who knew I would marry Lucille before I did. Father says pride is a sin but it felt good to think out loud just this once.

My child is on his way and when he gets here his bedtime stories will be about a wonderful place called Africa. As he grows, so will the information he is capable of understanding. His questions must be answered but always truthfully, with nothing more, but nothing less either. The history of captures and enslavements must never be forgotten. It must forever be told in the sad songs of prayer or the joyous songs of dance.

His grandmother, herself a captured slave of the past, will tell of the Great Lion, Armade'ous who she believes with all her heart, was born in America to protect her while she made her way. She will tell how, he lovingly, set her free because he knew she was strong. His cub was born to her and she taught him everything that was important in life. How to survive, to live with dignity, to have compassion, to have patience, to be truthful, to protect children and how to love life with all it has to offer. She will tell of how later in life a wise Warrior came to her and showed her the path to peace. They married and together witnessed the Cub turn into the free Lion he was meant to be.

It was so quiet for a few minutes it was almost scary. There was no breeze, no birds flying, no Cajun marshy bayou sounds, nothing. But if you listened closely you could hear the sound of a very, very faint heartbeat almost like the sound of an ancient drum in the distance. Suddenly Lucille was startled as she felt a slight pain. The new Lion Cub was making his presence known.

After hugs and tears all around the family made a root beer toast to Armade'ous thanking him for the part he played in their lives. Gabriele sang an African prayer song then asked her Lion to please help Daniel find his brother Al before it was too late. Uncle Bud thanked God for everything and added, " God, if there's anything I can ever do for you, you just let me know."

Uncle Bud licked his lips and rubbed his hands together because he suddenly remembered that the best of the food had not been eaten and the family could not let it go to waste. They over indulged again and again had to sit in the rocking chairs but this time they each took a nap in the shade as the rooted limbs of the old oak tree continued to work their slow, easy, peaceful, Cajun magic bayou style.

Uncle Bud was right about Lucille. She felt as though she was born again because she was so excited about everything. The next day she went to the general store and bought a large book with leather binding to write about their family history. It was rather expensive but she used the money her parents had given her before they died. That night after supper she told Daniel that next Sunday she would like to have the family over for coffee and cake after church services. They could sit on the back porch and visit, just a little visit not an all day thing. Daniel smiled, gave her a hug and said, "Sounds good to me."

Church service was very nice and as usual the family exchanged pleasantries with other members. Finally they were alone and Lucille invited Uncle Bud and Gabriele to her house for a short visit. They had been working hard all week and really weren't in the mood. The eagle was still emotionally drained from soaring last week. After all, it's hard to do the right thing sometimes it wears you out. But who could say no to Lucille. Lucille said, "Oh! Could you please bring your letter of freedom so we can read it while we have coffee and cake?" Gabriele looked a little puzzled but agreed and she and Uncle Bud went by their house to get it. Seems like it was their turn to wonder what was going on. That happy little daughter in law was wearing them out with all of her youthful enthusiasm. Life itself sets her off; always excited about making people happy. She sparkled like fireworks all the time. God help them all if the next generation is the same way.

Back porches sure play an important role in Cajun life. Ask any female what her favorite part of her house is and she will tell you that it's the back porch. It's her quiet place early in the morning when her family is still a sleep. She sits on the swing, enjoys her first cup of coffee and for a few minutes thinks about herself, the part known only to her. Then her thoughts merge into all the happy times of her life. Not family problems, not money problems, not stress of any kind, just little happy thoughts of childhood, early marriage and family. By the time she is ready for her second cup her loving husband is up and about. They snuggle, smile and enjoy the quiet morning. The porch is sacred and reserved for family and friends. Enemies are never allowed. Cajuns have a reputation for eating anything that moves and everyone knows that if he thinks something will do him harm he strikes first. Nobody has ever found out what would happen if an enemy dared set foot on the back porch.

Daniel greeted Uncle Bud and Gabriele and told them Lucille was on the porch. Everyone sat down and commented about the beautiful day as Lucille cut the cake and Gabriele poured the coffee. Finally Lucille told them how she couldn't stop thinking about last Sunday and she wanted the family's permission to write each story in a beautiful book she had bought. As she passed the book around she said it would be a wonderful recording of family history as each new family member added his or her life story to it. The first thing you would see when opening the book would be the hand written invitation to meet under the old oak tree for a family dinner and story time. The next page would display the title page "FIRST THERE WAS AFRICA". Then we could write the beautiful things Uncle Bud said about America followed by each of our stories exactly as we shared them and it would be so wonderful to add Gabriele's letter of freedom. As head of our family I believe Uncle Bud and Gabriele should keep the book in their home until the time comes to pass it on to the next head of the family. Our stories can be written on scratch paper as things are recalled then one of us can write them in our family's history book. I would love to have that honor.

Gabriele was totally surprised and began to cry. After finally composing herself she said that she felt she wasn't deserving of such a loving family and wondered why God blessed her so. Uncle Bud just sat quietly, smoking his corncob pipe and smiling, as he thought how Lucille never disappoints him. Daniel just about burst with pride as he hugged his wife. Everyone was in agreement to Lucille's proposal and after one more cup of coffee the heads of the family went home.

Lucille began to write the stories in her spare time. She didn't want to become obsessed with her project. It was something to be done right with care, with love and truthfulness. One day as she was washing dishes she began thinking about Gabriele's story. The part about Armade'ous having a son named Al seemed to nag at her. Daniel's friend, the cotton picker who had come to dinner a few years ago was named Al. The more she thought about it the more she was convinced that Cajun Al was Daniel's brother. There were too many noticeable similarities to be a coincidence. She finished the dishes and made a pot of coffee. When the coffee was done she poured a cup and sat on the back porch to relax on the swing. There was such a nice breeze that when she finished her coffee she lay on the swing for a short nap.

Lucille dreamed of sitting in the shade of the old oak tree writing in her book when an Indian suddenly stood before her. He said that he was Chief Spirit of the Oak and that Cajuns and Indians believe strongly in bloodlines. He said that the brothers must unite before death and that she is to tell Daniel he has to find the blue horse. When she woke up she wondered what could that mean, it had to mean something. Lucille was even more convinced that Daniel and Cajun Al were brothers dream or no dream.

Since she and Daniel had no secrets from each other, not even secret thoughts she decided to tell him what was on her mind. His reaction was surprising. Daniel said that the possibility made sense to him. There seemed to be an unexplained connection between him and Al, one of heart and soul, not just similarities. Daniel felt that when Gabriele described Armade'ous she was describing all Daniel knew about Cajun Al. This was one time that Daniel prayed and really meant it as he asked God to help him find his brother.

   Daniel decided the best place to start was by asking Uncle Bud for his help. He and Lucille went over to the house and told Uncle Bud and Gabriele everything. They also believed the man in the cotton field was there new son. Gabriele told Daniel to go and find him and that she would look after Lucille. Uncle Bud decided the best place to start was at CRABBYS because the OLD CRABS know everything that's going on in the area. Some had heard of a man named Al whose wife had drowned a while back but that's about it. Uncle Bud suggested they go to the neighboring town and ask a few questions. When they got there they stopped by the barbershop. The barber, Mr. As-if, said that he has known Cajun Al for a very longtime. As a matter of fact he was my first customer. We became good friends and I was best man at his wedding. He paused a minute as though deep in thought then said, " Boy those were some good times." He's a good man old Cajun Al. He was a loner for a while after his wife died, but now he's into horses and is the best judge of horseflesh around. Maybe if you check the racetracks on Sundays you might catch up to him. This information was helpful but yet it wasn't because there was a racetrack in every small town around here. However they weren't about to give up. They went back home but every weekend Daniel and Uncle Bud traveled Cajun country searching and searching for Cajun Al.

   Finally they heard that there was going to be a big race at the Cajun Country Track right here in Vermilion Parish on Sunday. Every trainer in the parish would be there because the purse was big and if your horse finished first at this track it meant that you really were the best. Every weekend the bragging rights were the same but the horses were always faster, stronger and more beautiful no matter where the race was held. Daniel and Uncle Bud went to the refreshment stand to ask a few questions when suddenly there was an argument between two horse trainers. These men were angry and trading insults about anything and everything. One would laugh the second one would get mad, the second one would laugh and the first one would get mad. It was mostly yelling but when the insults were directed at their racehorses as to which one trained a mule and which one trained a stud somebody hit a raw nerve and blows were exchanged. When the dust settled some Cajun loud mouth yelled the magic words, "The drinks are on the house" and everybody laughed, forgot the whole thing and went back to having fun.

Uncle Bud and Daniel decided to go their separate ways because the crowd was so large. Never had they seen so many people in one place. They would meet at the refreshment stand in one hour. There were several races scheduled for that day but the main race was the last one. Uncle Bud realized that the chatter was all about one horse. Some said it was the biggest, some said it was the strongest, some said it was the fastest most beautiful horse they ever hoped to see. Finally one trainer said," That Al, he's the best. That blue horse of his can't be beat. I bet on the blue horse every time." Uncle Bud asked the stranger if he knew where he could find the blue horse. The stranger just laughed and said, "No. He's well hidden and most likely protected by Jr. and trust me, you don't want to meet up with Jr. He laughed and said just wait for the last race."

Reunion

Uncle Bud went back to the refreshment stand just in time to see Daniel rush a man from behind, grab him around the upper body trying to stop the man from killing some loud mouth but the man was so angry that he never felt Daniels weight as he dragged Daniel along with him. At the same time people were yelling, "No. No Al. Don't. He didn't mean it. Stop." Finally Daniel was able to stand, brace himself, tighten his grip and stop the man from going any farther. The loud mouth ran for his life but that wouldn't save him because they would meet again and Al said he had a butt whipping coming to him and he had better just come and get it because it's coming sooner or later, makes no difference. You know what they say about a Cajun's word and Al had just given it.

The two men sat on a bench for a minute trying to catch their breath when Daniel said, "Al is that you? What got into you man"? Al thought a minute then laughed and hugged Daniel. Al said that he was buying a root beer when this loud mouth started taunting him. For a time Al ignored him but when he called the blue a plug and said Al drugged his horse, and cheated his way to the top Al just had to make him eat those words. Al thanked Daniel for stopping him because Al was blind with rage and may have killed the fellow but Al warned Daniel not to step in the next time because if he does he and the fellow will get a butt whipping. Daniel said that he understood, the Cajun had again given his word.

Daniel introduced Uncle Bud and they told Al that they really needed to talk to him about something important. Al asked them to stay for the last race so that they could watch the blue run. Daniel agreed and invited Al to his house for a few days of rest and good, hot gumbo. Al wasn't the only con in the family who had a little snake oil in him. Daniel knew that Al would never refuse a bowl of gumbo no matter what.

Although there were many strong, muscular horses at the track none stood out like Al's Chat. He seemed to have a fierce spirit and pride like an Indian as he held his head up right and pranced around. Daniel didn't know as much about horses as Al did but he knew enough to know Al's Chat had a good bloodline. Suddenly the call came for all horses to line up at the gate. The gates opened and the horses were off. At first Al's Chat was behind but when they neared the finish line the blue easily, without breaking a sweat passed them and won the race. That horse was much like Al; he liked to tease the people.

    They packed up and went home. Uncle Bud couldn't wait to tell the OLD CRABS all about his trip especially about the legendary blue horse and that he knew the trainer-owner personally. When they arrived Lucille and Gabriele happily began cooking gumbo because Lucille remembered that it was Al's favorite dish. After supper the men sat on the back porch and the women washed dishes but listened closely as Daniel began telling Al a story, a good story that held Al's interest. When Daniel finished Al drank his coffee, took a deep breath and said," That's not all of it. Want to hear more?" Gabriele and Lucille couldn't help it; they came out of the house and sat on the porch. Gabriele said, "Yes, we do." Al began with the story his mom told him about her slavery, her Privateer and her savior. He told his own story and how he unknowingly met his brother in a cotton field and felt a strong bond with this man that he knew could never be broken. We are brothers born of the same blood. Al and Daniel shook hands and everyone shed tears of joy. They brought out the good old root beer and once again toasted Armade'ous.

    Al felt so blessed to have found more family members especially since the loss of his beloved Mary. He talked about his children Roland, Steven and Lois. They were everything to him. Pain and joy come and go but family love is forever and ever no matter what. Al choked back tears as he said maybe one day he would find his other brother and sister. When your baby is born you'll see Lucille, you'll see what I mean. He visited for a few more days but it was time to go. Al's Chat needed more training, he couldn't be allowed to become fat and lazy. Lucille cried and said they would miss him and that he was always welcome at any time. Watch for my smoke signal from my gumbo pot then take a deep breath you old Indian, I know that will bring you back. Would you mind if I add your story to our family history book. Al smiled as he left in his old truck and said, " Be sure and put down who's the best."

Al was with the family when Daniel's baby boy was born. Lucille wondered if the old Indian Chief told Al that this was the day of the extension of the bloodline and that he should come home. The new Cub was to be called Daniel Armade'ous also known as Bud. Al held his head up and took a deep breath because he was just about to burst with pride. He told Daniel " Don't buck this young horse, especially while he is young. Walk him with a strong arm and just a little weight. Guide him but don't break his spirit. He is proud and has a strong will just like us. He's a Cajun Man. " Al and Daniel hugged each other as Al announced he had to leave. He knew this visit was a short one but he said a smoke signal from another gumbo pot was calling him. He had that little grin on his face as he said bye for now.

Time seemed to fly by and Bud was now a teenager who liked girls and dancing. That's all he talked about. Lucille tried to keep a tight reign on him but he was very strong willed. He always worked hard, helped anybody in need, never got in trouble and kept his word if given. When Saturday night rolled around it would be unfair not to let him go out but he had to be home by midnight. This night he came home early from the dance and was so excited he could hardly talk. Daniel told him to slow down and catch his breath. Daniel asked if he was hurt or in trouble. Bud said no but he had just seen his first real fight. There was blood everywhere, a man knocked out lying on the floor, a big man standing over him like some mad Lion ready to eat the man on the floor and another big man holding him back from behind. The big man who was so mad he didn't seem to even notice the big one holding him back; he just dragged him around like nothing. The mad man cooled off and both big men went outside so that the mad one could explain what had happened. I followed them and heard him say that a few people had been drinking and the man on the floor started talking louder and louder. He wasn't getting too much attention so he started insulting one of the big men while the other one was outside talking to a pretty girl. The big man inside tried to ignore the loud mouth but when he insulted the memory of the blue horse and its trainer, the big man let him have it. They exchanged lots of blows but the big man was so mad he seemed to have lost his mind and grabbed anything he could feel for to fight with, a bottle, a glass, another man standing in the way, even a paint can that was on the floor. That's when the big man who was outside heard all the noise, came inside and held the mad one back because the loud mouth was out cold, it was over. The big man who was in the fight told the big one who held him back, " Thank you for bringing me to my senses because I could have killed him but if you ever step in again I will give you a butt whipping you will never forget. You got my word on that." Afterwards I heard some people talking and they said the two big men were brothers and the mad one was called Roland and the one holding him back was called Steven.

    Daniel and Lucille began to laugh so hard that they both had tears in their eyes. When they calmed down a little Daniel told Daniel Armade'ous, " Let me tell you a story son".

Cajun Al Continues

Al's Chat continued to run like a hurricane, winning race after race but all good things come to an end. Al observed that his horse was not his old self. He developed a slight limp. So Al brought him to one final race in Texas. While sitting around the camp sight the night before the race Al watched and listened to the other horsemen. He noticed two of them admiring Al's Chat. They came over and asked a few questions. The next day Al told his jockey to run Al's Chat just ahead of the pack but hold him back and not to give him his reign. The jockey followed instructions and Al's Chat won. The two horsemen watched the race and knew what the jockey had done. They offered Al $5,000.00 for Al's Chat. He accepted but did not mention that Al's Chat was hurt and may never race again. Al knew in his heart and soul that his prize possession would retire on a stud farm where stories of his greatness would be told as long as the wind blows and the river flows.

Al allowed himself some quiet time. He had a piece of land South of Erath not far from the Vermilion Bay so he and Steven built Al's house. It was small, two rooms and a bath. But the thing he liked best was it had a small porch facing the setting sun. Al paid cash at the lumberyard and made sure there was no trapper involved. He visited here and there and had Sunday dinners with Lois and her family. He became bored so he built a few pigeon cages, acquired a few show pigeons and prizewinning rabbits to raise for his own pleasure. He and his friends Poppa Charlie who lived along the bayou and had a cattle ranch and Mr. Gaultier who also lived along the bayou and had a few shrimp boats would have coffee in the morning, gossip a little, reflect on the old days and trade rabbits and pigeons amongst themselves. But Al soon realized he had no more spark. No excitement in his life, nothing to bring forward the snake oil in him. So he decided cock fighting would be his new passion.

    His instincts were good. He could easily spot a good fighting rooster from a chicken rooster. After all they were just like men, you were a fighter or you weren't. Cock fighting was somewhat like horseracing. The game was the same, the hunger to win at all cost was the same, only this fight was to the death and weapons were used. Small gaffs resembling a large claw were attached to the feet of the rooster and they were trained to attack until only one was left standing. Al soon walked away. This was no sport. There was no joy in such cruelty. Animals and birds could breathe, think, learn and survive on their own just as humans. Al didn't feel that at all cost meant to the death. He felt it meant that in a fun, exciting game of wit and chance the winner takes all and it ends with a good laugh and friendly Cajun handshake. Cajuns then regroup and put a new, secret plan in motion, which by the way happens to be no secret. Cock fighting reminded him too much of slavery and he had no thirst for blood.

    Al was sitting on his porch one morning enjoying a cup of good, hot coffee and wondering what the poor people were doing on this beautiful day. Al always said that to Mary every morning because they had such a rich, full, happy life. While deep in thought he suddenly felt a tap on his shoulder. He looked up and saw that it was his friend Philip Landry. Hey, what you say Philip? Landry said that Hyram was having a lot of trouble with a breeding horse he had bought at the sale and didn't know what to do. It's a beautiful, muscular thoroughbred, black as night, stands 17 hands but it's the meanest beast God ever put on earth. He has a good bloodline and Hyram wanted to make money charging stud fees. Every time a man tries to take him out of the stall he bites, kicks and rears up. Hyram can't even pay a man to go in there. Al laughed and said I'll take care of it. Just as they were about to leave Steven arrived. They explained everything and Steven said he had to see this. So all three men headed out to Hyram's place. Hyram was pacing back and forth, all stressed out because some smartass young fool tried to go in the stall and got hurt. Al didn't have to ask which stall because the crazy horse was still crazy and showing off. Al told the men to wait for him near the walking wheel. Al had his bullwhip in hand as he entered the stall and closed the door behind him. Never in Hyram's life as a horseman had he heard so much noise. He was sure a murder was taking place. There was a clash of strong wills and only one could win. Suddenly everything was quiet, too quiet. The stall door opened and out comes Al sporting his silly little mischievous grin saying that you mustn't break a horse's spirit but you can't let him kill you. The men looked in the stall and there was the thoroughbred standing in the corner all calm and quiet. Al told Hyram to go in but Hyram said not me, I'm not crazy. Landry said, I'll go. He went in and rubbed the horse then took him out of the stall, hooked his halter to the walking wheel to cool him off before giving him a much needed bath. Steven was so very proud of Al. All those old stories he had heard about him were true, he knows no fear and is ready to help anybody at any time. Steven thought to himself, I love that old man.

Al The Old Man

The children, as he remembered Mary always referred to them, would visit and so would the grandchildren. One grandchild in particular, the new baby Steve, just loved cornbread and milk. Al smiled as he often prepared it for him. He also liked honey on his biscuits. This reminded Al of how when he and Mary were first married she would try her best but would always burn them. Al would add a little extra honey and tell her how these were the best biscuits he had ever eaten. It wasn't a lie, not even a little white one because the person he loved prepared them and the person she loved ate them.

Baby Steve became old enough to try his hand at cooking. So he decided he would B.B.Q. for him and Paw-Paw Al. Al furnished the meat and Baby Steve did the cooking. Because there was such a love connection it was remembered as the best meat they had ever eaten in their whole lives.

After much thought Al decided he would buy a gentle old horse for the grand children to ride. He still had his saddle and gear and figured what child did not like to ride a horse. He had a small barn on the property but needed a fence around the land so that the horse would not run away with a child mounted on his back.

Al's little granddaughter Dinah, baby Steve's older sister, would clean Al's house for him as best she could. One day after cleaning the three of them sat on the porch and began discussing what they would need in order to build a fence. The two children were very excited because they would have a horse to ride but building a fence was more exciting because it would make them real cowboys just like Paw Paw Al.

The day finally came. They all got up early, ate their biscuits and coffee milk then went outside. Baby Steve brought his old red wagon to put their drinking water and supplies in and his sister brought a chair for Paw Paw Al to sit in when he got tired. They used modern iron fence post and barbed wire. Somehow they managed to drive the post in the ground with a large hammer then clip the barbed wire to the post without too much difficulty. Al noticed he took longer to do this task then he use to but it didn't matter because he was having such fun with these excited children who loved him and saw him as someone special.

They worked hard, took many, many breaks and discussed how they were doing such a good job. They were happy and laughed a lot but none of them took the time to take a good look at the fence to make sure they were going in a straight line. By the end of the first day the fence that was to be installed from East to West was actually at a slight angle from East to South West. The children were really disappointed because they wanted it to be perfect. Al reassured them that this was the best little crooked fence he had ever seen in his whole life as a cowboy and not to worry because they could put the rest of it straight. He wanted this part to stay just like it was because it made him so happy. Al learned that a group hug sure was a wonderful thing.

Al always liked good food and family gatherings. He missed Mary a lot and figured this was the next best thing to being with her. It was mostly during these gatherings that Al realized how the children and grand children each had some little thing in them that kept her memory alive. So far all of the grandchildren had her kindness, Big Steven had her tenderness and patience, Roland had her sparkle and drive, Lois had her smile and loved telling stories. The whole bunch had Al's strength of character. They would take life like it comes, head on and never went around it. If there was a crisis the matter was resolved by any means necessary, peacefully or otherwise. Al figured he and Mary were a good team. She softened his heart and he brought to light her inner strength.

Christmas Eve was approaching and Al was looking forward to the party at Stevens' house. For some unknown reason he was just as excited as the children maybe more so. This was the happiest the family had seen him in a long time. The weather was cold, damp and dreary but this did not bother Al or anyone else because they knew there was lots of good, hot Christmas gumbo. It was sort of a little family joke and a well-known family fact that Al ate first. If he was hungry, he was hungry. It didn't matter if he ate alone but he ate first then hung around enjoying the company. Family and friends started to arrive and the fun began. Adults had a few drinks, then a few more and who knows, maybe a few more. The children ran around popping fire works, playing hide and seek in the dark and were very excited. They didn't care about cold, mud or the wild animals lurking about such as foxes, gators, or wolves. They were having fun. Finally, the parents ruined everything by making them come inside because the weather had gotten worse. The fun wasn't ruined for long. Those rascals began jumping in the beds, having pillow fights, eating treats and telling lies that they called stories.

    Suddenly there was a very loud pounding on the outside walls all around the house. Whoever or whatever was pounding did so with great force and went around the house several times. Everyone got quiet, including the stunned grown ups. The children feared it was Madame Long Fingers. They were always told that if they were bad and didn't listen, Madame Long Fingers would come in the night and steal them away and they would never be seen again. The children screamed in fear as the pounding stopped. Even the night sounds of frogs croaking and crickets chirping could no longer be heard. Everyone felt as though they had suddenly gone deaf. Finally there was a soft, gentle knock at the door and they heard,"Ho, Ho, Ho, Merry Christmas, Merry Christmas!" Much to everyone's surprise it was Santa Claus carrying a large, black bag filled with presents for one and all. The little children had never noticed how skinny Santa was in his red suit or that he was wearing black-rimmed glasses. The adults laughed and had to admit that they were just as scared as the grandchildren when they heard the pounding and just as happily surprised to see Santa. When asked how did he do that, you know slip away and get dressed and everything? All Al would say was, " Remember, I'm still the daddy around here."

Al was on Steven's mind a lot lately. He wondered, was it because of the holiday season, was it because he felt like a teenage kid who wanted to spend time with his dad, or was his Mom trying to tell him something? Steven got in his truck and went to Al's house for a morning cup of hot coffee and maybe a good, hot, buttered biscuit if he was lucky. Al was always happy to visit with any and everybody. They exchanged the usual pleasantries and after a little quiet time Steven asked Al if he still had his old pirogue, not the family boat, but the pirogue. Al said yes. His eyes lit up as though he suddenly had a flash of many happy memories. Why you want to know? Steven said because I thought maybe you could take it out and we could go to The Banker Ferry near the old hanging tree and shove off. Just you and me, tonight, just like old times. Want to? Al, with a sparkle in his eyes said yep. That's a good idea. Steven said let's not hunt or fish let's just go look around at some of our old spots and just talk. Al wanted to know what time they should leave. Steven said it's up to you. They decided on sunset. When they arrived they put the pirogue in the water and Al started laughing as he remembered how a long time ago his friend Father Andrico was so scared to leave by pirogue from this very spot on his first hunting trip. Steven laughed and said that Father told him that's how they first met and that he was afraid of Al but liked him very much. They drifted out slow and easy, Al sitting in the front and Steven in the back. Sometimes they used their paddles but mostly they let the current do the work. They talked and laughed and just looked around. The bayou was carpeted with water lilies, some white, some purple. Usually the marsh smelled like rotten eggs but this beautiful, foggy moonlit night it smelled like gardenias, honeysuckles, magnolias or any other wonderfully scented flower you could think of. The distant background sounds of the creatures that live here serve as a reminder of the Cajun code of survival which is, " take only what you need because this heaven has a little bit of hell". Here there are no lies, no cheating, no having to protect against evils of humanity and no responsibility except to whoever travels with you. You know Pop many people say how much you helped them over the years by teaching them how to survive out here. Al said, son we all help each other but I'll tell you like Armade`ous told your uncle Whit and me, "men are strong, wine is stronger, women are stronger still, but strongest of all is truth", be sure you remember that no matter what because it figures into everything. I was young at the time and didn't really understand until I was older but I never forgot those words. Al and Steven revisited many memories of their past before returning to Banker Ferry. While loading the old pirogue in the back of Al's truck Steven thanked Al. Al asked for what? Steven said, " Helping me understand what it really means to be a Cajun Man and I'm grateful to have learned from the best." The teary eyed Cajuns enjoyed one of Armade`ous's bear hugs then rode home in silence not knowing that both of them were saying a little grateful prayer to Sara Fina and Mary for teaching them the importance of kindness.

After the Christmas Holidays Poppa Charlie needed a good horseman to help get his cattle to the sale barn. They were scattered about the marsh and would be herded to the docking area where they would be loaded onto a barge and transported by bayou to the unloading zone. Several large trailers would be waiting at Don's landing to bring them to market. Al was always ready to lend a hand, especially to his life long friend. Al was just as excited as a little boy. How could anyone think this was work? What more could a good old cowboy ask for. Fresh air, sunshine, a good horse and freedom on the bayou. There is nothing better.

Several barges had been loaded but just as the last one was about to leave Al's horse was frightened by a snake. The horse suddenly reared up and Al was thrown to the ground. His hip was broken. He was taken to the hospital, had surgery and released after a few weeks but thereafter had to use a walking cane.

One day Poppa Charlie called Al and said he was coming to get him so that they could have dinner and spend the day together. Al never refused a home cooked meal. That afternoon after relaxing under an oak tree near the bayou they decided to walk in the pasture to have a close look at the cattle. As they slowly moved about Al sensed a bit of tension from one big bull nearby. Poppa Charlie noticed the bull was pawing the ground and was restless so he told Al they had better slowly walk away and not look back. Poppa Charlie started walking but Al didn't, he stood his ground accepting the challenge, you know, one old bull to another. Suddenly the bull charged at Al who continued to stand still looking the bull straight in the eye. The very moment the bull closed his eyes Al stepped aside and hit him along side the head with his walking cane. The two old bulls parted, one went back out to pasture and the other met Poppa Charlie on the back porch for some homemade ice cream. Poppa Charlie told Al that he was crazy but Al said no, I'm just not afraid of any animal. Poppa Charlie just shook his head and had nothing more to say about it until other friends came around.

    These days Al really enjoyed sitting on his porch. He sat up straight and proud, his large hands resting on his cane supporting his chin while he smiled looking at the crooked fence as he watched the setting sun .He missed Mary so terribly, but over all was satisfied with his life. One morning Poppa Charlie and Mr. Gaultier arrived for their regular coffee visit only to find Al asleep in his easy chair. Sadly they saw that he was not breathing. Al never realized he was a legend in his own time and is greatly missed.

The New Elder

It was Roland's birthday and the family gathered for a celebration. Roland's wife, Theresa, had a special surprise that she had been keeping secret all week. Everyone was catching up on the latest happenings in their lives when suddenly there was a knock at the door. Roland wondered who could it be but was excited because his belief has always been, the more the merrier! Silence filled the room as Roland opened the door, yelled like a Cajun and gave the person a big bear hug. Look who's here! The surprise slowly stepped forward, his frail, trembling body supported by his oak staff. Father Cornez Andrico was deeply touched by the excitement over his attendance and the love he felt from Cajun Al's family. Everyone mixed and mingled, sharing memories. Finally the call to dinner came. As always, when the family gathered for a meal there was a toast to the elders of the past. Usually it brought a moment of silent tears because the main dish was always gumbo, Al's favorite. Some Cajuns try to deny until they die that they eat too much but it's a funny thing that every one of them needs a nap or a moment of rest after a meal.

Father Andrico decided that now would be the time to speak up. Unfortunately, his health and his age hamper his abilities lately. In his mind he's far from the grave but he accepts the fact that in reality he has one foot in it! Father struggled to his feet and called the room to order. Children of Mary and Cajun AL, we will now begin an official ceremony with a short prayer after which you may be seated, please bow your heads. Some of you knew or heard about Eli and his stones. He was a good, kind fellow who sincerely believed in the power and meaning of his old Indian Stones. Who among us in our hearts and minds has not cast a stone by word of mouth with the intent that it does harm. Not so of Eli. Every person who was given one of his stones cherished it. As an elder, Cajun Al humbly accepted a Gray Stone. Eli said that it meant maturity and sorrow! Cajun Al kept it in a leather pouch hanging from his neck. Sara Fina had made the pouch for Armade'ous around the time Cajun Al was born. She removed it from his neck before burying him and placed it around Al's where it remained until he handed it to me and asked that I pass it on to his eldest child after the initial sorrow of his passing. Because Cajun Al was my best friend and helped me change some of my evil ways, I would like to make this an official ceremony in his honor. Roland was a tough bird, just like his dad but right this minute he was more like his mom, teary eyed. Father Andrico said, Roland, as of this moment you are officially set apart from the rest of the family for a purpose. He sprinkled warm water over Roland's head then placed the pouch containing the Gray Stone around his neck. You have maturity and the distinct honor of being the Elder. Each member of the family wanted to touch the pouch for their own personal reasons. Maybe they said a silent prayer or maybe they hoped to feel a spiritual connection because the gray stone had shades of gray in s swirl pattern much like gray smoke from a campfire rising to the heavens.

Afterwards everyone drank a toast to the official head of the family and wished him a very happy birthday. Steven pulled

Father aside and asked if he could really use holy water for a ceremony involving stones some believed held mystical powers. Father smiled and confessed that he had used bayou water. Would you expect me to use anything else in honor of your past elders? Steven laughed, raised his glass and said, "Here's to you Father".

Roland sat in his easy chair and asked Lois if she had any new stories to tell. She was always eager to tell what she knew, what she thought she knew and what she thought you knew! After all it takes a special person to tell a good tale. Lois says a good Cajun story is much like a good gumbo, you add to it until it has a little bit of everything and ends up being very good.

Did Daddy ever tell any of you about the time he took Mr. As-if gator hunting? Everyone said. "Let's hear it". Well, we all know Mr. As-if wanted to learn all he could about the life of a Cajun man. So every time he cut the hair of one of Dad's friends he would listen to their stories and get very excited to learn more and more. He envied their ability to meet anyone or anything head on. They weren't afraid of any beast, animal or human! He desperately wanted to see one of them in action. It wasn't his fault he was from the city where he grew up with too many civilized rules that made him deny most of his instincts. Everyone liked Mr. As-if. He was a good, kind man who helped people in his own way. One day Dad's friends got together and convinced him to take Mr. As-if on a gator hunt. Cajun Al was his hero and could make it more exciting and memorable. Well, Dad figured he would bite the bullet and go in for one of As-if's crazy haircuts and maybe a shave. They brought the barber chair outside as usual and as usual Dad asked," What's the latest and the straightest? " Mr. As-if said there was nothing new. In fact it was pretty boring the past few days because business had been a little slow. Dad said that it sounded like it was a perfect time to shut it down. And do what As'If asked? Well, I'm going back out at midnight, want to come gator hunting? Dad should never have asked that question when Mr. As-If had a straight razor in his hands. Every emotion experienced by man struck Mr. As-If all at once. He was so excited and nervous that he not only shaved the right side of Dad's face but cleaned the right side of his head just as slick as a boiled egg without even realizing what he was doing. Dad could never get angry with this man no matter what. When it came to Mr. As-if Dad had the patience of a saint, believe it or not! But he thought long and hard about what he would do when he met up with his so called friends! Dad told As-if to finish what he started and then they would make plans. They both laughed when Dad said that this time the crazy haircut wouldn't have any gashes! Needless to say Mr. As-if did not get a wink of sleep and was sitting in Dad's pirogue when Dad arrived at midnight. As-If said he had been waiting all night because he didn't want to miss a minute. Dad said it was the custom to give a big Cajun yell as you push off to warn the badass animals of the swampy marshes that you are coming and get ready for a fight. It really wasn't the custom but Dad wanted to add to the excitement of the story As-If was sure to tell in his shop. Dad's yell was loud and almost frightening, Mr. As-If's was weak at first but Dad made him try over and over again until he overcame his fear of maybe making a fool of himself. As-If, you can't have fun if you don't cut loose and leave your worries on land. Now, you paddle and I'll look for old red eyes, he's the biggest and the meanest gator out here and he's hard to find because he moves so quietly. As-If did as he was told. Suddenly from out of nowhere, there was a thump and another thump against the bottom of the boat. Dad yelled, it's red eyes and he's turning us over, swim! There was just enough daylight to see the fierce battle taking place between two killers, one with green eyes and the other with red eyes. Red eyes had a lot of bite strength in his jaws and strength in his massive tail, which he sometimes used to knock his opponent off his feet. If given the chance he bites then rolls over quickly in order to tear a limb from his prey but old green eyes was much meaner and he was fearless. He also had strength and rolling power. The difference was he had a sharp knife and he was the one hungry for alligator meat. Finally it was over! Dad right sided the pirogue, tied red eyes to it and started looking for Mr. As-If. He looked in the water then further out towards land. He saw what he believed to be a live man and hoped it was not the ghost of a dead Indian standing on shore with his arms crossed over his chest. Dad put the end of the pirogue rope between his teeth and swam to shore. Sure enough it was As-If standing there just as dry as a bone except for his shoes and the very bottom edge of his pants. Dad asked him how did he get there so fast and how could he possibly be dry, had he walked on water? As-If said all he remembered was that he saw red eyes and he ran! When he turned around he was standing on land and watched the fight but all he could say was "WOW". They had not planned to stay the night but Dad was tired so he taught As-If how to skin a gator. They built a small campfire, cooked and ate old red eyes. As-If kept saying how wonderful it was to know that the stories about the Cajuns are real just like he hoped they were and not just made up stuff. Dad told Mr. As-If that he believes that the real mystery here is how did he get from the middle of the bayou to shore without getting wet, that's what I would like to know. Well little buddy, since this was your first hunt and your first taste of gator I believe you should hang this bad boy in your shop to prove you brought in old red eyes.

The younger children asked Lois if this was a true story. She said that she tells it as it was told to her. Believe what you want. After a few minutes she turned to Father Andrico and asked that he please not anoint her as the Old Veuve of the family. Everybody laughed including Father. Steven laughed but didn't say that he had also been told that very same story.

This wonderful day was coming to an end as the family said their goodbyes. Roland asked Father Andrico to stay just a little longer if he didn't mind. They sat on the back porch and enjoyed some good, hot, black coffee. Roland told Father that he was touched when Father said that Cajun Al helped him change his evil ways. Father said that it was the truth. Well Father, if it weren't for Dad riding me hard, I would have ended up in prison. I really like, I mean, liked to fight, liked any excitement, and I must confess I liked women and frankly, still do! But being the popular bad boy in town I just had to be the best bad boy. It seemed important to me and I didn't want the good times to end! Dad had the good sense to tie his heart and let me have the razor strap across my back a few times no matter how much pain it caused him and me. It was the only way he could put the brakes on me and get my attention. He had to make me understand what a man has to see when he looks in the mirror. Thanks to him I believe I like what I see! Father said, " back at you". You, my son, are a chip off the old oak tree. I think, for me personally, this may have been the best part of the day. Roland took a deep breath and smiled. They shook hands and Roland walked Father down the steps to his car.

The Children

Every Cajun man or woman loves a little quiet time alone whether they admit it or not and Lois was no different. She liked to get up early in the morning, brew a pot of coffee, sit on the back porch and reflect on her life, past and present. She knew that today was not going to be a good day. The cold hard facts that her parents are dead and her husband is also dead made her realize that she can no longer say what she put off saying, she can't go back for one more visit. It seems that lately she is in constant sorrow. Most of the time she doesn't know if she wants to sit down, stand up, cry or die! She hoped that in order to have peace, she wouldn't sell her soul. She understands that she has to find a way to let the sadness go, just let it go.

As she drank her coffee and gazed at the wooded area in her back yard she watched the beautiful mosquito hawks flying happily everywhere. She envied their freedom. She watched them so long that she began to relax and thought the sound of their wings kept saying softly, over and over in Cajun Al's voice," A Cajun Spirit Is Never Broken". She had never realized that she could talk to her loved ones in heaven about her feelings and that they would find a way to help her. She cried a little then thought about her brothers when they were younger. Roland the fighting party animal who lived for today and was content to let tomorrow take care of itself and Steven, the free spirit who preferred to roam the woods and always questioned the why of anything.

I want to go home, the home of our childhood but that's impossible so the next best thing is to invite my brothers to join me down memory lane. I love them very much and want to tell them so while I still can. We decided that only the three of us would meet next Sunday at Roland's camp on Tiger Bayou. Good choice because after too many drinks, too much dip and chips we may have to stay the night. When a Cajun decides to let his hair down, sometimes the whole body goes down before the party ends.

They couldn't have picked a better place on this beautiful, sunny, breezy day. It really was the next best thing to going home. Roland had built his camp with Dad in mind. Everything about it was just like when we were little, including the deerskin rug near the bed. There was even a potbelly stove in the corner. Hey guys, that reminds me, did you know that Mom's secret weapon was food? Anytime she wanted to find out what the two of you were up to she would bring out her pots and pans or her cookie sheet. You could smell her good cooking a mile away. The two of you would come running and while you ate you told all your secrets and she would pretend she wasn't even listening. Us! You little tattle tail, you story teller. You were waiting at the table while the pots were still in the cabinet telling Mom just enough to make her want to know more. Lois smiled and said, "BEER TIME".

The more they looked around the more they thought about Cajun Al. There were crab traps, animal traps, a pirogue, etc. There was a big old oak tree along the edge of the bayou so they brought their chairs and sat under it as they enjoyed the scent of the sea. By now they had a few more beers under their tight belts and loose tongues. They were starting to laugh out loud for no particular reason, maybe just out of happiness.

Roland said, hey, remember Mr. As-if's haircuts. I liked them! I use to go there a lot with Dad. Steven said not me! They couldn't make me go. People waiting their turn would get him talking and he didn't stop cutting until he finished his story. It seemed as though one of his haircuts lasted me a year because I had to let all those gashes grow out. Lois said Steven should be ashamed of himself. Mr. As-If was a nice man. I know he was, but remember how Roland and Dad looked when they came home? Lois laughed and said you're right. They scared the daylights out of Mom when she laid eyes on them.

Those cold beers tasted better and better as the children went home by memory. It was almost like Cajun Al and

Mary were sitting near the oak tree laughing with them, watching as they dangled their feet in the bayou.

   Lois was drinking a little faster than her brothers but nobody was really keeping track because this was their day off from life. Lois kept pointing her finger at her brothers saying, you did this and you did that. Steven wasn't feeling any pain either so he said, "Wait a minute Saint Lois." Roland and I remember a certain sister of ours getting into a big fight one night after a few drinks. Yeah, you're right. Drinking brought out the Roland in me and I just had to fight when I saw somebody being bullied. The Steven in me came out too because I became the champion of the underdog, defender of the weak, savior of the day. Do you think maybe I really was Saint Lois? Steven said, no! How could that be when the devil made you do it.

   All kidding aside, we love you Lois and we know you are a goodhearted person. We can always count on you to come running, no matter what the call! You were Cajun Al's pride and joy with your blue eyes and blonde hair. Roland and Steven looked Lois straight in the eyes, raised their beers and said nothing. She smiled, raised her two beers and said, "Mom use to tell me that after all her years on earth she learned one thing. I asked, what? She said she couldn't tell me, I had to find out for myself." Well brothers, I know what it is, " Love doesn't die".

The Treasure

Steven's young grandson Matthew is a lot like him; he marches to the beat of his own drum. The family doesn't understand his obsession with walking the same, long path in the yard over and over almost as though he were in a dream state at times. When he goes in the house all he talks about, when he does talk, are Indians. Maybe he hears something in his mind, like a whisper, and sees himself as walking the walk of Indians past.

Steven decided he would ask Matthew to spend some time together, maybe go for a horseback ride in the country. Matthew was very excited because Indians and horses go together. When you think of one, you think of the other. They rode slowly and Steven began to talk about a dream he had last night. In this dream God was an Indian Chief who told him that there is no such thing as the future or the past. These words are used to explain the rising and setting of the sun. Otherwise it would always be day or always be night. The Old Chief said it is always now, never tomorrow, never yesterday. Humans have no need for time. If you are happy, live that way! We all face the same end. Steven asked Matthew what he thought about the dream. Matthew said that the Chief is a wise man. Steven felt that maybe this was something they should think about more.

They continued to ride when suddenly they came across a sign that said," SANCHEZ LAND FOR SALE, NAME YOUR POISON." Matthew asked what does that mean?

Steven said that he heard tell that Mr. Sanchez was an evil man who was a pirate, a swamper, a gambler and very cold hearted. He ruined everything he touched and he knew it but he never loss sleep over it. For some reason he never got sick so he took care of people who were. Matthew said that sounds like a nice thing to do. Steven said yes but he never did anything for the right reason. There was always something in it for him, always! Maybe after he died the family considers anything and everything to do with him poisonous. Anyhow, lets take a look. Matthew said yeah, lets take a look. We won't ruin anything we're the good guys.

They got off their horses and walked around. The place was beautiful. It was full of oak trees with branches that touched the ground and seemed to creep along like a spider. There was a small bayou that ran through it. They saw deer tracks, raccoon tracks, live rabbits, and many other wild creatures. Matthew even saw a bobcat. When Steven saw Matthew's excitement and the twinkle in his eyes it was as though Cajun Al's spirit had awakened. Matthew said, " Let's buy this place. Maybe we can call it TWO-DOGS, you know, like you and me. Steven said that if he really thought it was a good idea and if he really wanted to spend more time together they would buy it today. They decided that they would offer a reasonable dose of poison, not the usual expected overdose; after all they didn't want to kill anybody! They laughed, mounted their horses and rode out towards the setting sun.

The next morning Steven took care of the legal business for a moderate but fair sum and the land was theirs. He headed out to Matthew's house to share the good news and as usual found him walking his path deep in thought. Steven sat on the porch and waited. He had learned that it was better to let Matthew come to him when he was ready. Well, TWO-DOGS is ours. Are you ready to explore our land? Matthew ran inside and told his Mom he would be spending the day with Gramps.

Steven didn't realize that by trying to draw Matthew out, what really happened was that Matthew drew him in. Steven the young kid is dead but the old kid is alive. A free man has no end, only a beginning. He has to grip life and shake it like a tree. Roots are the secret, human or oak.

They stood on their land; their very own land just like the Indians did a long time ago. To help insure that the woods live on, they planted a few acorns along the bayou and other areas in memory of Cajun Al and Armade`ous. Steven seemed to tire out a little quicker than he use to so he said that's enough for today. Ready to go home? Matthew said O.K.

On the way home Matthew asked if Steven had a bow and arrows. I sure do but I'll have to look for them, why? Because I thought maybe I would buy my own and you could teach me how to use them. Now that we own land we could hunt together. Sounds good to me. Let's go shopping, that way you can get the one that is most comfortable for you. It will be my gift. Your first lesson will be tomorrow. Thanks Gramps. Maybe I'll buy two pairs of moccasins, one pair for you and one pair for me. We can exchange gifts then wear our stuff when we go on our land just like Armade`ous and Cajun Al probably did.

The next day they practiced a little and Matthew luckily speared a good size fish. They were both surprised and very excited because they now had a reason to build a campfire. They would cooked and eat their first meal on TWO-DOGS land. Steven figured what better time than now to tell Matthew he has Indian blood running through his veins. Matthew said, "I know." How do you know this? Oh, I just do. We come from the ashes and live slow and easy, appreciating the journey, somewhat in the past but always trying to slow down the present. Steven was speechless. Nothing more was said for a little while as they enjoyed their meal.

Matthew sat looking down at the dirt as he dug with an oak branch. Gramps, tell me more about Mr. Sanchez. I had a dream that he was angry and mean because he was always looking for something and couldn't find it. What was it Gramps? It was a treasure map. You see, a long time ago he was a privateer and had stolen a sheepskin with a map drawn on it showing the location of buried treasure. When his ship was attacked he asked a beautiful young Spanish woman who was a captured slave on his ship to hide it in an oak tree near where the battle took place if she was able to survive, which she did. But, she was so scared that she couldn't remember which tree she hid it in. Over the years Sanchez tried to find her or the oak tree but never did. All he knew was where the ship went down so he began buying land. The same land not very far from where the battle took place. Now we own his land. We can hunt for the treasure map if you want to but we must not go crazy like he did. We should have fun, agree? Agree.

  Matthew and Steven never, ever tired of hanging out on their land. Every day, every day they were out there but never before Matthew finished his walk. The family didn't worry as much anymore about the why of it because he was in good hands most of the day. Steven was more interested in treasure hunting and Matthew was more interested in developing his Indian bloodline. There was such a great love connection that they willingly shared their time, each one learning from the other. Gramps, what you say we go to TWO-DOGS at night and see how it is out there. Tonight would be good, because there's a full moon. That means the crabs are full. Maybe we can bring our nets and try our luck. Don't worry about a cooking pot because after you got that fish I decided I best keep water, a pot, a box of salt and even some hog lard for frying, in my toolbox of my truck. Matthew said, "I sure like your tools." Ask your Mom and Dad for permission then call me early and let me know. I have to take a little nap so that I won't be so tired tonight. O.K. Later Gramps.

  Well these two little boys couldn't stop thinking about the nighttime adventure. It was barely dark when Matthew heard the old truck drive up and off they went. They walked around very slowly just like Cajun Al and Armade`ous did, enjoying the wonderful, scary sounds of the woods and bayous. Steven told Matthew it reminded him so much of times he spent with Cajun Al a very long time ago. Matthew said he wishes he could have been there. It must have been great. Matthew had brought a metal rod with him because he thought maybe the treasure was not in a tree but buried in the ground. He began poking the dirt hoping to find it when something or someone pulled on the rod and tried to drag him down into hell. It scared Matthew to death and he screamed almost like a girl. He began running and yelling, I found Mr. Sanchez! He's buried but he's not dead! He's warning us to keep our mouths shut or else next time we'll be lying right next to him forever! We found the treasure but he says he found it first! Gramps! Gramps! Where are you! Finally poor old winded Steven caught up to Matthew, grabbed him and held him close for a while. It's all right son. I'm fine and so are you. Let's sit a minute then we'll build a campfire. I'm pretty sure that was the home of an alligator. I should have told you before we came out that alligators are in these bayous. They dig a hole at the edge of the water, but underground, and sometimes the ground caves in if it's disturbed. You and your metal rod must have jabbed the gator and he was ready for a fight. I'll teach you how to handle that rascal just like Cajun Al taught me. The next time the two of you meet, I promise, you will eat fried alligator. Steven placed a head feather from a night owl and two tail feathers from a night Hawk in his hair and also in Matthew's hair. Steven stood up and gave a Cajun yell or two. Then screamed, "Did you hear the warning son of red eyes! I, son of green eyes tell you this is our land!" Matthew yelled, "Yeah!" Then Matthew started an Indian dance around the campfire singing and yelling in preparation for war. Since Steven is a warrior, has long, white, hair and is of the same bloodline he had to save face and do a little high steppin himself. Finally the fire went out. The message had been delivered and it was time to go home. Matthew ran around the truck and reached inside, gave his Gramps a bear hug and said, " Thanks for helping me tonight Gramps. I love you."

    Matthew got up early the next morning and did not go for his walk. Instead he asked his mom to bring him to Steven's house. She was surprised at the urgency of his request but something told her not to ask questions just yet. Steven was awakened by the knock on his door. Good morning my favorite Grandson. He laughed then said that he could say that because not only was it the truth but also because he only had one grandson. Do you want to cook breakfast? Yeah, but let's eat outside under your oak tree. They began eating but Matthew was so excited that he talked faster than he ate. This was unusual because although Matthew was tall and thin, he usually ate a lot and talked a little. Gramps, Uncle Stevie gave me a deerskin hide yesterday, a real one. He just gave it to me for no particular reason. I put it near my bed last night and this morning I feel different some how. I can't explain it but I know something about me has changed. Well Matthew, all I can tell you is that you are the fifth generation to own a hide. Keep it someplace special in your room along with your bow and arrows and soon you might get your answers. Maybe, because you are the fifth generation, everything will be made clear to you in five days.

After breakfast they went inside the house to wash the dishes. Matthew went in the bathroom and removed as many of Steven's long white hairs from his hairbrush as he could, wrapped them in tissue and carefully placed them in his pocket without saying a word. He came out and asked if they could go to the woods but just for a little while because he might have other things to do today. Steven was always ready to hang out there. He loved the peace and quiet, sunshine or rain, animals wild or tame, the beauty of nature itself. He believed everything God made was of value. Since Matthew loved their land as much as he did it made all of it so much more meaningful.

When they arrived Steven sat and relaxed while Matthew looked here and there gathering owl feathers, hawk feathers, a snakeskin, a few dried herbs, some animal fur, five acorns and several willow branches. Steven watched him and was sure in his mind that Matthew would return with a million questions about the why of it all. He couldn't be more wrong. The only question was, " Do you have a bag in your tool box that I could borrow?" Steven gave him a paper sack and just had to ask what the gathering of feathers was all about. Matthew said that he didn't know but he just had to do it. Matthew said that he was ready to go home now.

That night after supper he asked his parents if he could sleep in the attic. He said it would be fun and he promised to be quiet. They could think of no logical reason to say no. After the family settled in for the night, Matthew brought all of his Indian stuff up there with him. He thought something big could happen and he might need the extra room. He didn't turn on the light because the moon shone bright and clearly through the window. He lay on his deerskin hide on the floor wearing his moccasins and a pair of jeans with his bath towel resting across his lower waist and no shirt. He looked up at the moon as the man in the moon looked back at him with a smile. Did he know why Matthew felt different? Was he about to release a family secret?

It was past midnight and it was now the morning of the fifth day! Matthew was not afraid when he realized that suddenly an Indian Chief stood quietly in the moonlit room with Armade`ous and Cajun Al. These Elders of Matthew's family had returned for a sacred spiritual ceremony. They sat on the deerskin hide while Chief Spirit of the Oaks stood guard. Matthew thought, " He looks like a big oak tree himself". Armade`ous and Cajun Al were alike, big and strong like Gramps, but different somehow. Matthew sure wished Gramps could be here now.

Armade`ous and Cajun Al told Matthew all the important things they had learned about survival in the woods and the importance of cleansing your mind, body and spirit by dreaming. They asked if he had gathered all the things they had called for. He said he had and handed them to the Chief. The ceremony began with a chant, then as a symbol of unity, the Chief, Armade`ous and Cajun Al, assembled the things gathered in a special order tying them with strands of Steven's long, white hair. Chief said that these Furriers were the best and this gift is one from their hearts to protect him as he will protect other dreamers. Chief Spirit of the Oaks hung the gift around Matthew's neck and announced to all seers of spirits that Matthew is a DREAM CATCHER. Matthew was very proud and honored. When he finally stopped saying thank you and stopped admiring his gift he reached out to give each of them a bear hug but they were no longer there. They had gone as quietly as they had arrived.

The next morning Matthew, the Dream Catcher came down stairs wearing his ceremonial outfit including his moccasins, deerskin hide and bow and arrows. The family stared but saved the questions for dinner conversation as they watched Matthew go out the door for his usual walk. Afterwards he called his Gramps and asked if they could go to the woods today so he could tell him a story. Steven said he was on his way.

Steven was not at all surprised when he saw what Matthew was wearing or when he heard his story. You see nobody knew that Steven was a seer of spirits. He saw the whole ceremony in his dream. How did you like my dad, Cajun Al and my grandpa, Armade`ous? Weren't they the best? Matthew said, "Yeah! Just like you."

The two dogs sat in silence, each remembering the Elders in his own special way. Matthew thanked Steven for his patience, for teaching him, for sharing with him, for listening and not laughing at his dreams. I love you Gramps and I want you to know that you are my treasure. I will keep you buried in my heart for the rest of my life.

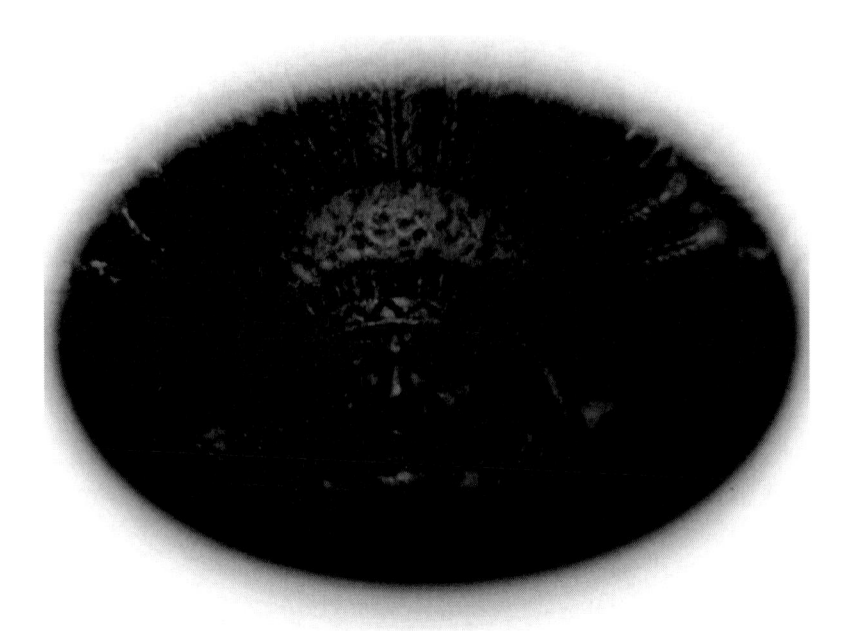

Chief Spirit of the Oak

    Oddly enough Steven began having a dream about Chief Spirit of the Oak. In this dream Al was sitting up straight and proud in a chair resting his large hands on his cane supporting his chin. But now he was sitting along the bayou not far from the oak tree he called home so very long ago. He was wearing his Stetson Cowboy hat, his white western shirt, blue jeans and his good cowboy boots he loved so much. A quiet breeze rustled the leaves of the mighty ancient oak trees as the moss gently swayed back and forth allowing the scent of the good cologne Al always wore to fill the air. The cabin he and Mary shared was no longer there, only Al. He smiled that silly little mischievous grin he had when he pulled a bluff on someone. He seemed so happy and peaceful as he watched the current in the bayou while reflecting on his life.
    Chief Spirit of The Oak would fade in and out. Although he said nothing his presence was felt and seen only in a fog. He majestically towered over and behind Al, waiting, just waiting. While still dreaming, Steven was in awe of the old Chief. His facial appearance projected great strength of character and wisdom. His dress projected dignity. His

waiting projected patience. The dark, leathery skin told that he braved the elements as a man. Steven knew that the Chief and Al were friends.

Al sighed and said, "We did good Mary." Chief Spirit of the Oak stepped forward out of the fog and into the clear light of the moon. He held Al's Chat's reign while Al mounted. Al paused, took one last look around and rode off into the foggy, marshlands of the bayou.

Steven awakened with peace in his heart realizing that when all is said and done, like many others before him, he too has a TRUE CAJUN SPIRIT.

ABOUT THE AUTHOR

For as long as I can remember I tried to keep the peace. Even as a child I didn't like confrontation and some of the results I witnessed. I avoided directness and went around the problem to achieve a result, never realizing that made me a coward.

Our family lived in Abbeville, Louisiana during some of my teenage years and we visited friends in the neighboring town of Erath. There I met Mr. Alphe Peltier. After he left, some gossiping women began to talk about him. What they said about the man and what I saw were two different things. They seemed to be jealous of his freedom and his courage to tell it like it is no matter what people thought. Maybe they just didn't understand his sense of humor.

I never dreamed that just a few days later I would go to this man with a personal problem. He was tending to his horses as I arrived at his stables. He seemed to do this with so much love and pride that I hated to bother him. I talked and he listened. He was really the first person in my life to ever listen to me with compassion and understanding, not with tolerance because they had to. Neither of us ever spoke of this meeting to anyone.

In time I married into his family. Al and I were sometimes at odds but I felt more like I was born into the family rather than lovingly welcomed into it.

Because my husband, Steven, always went straight to the truth of any matter and never around it, people had respect for him. I wanted to be just like that so I began working on myself.

I always secretly wanted to be a police officer. So, I decided that since I was no longer a coward I would go for it. At fifty years of age I graduated from the police academy and became the first female patrolman of Erath.

After I retired I began thinking about Cajun Al and how it was a miracle that he survived everything life threw at him. He never let any of it make him bitter. He was a better man than most because he helped friends and enemies, never holding a grudge against anyone.

I have written this story based on his life and some of the characters, most were real and some imagined. He was no coward and thanks to him, neither am I.

Mary Jane Fitch Peltier

Manufactured by Amazon.ca
Acheson, AB